# The Really Simple, No Nonsense Nutrition Guide

**Edward R. Blonz, Ph.D., M.S.**

Conari Press
Berkeley, CA

# Dedication

This book is dedicated to wholesome foods and those who take the time to grow or prepare them in a way that contributes to good health, the joy of eating, and the health of our environment.

Cover: Andrea Sohn Design.
Illustrations and charts by Tina Cash.

ISBN: 0-943233-45-3

**Library of Congress Cataloging-in-Publication Data**

**Blonz, Edward.**
     The really simple, no nonsense nutrition guide / by Edward R. Blonz, Ph.D.
       p. cm.
  Includes bibliographical references and index.
      ISBN 0-943233-45-3 : $8.95
      1. Nutrition.  2. Health.  I. Title.
RA784.B58 1.993
613.2—dc20                92-47223
                           CIP

# Contents

# About the Author

Edward R. Blonz holds a Ph.D. and M.S. in nutrition from the University of California at Davis, where he worked on the role of insulin in the development of obesity. He also holds a B.A. in psychology from the University of Wisconsin at Madison. His career has included roles in academia as faculty member, researcher and educator, and he has held administrative positions in the business sector. At present, Dr. Blonz is the president of Nutrition Resource, a company he formed to help fill the growing void between scientific research and public understanding.

# Acknowledgments

I want to thank my family, friends and food editor for their unflinching support and encouragement. Thanks to Paula Hamilton for the fertile soil that allowed me to plant and grow a journalistic voice. My appreciation to the readers of my syndicated weekly newspaper column for their stimulating questions, and a thanks to the dieticians and health educators of Kaiser Permanente for their helpful input. Thanks also to Conari Press for their thoughtful suggestions and energy. My love to Ruth and Lillian, without whom this wouldn't have been possible. And finally, most of all, my special thanks and love to Kay and Joshua, my wife and son, for giving me the space, the time, and the understanding to complete this project.

# Introduction

This is a book about food. It's designed to help you decide which foods are best for the health of you and your family. More important, though, this book is designed to give you the lowdown, in plain English.

These days, food, nutrition, and health information comes at us from all sides—often with contradictory advice. How are we expected to cope, let alone decide? We're usually left to figure it out on our own, and for some of us that's like being a stranger in a strange land. How unfortunate that many people get so frustrated that they simply give up, rather than gain any understanding of the science (or lack of science) behind what they hear in the media.

Most nutrition articles are not written by scientists; they come from journalists who write about science. Although many are excellent writers, it's questionable whether they have the scientific savvy to critically examine the basic research behind the story. This has always been a source of frustration for me throughout my career in nutrition. So after years of suffering on the sidelines, I was given an opportunity to do something about it. I began writing a weekly newspaper column on food, nutrition, and health that is now syndicated around the country.

This book is a compilation of those writings. Its down-to-earth approach takes on the complexities of popular nutrition science and breaks them down into digestible bites, palatable even for the most science-phobic reader. You'll learn what your body needs, how foods can improve your health, what the potential problems are with what you eat, and how to be a wise consumer. Many chapters provide valuable referrals to books, products, and key organizations that can be of further assistance. Finally, there's an easy-to-follow eating plan and a really simple chart.

As you read, keep in mind that nutrition is a dynamic science. Although this book is based on the latest scientific findings, nutrition will always be subject to review and revision as new research is done. About the only constant is the healthfulness of fresh, wholesome food.

The ultimate choice of which path to follow is yours. This book is not intended to dictate or be dogmatic. My purpose is to present science in a clear, concise, and upbeat format; what you do with the information is your decision. When it comes to the health of yourself and your family, however, it should be an informed one.

# What Your Body Needs

# Protein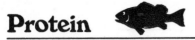

*The stuff we're made of*

## First Things First

The word *protein* comes from the Greek *proteos*, which means "to come first." It's a fitting name because protein is a primary ingredient in every cell of the body. The protein from our diet is needed to make hair, skin, nails, muscles, organs, blood cells, nerve, bone and brain tissue, enzymes, hormones, antibodies, chemical messengers, and the DNA and RNA used to form the genetic code of life. That's quite a lineup!

## Building Blocks

All proteins are made from building blocks called amino acids. While there are many different types of protein, there are only about 22 kinds of amino acids. Of these 22, our body can manufacture all but nine. The reason we need protein in our diet is to supply these nine essential amino acids (EAAs). Because most dietary proteins are too large to be absorbed, the body uses its digestive enzymes to separate the food proteins into their individual amino-acid building blocks. Only then can they be absorbed and used by the body as raw materials to make the variety of proteins necessary for good health.

## Too Little Can Cause Problems

In the developing countries of Africa, Asia, and South America, protein foods are scarce, and deficiencies are not only present, they can be life threatening. For generally well-nourished people, a protein intake below required levels will not pose problems if it's only for a day or two now and then. But if the body consistently fails to get enough protein, it will begin showing signs of deficiency.

Depending on the length and degree, symptoms of an ongoing protein deficiency could include: increased susceptibility to disease, fatigue, anemia, hair and skin problems, mental confusion, pallor, digestive disturbances, muscle wasting, weight loss, and eventually death.

## Too Much of a Good Thing

As essential as protein is, an excess can cause problems—and in the U.S., overconsumption is the norm, not the exception. The average individual does *not* benefit from extra protein, mainly because there is no way to store it for later use. When overindulged with this relatively expensive food, the body, for the most part, has no option but to turn it into body fat. This conversion places an extra demand on the liver and kidneys, the two organs responsible for converting excess amino acids into fat.

The high-protein American diet also likely contributes to high incidence of osteoporosis in our society, because chronic protein excess can prevent dietary calcium from being absorbed.

## What If You Don't Eat Meat?

Most foods have some amino acids. Animal proteins, such as meat, fish, eggs, and dairy products, are *complete* proteins because they contain all the EAAs. Except for soybeans, vegetable proteins such as grains and legumes are *incomplete* proteins because they lack one or more EAAs. You can easily meet your daily protein requirement by eating only vegetable proteins, however, by combining different foods so that sufficient amounts of all the EAAs are consumed.

There are three basic types of vegetable protein: whole grains, such as rice, corn, oats, and barley; legumes, such as beans and lentils; and nuts and seeds, such as almonds and peanuts, and sunflower and sesame seeds. By planning your meals to include foods from two or more of these groups, you end up creating a complete protein. For example, by eating both rice (grains) and beans (legumes), you supply the body with the daily EAAs it needs.

Putting together this type of "complementary protein" is the essence of vegetarianism. At one time, it was thought that the body needed all the EAAs to be consumed at the same meal. Recently, however, scientists have determined that the body can successfully make protein so long as the full complement of EAAs is present over the course of a day.

## How Much Do You Need?

A quick way to estimate your daily protein requirement is to count 11 grams of protein for every 30 pounds of body weight. By this method, a 150-pound adult needs about 55 grams of protein per day. (Note: If you're overweight, use your ideal body weight for this calculation.) Pregnant women should add an extra 10 grams of protein per day, and nursing mothers an extra 12 to 15 grams during the first six months. Requirements for children are higher. Check the table on RDAs in the Appendix.

Understanding what a gram of protein is can be confusing. The following examples should give you some perspective:

### Protein Content
*Grams*

| | |
|---|---|
| 1 slice sandwich bread | 2 |
| 1 cup broccoli | 3 |
| 1 oz. (20-30) almonds | 6 |
| 1 cup white rice | 6 |
| 1 large egg | 6 |
| 1 cup cooked pasta (no sauce) | 7 |
| 1 oz. cheddar/jack/swiss cheese | 7 |
| ½ cup kidney beans | 8 |
| 2 Tbs. peanut butter | 8 |
| 1 cup lo-fat milk | 9 |
| 1 cup fruit yogurt | 10 |
| 1 cup tofu | 18 |
| 4 oz. hamburger patty | 28 |
| 4 oz. fish (trout) | 30 |
| 4 oz. roast chicken breast | 34 |

## Related Topics

See also: Vegetarianism Explored and The Wonderful World of Digestion.

# Dietary Fat

*Jack Sprat was ahead of his time*

## Fat Facts

Fat, a member of the lipid family, is the most concentrated form of energy in living things; it contains over twice the calories (energy) of protein or carbohydrates. Similar to those of other mammals, human bodies are designed to turn virtually all excess dietary energy into fat and store it as an energy reserve.

Fat provides insulation for the body and padding around sensitive internal organs. Several nutrients are found in fat, including vitamins A, D, E, K, and the essential fatty acids. When eaten, fats slow the rate at which the stomach empties, causing a feeling of fullness and satisfaction. And for some people, the most important quality of fat is that it contributes some of the most wonderful tastes and textures to our food.

Although there's nothing inherently "wrong" with fat, scientific studies have consistently linked its overconsumption to some of our most troublesome health problems, including heart disease, cancer, obesity, and hypertension (high blood pressure).

## Fat's Ins and Outs

There are three basic types of fat: saturated, monounsaturated, and polyunsaturated. Saturated fat is found primarily in animal products, such as butter, lard, eggs, meat, and poultry. Vegetable sources of saturated fat include coconut oil, palm oil, palm-kernel oil, and cocoa butter.

Monounsaturated fat is found in different quantities in most vegetable oils, some of which are primarily monounsaturated; these include canola (rapeseed), olive, almond, avocado, and peanut oils.

Polyunsaturated fat is found in the oils of seeds and some nuts, including corn, soy, safflower, sesame, and walnut. Polyunsaturated fat is the only type known to be required by the body. Fish oils are unique in the animal world because they also contain significant amounts of polyunsaturated fat.

## Which Should We Eat?

Over the past decade unsaturated fats have mistakenly been given a clean slate while saturated fats were viewed as the problem child of the fat family. Recent research, however, points to a need to change this particular good fat/bad fat approach.

Certain saturated fats, such as the stearic acid found in cocoa butter and some animal fats, has been shown to have little effect on the blood cholesterol level. Even the saturated tropical oils— coconut, palm, and palm-kernel—are not the dietary demons they once were thought to be.

Polyunsaturated oils, once touted for their cholesterol-lowering ability, were long considered to be the ideal fat. Recent research, however, has linked an elevated intake of polyunsaturates with undesirable side effects such as suppression of the immune system, increased risk of cancer, and gallstone formation.

There's one type of fat that should be either completely avoided or kept to an absolute minimum. It's called partially hydrogenated fat and it's used to make margarine, shortening, and many processed foods. (For a complete discussion of why they are dangerous, see "The Dangers of Once-Friendly Fats.")

Monounsaturated oils are the only category of fats that continue to receive a clean bill of health. As such these should remain the focus of your low-fat diet.

## Why Is a Low-Fat Diet Important?

Scientific research has found a strong association between the amount of fat consumed and the risk of developing heart disease and cancer. But notice that word *association*. There are also associations between those killer diseases and physical inactivity, stress, smoking, blood pressure, obesity, and low fiber intake. Your level of risk also depends on whether the disease runs in your family.

If you eat a high-fiber diet, don't smoke, have normal blood pressure and weight and an active, stress-free lifestyle, and are lucky enough to have healthy parents, the "riskiness" of your fat intake shrinks dramatically.

So why pick on fat? One reason is that we can eat only so many calories in a day. Because fat is such a concentrated source (it has over *twice* the calories of protein or carbohydrates), too much fat means too little of the other foods we need. A lack of these other foods—fruits, vegetables, and grains—deprives the body of the nutrients and fiber it needs to remain healthy.

Another reason is that fat has a nasty habit of changing into "free radicals"—reactive compounds that can damage the cells in the body in a way that leads to heart disease, cancer, and other degenerative diseases. The higher the fat consumption, the greater the risk of this happening. The body's best hope of protecting itself is through a low fat intake and a plentiful supply of the nutrients found in fruits, vegetables, and grains—the very foods that a high-fat diet knocks off the plate.

## Where Does Cholesterol Fit In?

There's often confusion over the relative roles of fat and cholesterol. Cholesterol is not the same as fat, but they both belong to the lipid family. Cholesterol is a waxy, fat-like substance with a complex structure resembling honeycomb. Unlike fat, the body does not use cholesterol for energy; this complex compound is an essential structural component in every cell of the body. In addition, cholesterol is a raw material for a number of hormones, including estrogen and testosterone. (See "Eating for a Healthy Heart" for a discussion of the relationship between cholesterol and heart disease.)

### What's a Triglyceride?

For simplicity, you could almost use the terms *fats* and *triglycerides* interchangeably. A triglyceride is the way that nature bundles fats together—the fats in the diet, in the bloodstream, and even those fats in the body's energy storage depots. Triglycerides look like a squat letter *E*, the three prongs representing the individual saturated or unsaturated fatty acids that make up the triglyceride.

The blood triglyceride level usually goes up after eating—even if there's a limited amount of fat in the meal—because the body is programmed to convert most excess protein or carbohydrates into triglycerides, the energy form best suited for storage. A high intake of alcohol or sugars such as fructose, sucrose, or glucose also increases blood triglyceride levels. Not much is known about how an elevated triglyceride level impacts health. In general, people with high triglycerides tend to be at higher risk for several disorders, including heart disease, but it's unclear what role, if any, triglycerides play. Suffice it to say, any abnormal readings should be closely monitored.

## Is There a Minimum Fat Requirement?

There is no minimum requirement for fat, per se, but there is a need for a certain type of polyunsaturated fat. Called essential fatty acids (EFAs), they're found in polyunsaturated vegetable oils, such as sunflower, safflower, corn, and soy. (Olive and canola oils also contain essential fatty acids, but in lesser amounts.) An average adult needs 3 to 6 grams of EFAs every day—the amount found in 1 to 2 tablespoons of any polyunsaturated vegetable oil. You needn't go out of your way to add polyunsaturated fats; a healthy diet that includes vegetables, grains, and legumes will usually supply the needed amount. It's rare for an EFA deficiency to develop in anyone eating a varied diet.

## Figuring Your Fat Allowance

Your fat allowance is the maximum amount of fat, in grams, that you aim for in your daily diet. There are two quick methods to determine it, each based on current health guidelines that fat be no more than 30 percent of daily calorie intake.

The first method is to divide your ideal body weight by half. (Ideal body weight is that listed in height/weight charts found in doctors' offices, health clubs, or diet/health books.) That number in grams is your fat allowance. For example, according to the Metropolitan Insurance Table, a 5'4" woman of medium frame, 25 to 29 years old has an ideal body weight of about 130 pounds, and thus a daily fat allowance of about 65 grams (130 divided by two). This method assumes a light to moderate activity level. While not very precise, the method does provide an answer with a minimum of math.

Another shorthand method relies on daily calorie intake. Divide the number of calories by 30 to get the maximum number of fat grams recommended. For example, someone on a 2,100-calorie diet should have no more than 70 grams (2,100 divided by 30) of fat per day. Here are some common foods and the number of fat grams they contain:

## Fat Content
*grams*

| | |
|---|---|
| 1 cup broccoli | 0 |
| ½ cup red kidney beans | 0.4 |
| 1 cup rice | 0.6 |
| 1 cup cooked pasta (no sauce) | 1 |
| 1 slice sandwich bread | 1 |
| 1 cup fruit-flavored yogurt | 2 |
| 4 oz. fish (trout) | 5 |
| 1 cup 2% low-fat milk | 5 |
| 1 large egg | 5 |
| 1 cup marinara sauce | 8 |
| 4 oz. roast chicken breast | 9 |
| 1 cup tofu | 9 |
| 1 Tbs. butter | 12 |
| 1 oz. (20-30) almonds | 14 |
| 2 Tbs. peanut butter | 16 |
| 4 oz. hamburger | 21 |
| 12 Oreo-type cookies | 24 |

## Calculating Fat Percentage

Although percentage of calories from fat is not indicated on food labels, determining it is easy. The most accurate way is to divide the calories from fat by the total calories (both figures are listed under Amount Per Serving on the nutrition panel).

Another method uses grams of fat and calories per serving. If there are no more than 3 grams of fat for every 100 calories in a serving, then no more than 27 percent of the calories are from fat—just below the recommended level. This formula works regardless of serving size.

## Keeping Some Perspective

As healthy eaters, we should be mainly concerned with total fat intake, rather than specific types of fat. As a general rule, however, avoid partially hydrogenated fats whenever possible and rely more on monounsaturates. But if you're supposed to be restricting your total fat intake, even these should be limited.

## To Learn More

There are a number of resources that can help you plan and enjoy a low-fat approach to eating. I recommend: *Controlling Your Fat Tooth* (Workman Press, NY 1991) by J. Piscatella, and *Fight Fat and Win* (DCI, Minneapolis 1990) by E. Moquette-Magee, M.P.H., R.D. I also recommend *Cooking Light: The Magazine of Food and Fitness* (bimonthly), (800) 336-0125. See also: Eating for a Healthy Heart and The Dangers of Once-Friendly Fats.

# Carbohydrates

*Heavy on the starch, please*

## The No-Limit Nutrient

While fats and protein are preceded by the advisory to "avoid too much," there are few constraints placed on carbohydrates. This is ironic, for it wasn't too long ago that carbohydrates—especially sugar—were on the hot seat, saddled with the blame for such common ailments as obesity, heart disease, and hyperactivity in children. Recently, however, science has cleared carbohydrates of their alleged nutritional misdeeds.

As a group, carbohydrates constitute the body's most important source of energy. There are three basic types: simple carbohydrates, complex carbohydrates, and fiber.

## Simple and Sweet

The most important simple carbohydrate, glucose (also called blood sugar), is the body's basic fuel: It's the preferred fuel of the brain and nervous system, and the only fuel that the red blood cells can use. Indeed, there are entire body systems dedicated specifically to maintaining the level of glucose in the blood.

Glucose is referred to as a single sugar or a simple carbohydrate because it exists as individual, unattached units. Other common single sugars include fructose (fruit sugar) and galactose.

Simple carbohydrates can also be double sugars, which are two single sugars attached to one another. The most common of these is sucrose, or table sugar (glucose and fructose); lactose, or milk sugar (glucose and galactose); and maltose (glucose and glucose), found in grains and malt beverages such as beer. The sensation of sweetness comes from the ability of the single and double sugars to stimulate the sweet taste receptors on the tongue.

Simple carbohydrates undergo little in the way of digestion. Single sugars are absorbed intact whereas the double sugars must first be split apart. Then the liver changes both fructose and galactose into glucose.

## It's All in the Build

Glucose also serves as the building block for the complex carbohydrates, which are found in foods such as beans, rice, pasta and potatoes. These complex carbohydrates, or starches, consist of hundreds to thousands of glucose units connected to each other in straight line or branched formations. They are too large to be absorbed through the wall of the digestive tract, so the body releases a set of enzymes designed to break the starch apart, piece by glucose piece.

Cellulose, such as that found in hay and wood pulp as well as many vegetables, is also made from glucose. The big difference, though, between digesting a meal of mashed potatoes and one of mashed wood is that the body lacks the enzymes needed to separate the glucose units of cellulose. As a result, starch gets digested and absorbed, and the cellulose passes through the system. Because the body cannot digest cellulose, this complex carbohydrate is classified as a dietary fiber.

*Fiber* is an umbrella term referring to a group of complex carbohydrates that have no nutrient value because they're not digested. Despite this fact, this group, which includes cellulose, pectin, and vegetable gums, has taken on increasing importance as a crucial component in a healthy diet. (For a detailed discussion, see "Fiber and Health.")

## The Fuel With Something Extra

Normally, muscles require oxygen from the bloodstream when they work. This is why our breathing rate picks up during physical activity. Carbohydrates, though, are exceptional in that they're an anaerobic fuel (*an*=without; *aerobic*=requiring oxygen). There's a small amount of stored carbohydrate, called glycogen, in the muscles and liver, and the body relies on this fuel to meet special demands. It's this fuel and the anaerobic ability of carbohydrates that enables us to dash across a room and grab a falling child or sprint down the street to catch a bus. This carbohydrate provides a vital source of energy that keeps the muscles working until the lungs gear up to provide the needed oxygen.

## Focus on the Complex

When thinking about carbohydrates in your diet, focus on the complex rather than the simple sugars. Why, if all carbohydrates end up as glucose? The answer is in the nutrient company the different carbohydrates keep. Except for fruits, foods high in simple sugars tend to be high-calorie and often high-fat processed foods where intense flavor or a sweet taste is the main offering. In contrast, complex carbohydrates are generally found in grains, vegetables, and legumes—whole foods with a wide array of valuable nutrients and fiber.

## How Much Is Enough?

One-half to two-thirds of the calories you eat every day should come from carbohydrates. For an individual on a 2,000-calorie diet, this translates to 250 to 335 grams of carbohydrates per day (there are four calories in each gram of carbohydrate). The "bulk" of your intake should be from complex carbohydrates. Here's the carbohydrate content of some common foods:

## Carbohydrate Content
### (grams)

|  | Complex | Simple | TOTAL |
|---|---|---|---|
| 1 cup rice | 59 | 0 | 59 |
| 1 medium potato | 48 | 3 | 51 |
| 1 cup red kidney beans | 40 | 0 | 40 |
| 1 cup cooked pasta (no sauce) | 40 | 0 | 40 |
| 1 medium sweet potato | 15 | 13 | 28 |
| 1 cup Cheerio's cereal | 15 | 1 | 16 |
| 1 slice whole-wheat bread | 12 | 1 | 13 |
| 1 cup Sugar Smacks cereal | 12 | 21 | 33 |
| 1 medium banana | 9 | 18 | 27 |
| 1 medium carrot | 3 | 4 | 7 |
| 1 medium orange | 3 | 12 | 15 |
| 12 oz. cola soft drink | 0 | 38 | 38 |
| 1 Tbs. granulated sugar | 0 | 12 | 12 |

## Our Link to the Sun

In essence, carbohydrates deliver energy from the sun to satisfy the needs of the body. In the process called photosynthesis, plants take energy from the sun and produce glucose from carbon dioxide and water; they then use this glucose as a building block for growth. When we eat plants for food, the cells in the body use the glucose as fuel and break it back down to carbon dioxide and water. The energy in the glucose is then released and used by the body. The water is either exhaled in our breath or excreted as urine, and the carbon dioxide returns to the air—both again available to be used by plants.

## Related Topics

See also: Fiber for Health and The Wonderful World of Digestion.

# Water

*At the roots of life*

## Drink Up

Our bodies require more water than any other thing we ingest. We might survive for many weeks without food (if you call that living), but we would last only a few days without water. Despite this, perhaps because of its wide availability, water's importance as a nutrient is often overlooked.

## Life Begins in Water

Water is the medium in which human biochemical life exists. All our chemical reactions take place in and around this vital fluid, and oftentimes water is an ingredient or product in these reactions.

A human embryo is approximately 97 percent water by weight. At birth the body is about 77 percent water, and by adulthood, it's down to around 60 percent. Water content varies according to gender and the respective amounts of bodily tissues. Muscle, for example, is about 75 percent water by weight, whereas adipose (fat) tissue is about 25 percent water. Even bones are more than 20 percent water by weight. This means that a muscular, heavy-boned individual tends to have a higher proportion of body water.

## Hot and Cold Running Water

Water helps maintain the body's operating temperature. Those who live near a lake or ocean are familiar with the temperature-moderating effects that water can have on the environment. We also rely on this effect in our bodies. The water in our tissues helps to keep our body temperature relatively constant. This is important because essential organs, such as the brain, are sensitive to changes in temperature.

Aside from buffering the effects of climate, water also helps the body to release heat—that which is produced internally as a byproduct of muscular work and biochemical activity. To make sure things don't get too hot, the body relies on evaporation, a process that uses up heat energy. The relief comes through exhaling water vapor through the lungs, or through the cooling effect of perspiration on the skin.

## A Multi-talented Liquid

The articulating surfaces in our joints are "oiled" by water-based solutions. Our eyes are constantly bathed to keep the tissues moist and clean, and the digestive tract and lungs also experience the lubricating and cleansing effects of water.

Water is the transporter of supplies and byproducts to and from various points in the body. Nutrients and other essentials are usually in water-soluble forms so that they can ride through the major fluid pathways to their various destinations. Water also dilutes toxins and waste materials, and helps usher them out of the body. Even those materials that don't dissolve in water, such as fats and cholesterol, have special water-based transport proteins (lipoproteins) that help shuttle them around the body.

The water in the body also functions as a shock absorber. A developing fetus is cushioned by the fluid environment of the uterus. The brain and spinal cord are also surrounded by water-based compartments that help shield these vital organs from concussion.

## How Much Do We Need?

It's estimated that the body needs from 1 to 1.5 liters of water for every 1,000 calories in our diet. This translates to a minimum of about eight 8-ounce glasses of water every day for the average person. Individuals who live in hot or dry climates are likely to need more, as are those who engage in physical exertion.

Your daily fluid intake can come from drinking water or other beverages such as juice, milk, or soft drinks. Fruits and vegetables can also be counted, as they're about 80 percent water by weight. Don't count your intake of coffee, tea, or alcohol though, as these have a diuretic (water-removing) effect that tends to cancel out their contribution.

# Water Glossary

Once you get past tap water, there's a sea of possibilities and prices:

## Still Water

*Mineral water:* Has no legal definition, as all water except distilled and purified water contain some minerals. Industry standards, though, specify 500 milligrams of minerals per liter.

*Spring water:* Water that naturally flows out of the ground.

*Natural spring water:* Spring water collected without pumping or processing.

*Hard water:* Contains the minerals calcium and magnesium.

*Soft water:* Calcium and magnesium have been removed and replaced by sodium.

*Drinking water:* Non-carbonated water with no guarantee that it comes from a particular source or *has* been given a special treatment.

*Purified water:* Minerals removed.

*Distilled water:* The condensed steam of boiled water, a process that removes all minerals.

*Deionized water:* Minerals removed by a deionizer.

## Water With Gas

*Carbonated water:* Carbon dioxide gas added to the water under pressure.

*Sparkling water:* The same as carbonated water.

*Club soda:* Carbonated, filtered tap water with minerals added for taste. Can contain small amounts of caffeine or alcohol, so be sure to check the label.

*Seltzer water:* Carbonated, filtered tap water that has no added minerals.

## For More Information

See also: Getting the Lead Out and Keeping Pesticides off Your Plate.

# Vitamins & Minerals

*Essential factors from A to zinc*

## Tales of Discovery

It wasn't until 1860 that scientists discovered that germs could be responsible for disease. Following that development, they focused on finding the bugs behind every illness. This approach wasn't always successful, however, as some illnesses seemed to persist even though the germs were under control. That the answer might lie with what people were eating (or not eating) was not as popular a concept as the "germ theory." But as time went by, more and more scientists began to look to food for their answers.

The history of vitamin and mineral nutrition contains many colorful tales of discovery. Some began with an investigation of the power certain foods seemed to have over disease; others came from failed growth experiments, where all the nutrients thought to be essential were present in the diet.

## "Funk-y" Beginnings

The word *vitamin* was coined in 1912 by Dr. Casmir Funk, a Polish scientist who was searching for a cure for beriberi, a paralyzing disease that was common in regions where white rice was the main staple in the diet. Earlier work had zeroed in on rice polishings—the husk and bran that are removed when brown rice is made into white—as containing some factor that could combat beriberi. Funk eventually identified the key compound, called thiamin, and dubbed it a "vital amine." This was shortened to "vitamin," which continues to stand for the entire class of essential compounds.

## What Are Vitamins?

Vitamins are a diverse group of chemicals, but they have a few things in common:

• Compared with other nutrients, vitamins are needed only in trace amounts. All the required daily vitamins could fit in one-eighth of a teaspoon.

• Vitamins don't provide any calories.

• All vitamins are "organic," because they're based on the element carbon.

• Vitamins perform specific metabolic functions in the cell—the basic unit of life.

• Vitamins cannot be synthesized by the body in quantities large enough to meet the body's needs.

• Their absence from the diet leads to a failure to thrive and the development of a deficiency disease.

• All vitamins can be found in food.

Not all animals require the same vitamins. For example, humans are among the few animal groups that cannot manufacture their own vitamin C (ascorbic acid). This means your dog or cat does not need a daily ration of ascorbic acid, but you do.

## Water-Soluble Vitamins

Vitamins are divided into two main categories, based on whether they dissolve in water. Here are the water-soluble vitamins, what they do in the body, and a list of good foods sources:

**Thiamin** (vitamin $B_1$): Needed for carbohydrates to release energy; also required for normal functioning of heart and nervous system.

*Sources: pork, liver, meat, fish, poultry, eggs, whole grains, legumes, nuts and potatoes.*

**Riboflavin** (vitamin $B_2$): Required for metabolism and energy release from food; important for health of the skin, the lining of the digestive system, and the lungs.

*Sources: liver, milk (enriched) and milk products, meats, seafood, enriched grains, asparagus, broccoli, avocados, Brussels sprouts, eggs, and green leafy vegetables.*

**Niacin** (vitamin $B_3$, nicotinic acid, and nicotinamide): Required for normal cell metabolism and energy release from carbohydrates; also plays a role in the synthesis of hormones and DNA.

21

*Sources: organ meats, poultry, seafood, nuts, green vegetables, and legumes.*

**Pantothenic acid** (vitamin B$_5$): Needed for energy release from food and for the synthesis of adrenal hormones and other chemicals involved in the nervous system.

*Sources: organ meats, milk products, egg yolk, poultry, mushrooms, nuts, green vegetables, and whole grains.*

**Pyridoxine** (vitamin B$_6$): Key vitamin in protein metabolism; also plays a role in fat and carbohydrate metabolism.

*Sources: blackstrap molasses, meat, organ meats, poultry, wheat germ, brewers yeast, whole grains, fish, soybeans, bananas, avocado, green and leafy vegetables.*

**Vitamin B$_{12}$:** With folic acid, helps to form red blood cells; needed for healthy nervous tissue and manufacture of genetic material.

*Sources: meat, poultry, fish, shellfish, eggs, dairy products, vit.B$_{12}$ fortified foods, and fermented soy products.*

**Ascorbic acid** (vitamin C): Needed for healthy gums, wound healing, and to make collagen (the "cement" that holds body cells together). Also serves as an antioxidant, and plays a role in the immune system, protein metabolism, and other body systems.

*Sources: citrus fruits, peppers, melons, berries, Brussels sprouts, green vegetables, tomatoes, and potatoes.*

**Folic Acid:** With vitamin B$_{12}$, helps make red blood cells; important for the manufacture of genetic material.

*Sources: green leafy vegetables, organ meats, legumes, orange juice, beets, avocado, and broccoli.*

**Biotin:** Needed for metabolism and synthesis of fats, amino acids, and carbohydrates.

*Sources: organ meat, oatmeal, egg yolk, milk, soybeans, peanuts, whole grains, fruits, and vegetables.*

The missing numbers in the B series reflect the inexactness of science. Over the years there were many "discoveries" of water-soluble vitamins that later turned out to be false. Some had already been assigned a number in the B series, so when they were finally rejected, the number was discarded as well.

## Fat-Soluble Vitamins

There are four fat-soluble vitamins: A, D, E, and K. Beta-carotene, which can be transformed by the body into vitamin A is not considered a vitamin in its own right. Unlike water-soluble vitamins, fat-soluble vitamins are not excreted through the urine; they remain in body tissues until they are either used up or broken down. Here a description of their functions in the body, along with some good food sources:

**Vitamin A** (retinol or beta-carotene): Needed for proper vision and skin health; has antioxidant abilities and may protect against infection and certain cancers.

*Sources: liver and fish liver oils, vitamin A fortified foods, egg yolk; beta-carotene found in carrots, leafy green vegetables, sweet potatoes, squash, apricots, and cantaloupes.*

**Vitamin D:** Needed for healthy bones and teeth—necessary for the absorption of dietary calcium.

*Sources: fortified dairy products, fish, fish oils, egg yolk; also manufactured by body when directly exposed to sunlight.*

**Vitamin E** (tocopherol): As an antioxidant, vitamin E protects fats and cell membranes from free-radical destruction; also helps form red blood cells.

*Sources: wheat germ, nuts and seeds, whole grains, vegetable oils, and green leafy vegetables.*

**Vitamin K:** Required for normal blood clotting.

*Sources: turnip greens and other leafy vegetables, cruciferous vegetables, whole grains, and green tea.*

## Too Much Is Not Good

When present in greater-than-required quantities, excess water-soluble vitamins are extracted by the kidneys and excreted in the urine. As a result, there is little danger from a long-term build-up of these compounds. With fat-soluble vitamins, however, the body stores any excess in areas such as the liver or the fat tissue. If excessive amounts are continually taken, there's an increased risk of buildup to a toxic level.

## Neither Animal nor Vegetable

A mineral is loosely defined as anything in nature that is not animal or vegetable. For nutrition purposes, though, minerals are defined as follows:

• Minerals are inorganic chemical elements.

• Relative to protein, fats and carbohydrates, minerals are needed only in trace amounts.

• Minerals don't provide any calories.

• Minerals are required for use in specific structures or metabolic functions.

• Minerals are neither synthesized nor changed by the body.

• Their absence from the diet leads to a failure to thrive and the development of a deficiency disease.

• All minerals can be found in foods.

## The Minerals We Need

Of the 15 required minerals, six are required in relatively large amounts. These include calcium, phosphorous, magnesium, potassium, chloride, and sodium. The remaining nine are equally essential, but are needed in only trace amounts: iron, zinc, iodine, manganese, selenium, copper, fluoride, chromium, and molybdenum. Here is a list of the minerals, their functions in the body, and good food sources:

**Calcium:** Needed primarily for bones (99 percent of body calcium is in the bones) and teeth, but also for muscle contraction, normal heart rhythm, blood clotting, enzyme production, and nerve transmission.

*Sources: milk and milk products, green leafy vegetables, sardines and other small fish with edible bones, oysters, almonds, broccoli, dried figs and apricots, navy beans, tofu, almonds, brazil nuts, and blackstrap molasses.*

**Chloride:** Forms digestive acid in the stomach; needed for fluid and acid/base balance in the body.

*Sources: salt (sodium chloride), meat, fish and poultry.*

**Chromium:** Functions as part of glucose-tolerance factor, a substance that works with insulin to regulate blood-sugar level.

*Sources: whole grains, peanuts, organ meats, legumes, molasses, cheeses, and brewer's yeast.*

**Copper:** Helps in the formation of red blood cells; essential for normal hair and skin; needed for antioxidant enzyme production and normal respiration.

*Sources: organ meats, shellfish, meats, legumes, nuts, raisins, and mushrooms.*

**Fluoride:** Encourages hardness of bones of teeth and helps prevent tooth decay.

*Sources: fluoridated water, fish, and tea.*

**Iodine:** Needed for normal activity of thyroid gland and is essential for normal cell activities.

*Sources: seafood, sea vegetables, iodized salt, and foods grown on iodine-rich soil.*

**Iron:** Key mineral for two oxygen-carrying compounds—hemoglobin in red blood cells, and myoglobin in muscle cells; also involved in immune system.

*Sources: red meats, liver, egg yolk, poultry, fish and eggs, iron fortified cereals, breads or rice, nuts, seeds, legumes, dried fruits, and some dark green leafy vegetables.*

**Magnesium:** Needed for normal bones (half of body's magnesium is in the bones), and required for normal nerve transmission, muscle relaxation, and normal heart rhythm.

*Sources: nuts, bananas, legumes, whole grains, avocado, dark leafy greens, milk, and oysters.*

**Manganese:** Helps in the formation of bones and connective tissue, and needed for normal metabolism, reproduction, and digestion.

*Sources: whole grains, tea, raisins, nuts, legumes, and leafy vegetables.*

**Molybdenum:** Needed for key metabolic enzymes, helps form compounds required for iron utilization, and required for normal growth and development.

*Sources: whole grains, legumes, milk and dark green vegetables (depends on soil content).*

**Phosphorous:** Primarily found in bones and teeth, but widely distributed throughout body for general metabolism.

*Sources: meat, poultry, eggs, legumes, fish, whole grains, and nuts.*

**Potassium**: Works with sodium to help regulate the body's fluid balance; also needed for muscle contraction and normal heart rhythm.

*Sources: most fruits, legumes, vegetables, meats, and fish.*

**Selenium**: Needed to create key antioxidant enzyme that acts as a free-radical scavenger designed to protect against cell damage.

*Sources: seafood, whole grains and vegetables grown in selenium-rich soil, and organ meats.*

**Sodium**: Works with potassium to help maintain fluid balance; also is involved in the regulation of blood pressure.

*Sources: salt, seasoning salts, smoked and other cured foods, and most processed foods.*

**Zinc**: Plays a role in many enzymes, including those involved in detoxification, sex-hormone production, and wound healing; also involved in taste and smell.

*Sources: shellfish, seafood, liver, meat, nuts, legumes, milk and milk products, eggs, whole grains, corn, and wheat germ.*

## Mineral Overdose

It's dangerous to take too much, especially where the trace elements are concerned. For example, there is a narrow margin of safety between the RDA for iron (18 milligrams for women) and the minimum adult toxic dose of 100 milligrams. Another reason to use caution is because minerals often work in conjunction with each other; taking an excess of a single mineral can throw off the body's delicate balance.

## Fortified Foods

Most of us take vitamin and mineral supplements without even knowing it. Through fortification and enrichment, vitamins and minerals are added to processed foods. Breakfast cereals are a good example. The vitamins and minerals flaunted in ads don't come from the grain—they're added to the cereal formula before the final product is made. Cereals are not alone. Vitamin D is added to milk, fruit juices contain added vitamin C, and rice and most flours are enriched with thiamin, niacin, iron, and riboflavin.

Any vitamin or mineral listed on an ingredient statement, is an indication that the nutrient was purposefully added to the product. The reason? Often it's to replace nutrients that were lost during processing. Sometimes, however, critical nutrients are added to commonly consumed food staples to reduce the danger of widespread deficiencies.

## To Go Further

See also: To Pill or Not to Pill and Recommended Daily Allowances.

# How Food Works
## in Your Body

# The Wonderful World of Digestion
*It all begins when you swallow*

## Understanding Is Key to Eating Right

The body likes things simple. Food, by contrast, is a complex combination of different types and sizes of nutrients and nonnutrient ingredients. In order for your body to absorb what food contains, it first has to take it apart piece by piece. This assembly line, or should we say *dis*assembly line, is our digestive system.

The "workers" along your digestive tract are enzymes—chemicals with specific abilities to pull apart the proteins, carbohydrates, or fats in food. The digestive system is the epitome of specialization in that each of its enzymes can perform only one type of action on one type of nutrient. For example, one enzyme specializes in splitting big proteins into smaller pieces, but a different one is needed to complete the job. As a result, the normal digestive system requires over a dozen different enzymes to digest a typical meal. The beauty of the human digestive system is that it's specifically designed for a mixed diet. Different types of food are handled in specific areas. That's the reason we don't have to eat our foods one at a time.

## Before the First Bite

Digestion starts even before we begin eating. When you're hungry, just thinking about food is enough to start the saliva running into your mouth, the fluids into your stomach, and to prime the muscles of the stomach for the meal about to head its way.

Saliva is mostly water, but it also contains enzymes that begin the work of breaking down carbohydrates. Giving each mouthful a good chew aids digestion because it mixes the food with saliva. This not only helps carbohydrate digestion, it makes the food easier to swallow through the esophagus and into the stomach.

30

## Entering the Stomach

The muscular stomach churns the food into chyme, a liquid mass with a creamy consistency that then enters the small intestines. While in the stomach, food is exposed to strong digestive acids and enzymes. This causes the structure of food to crumble and prepares it for further digestion and absorption.

Carbohydrates tend to pass through the stomach quickest, followed by proteins and then fats, which take the longest to be released. The stomach protects itself from its own corrosive chemicals with a mucous layer that insulates it from the food being digested.

## The Small Intestine: An Enzyme Factory

As the chyme departs the stomach, it is immediately doused with the body's own antacid solution. Your meal is now in the small intestines—a virtual enzyme factory where the main part of digestion and absorption takes place. Enzymes and other digestive aids produced in the liver, pancreas, and small intestines are unleashed upon the chyme in an orderly fashion. There are specific areas in the small intestines where different nutrients are absorbed. If all goes well, by the time your food reaches its respective absorptive surfaces, digestible carbohydrates have been broken down into simple sugars, proteins have been reduced to amino acids, and fats have been separated into individual fatty acids.

## What About Vitamins, Minerals, and Fiber?

Vitamins and minerals don't require digestion, but to be absorbed by the body, they need to be separated from the food in which they came. Some vitamins and minerals are absorbed alone, but others have to be ushered in with a special carrier substance that's produced by the body and released into the digestive tract.

For example, the fat-soluble vitamins need to hook on to a fatty acid to gain entrance. Vitamin B12 needs to link with a protein called "intrinsic factor," which is released by the stomach. And calcium and certain forms of iron have to find their respective "binding proteins" before they can be absorbed.

Fiber is unique in that the digestive system lacks the enzymes to break it down. As a result, the fiber in our food makes the complete trip from the mouth, through the stomach and small intestine, and into the large intestines. This undigested fiber adds to the bulk of the stool which is eventually eliminated from the body.

## Finishing Up the Job

Once food enters the large intestine, which includes the colon and rectum, most of digestion is over. The remaining task is to absorb water. This action prepares the undigested residue of the chyme for eventual elimination through the rectum.

The large intestine is not an empty tube, however; it is inhabited by a host of bacteria, called the intestinal flora, that live off the part of food our body does not absorb. Occasionally, food arriving in the large intestines includes carbohydrates that the body had trouble digesting. This might include some of the complex carbohydrates found in beans and other legumes, or the milk sugar (lactose) in those who have trouble digesting milk. When this happens, the intestinal flora devour these compounds and give off methane and other gases as a byproduct. This can contribute to bloating and the production of gas, or flatus.

## Flatulence Facts

Since foods affect people differently, any of a wide variety can appear on a particular person's "gas" list. Common culprits include dairy products, beans and other legumes, as well as certain grains, cereals, vegetables, nuts, and seeds. Beans, lentils, and other legumes have a notorious reputation for gas because they contain a type of carbohydrate the body does not completely digest.

The gassy nature of foods, though, can even vary from meal to meal. For example, a large glass of skim milk or a bowl of beans on an empty stomach would probably produce more gas than the same serving eaten with a meal. This is explained by the slower rate at which a meal's combination of protein, fat, and carbohydrates travels through the digestive system. When it finally arrives at the large intestines, there's a mixture of materials to occupy the attention of the bacterial flora. On the other hand, when a single gassy food is eaten, though, the flora focus on the one, problem-causing material.

It's also known that some people tolerate large servings of foods that cause excessive gas in others. It's unclear how much of this is due to differences in digestive ability, how often we eat a particular food, or even such factors as whether we're relaxed or anxious, the speed at which we eat, or how completely we chew.

If you are constantly bothered by gas, start keeping a food diary. On the days your problem is most bothersome, make a note of the foods you have eaten, the meal conditions, and even your state of mind. Often a pattern emerges that can give you hints about ways to eat, methods of preparation, or more tolerable serving sizes. In addition, over-the-counter food supplements can help with a couple of the more troublesome carbohydrates. Lactase pills or drops supply the enzyme that digests the gas-causing lactose. Or you can simply drink lactose-reduced milk.

As with any physical complaint, be sure to discuss the situation with your health professional. Although food is usually the cause of flatulence, any digestive upset may be a reaction to medication or a sign of other problems that should be investigated more thoroughly.

## Related Topics

Recently, a New Jersey company began marketing a liquid product called Beano, which they claim breaks apart the gas-causing carbohydrates in legumes and other vegetables. They offer free samples via their toll-free number (1-800-257-8650).

For an in-depth focus on digestive problems, try *Your Gut Feelings* (Consumers Union, Mt Vernon, NY 1987) by H. Janowitz, M.D. See also: Allergies and Other Adverse Reactions, Benevolent Bugs, Carbohydrates, and Protein.

# How What You Eat Can Improve Your Health

# Eating for a Healthy Heart

*The facts may surprise you*

## Heart Disease Is With Us

We're still losing the war against heart disease. There has been some progress, in that fewer people are dying, but the prevalence of the nation's number-one killer disease remains unchanged. Optimistic statistics may be nothing more than a reflection of improved methods of diagnosis and medical treatment.

The reason for the lack of progress is as simple as it is profound: We're not focusing on the real problem. The American public has been persuaded to wear blinders that only let them see fat and cholesterol as *the key dietary factors causing heart disease.* While there's little question that fat and cholesterol play a role in heart disease, they are not the unqualified culprits we've been led to believe.

## Cholesterol's Split Personality

Cholesterol is a waxy substance that does not dissolve in the human body's water-based blood. As such it has to be shuttled around the blood inside fat-carrying proteins called lipoproteins. Most of the cholesterol in the body is manufactured in the liver. When cholesterol is present in the foods we eat, the liver is programmed to make less.

There are four basic types of lipoproteins, but two appear to play important roles in heart disease. The first, called low-density lipoprotein (LDL), can be thought of as the carrier of cholesterol into general circulation. The second, called high-density lipoprotein (HDL), shuttles cholesterol on its way out of the body. As the proportion of blood cholesterol traveling in the LDLs goes up, so does your risk of heart disease. By contrast, as the cholesterol in the HDLs goes up, your risk decreases. Because of this, it's convenient to think of LDLs as the "least desirable" and HDLs as the "highly desirable" forms of cholesterol.

## The Real Lowdown on Cholesterol

Heart disease results when there's a blockage preventing blood flow through the arteries that service the heart muscle. A stroke occurs when there's a blockage in the blood vessels that supply the brain. In both cases, such blockages often begin as a kind of scratch, or lesion, on the inner lining of the artery. The failure of a blood vessel can be life-threatening. So after such an injury is detected, the body immediately takes steps to repair the damage and wall off the affected area.

Cholesterol is a key ingredient in this repair process. It makes up part of the "plaster" over the injured area. The amount of cholesterol "blockage" in the blood vessels depends, in part, upon the level of injury to the tissues. As the damage to blood vessels increases, so to does the blood cholesterol level. The level of LDLs also will be high as LDL is the carrier for cholesterol when it's on its repair missions.

As you can tell from this scenario, cholesterol is not the responsible party; it's only present because of the problem. Thus our continued focus on cutting cholesterol out of the diet and lowering blood cholesterol as ends in themselves may help explain why our efforts against heart disease are going so poorly.

## Oxidized Fats: The True Culprits

The real villains in heart disease are those agents responsible for blood-vessel damage in the first place. It now looks as though the main source of this damage has to do with oxygen. Although necessary for life, oxygen in the wrong place at the wrong time has a nasty tendency to react with fatty substances and turn them into harmful compounds. Scientists have discovered that these "oxidized" fats are directly responsible for the lesions that initiate the artery-clogging buildups.

Oxidized fats enter the body in two ways: through diet, or when oxygen reacts with fats already present in your system. Dietary sources of oxidized fats are foods containing rancid fats, those fried in unsaturated oils, and cholesterol-containing dried-food products, such as powdered eggs.

## Diet for a Healthy Heart

There is no way to avoid all oxidized fat. So before you cease your sauteing and throw out your frying pans, it's important to appreciate that there's a sophisticated two-pronged defense system set up to protect the body from this type of harm. One aspect prevents fats from being oxidized, and the other neutralizes those fats that have already had their deleterious dose of oxygen.

To be at their best, these defenses depend on a daily supply of antioxidant nutrients from the diet. Here's a list of these antioxidant nutrients together with their food sources (check the Appendix for a listing of recommended amounts):

• Vitamin E: Wheat germ, nuts and seeds, and their oils.

• Beta-carotene: Sweet potato, papaya, apricots, and dark yellow and green vegetables.

• Vitamin A: The body makes vitamin A from beta-carotene; preformed vitamin A is found in fortified foods, egg yolks, and liver.

• Vitamin C: Citrus, tropical fruits, melons, berries, peppers, broccoli.

• Selenium: Seafood, cereals, meats, whole grains, brazil nuts.

• Zinc: Oysters, whole grains, seafood, organ meats.

## Other Dietary Considerations

Cutting back on dietary fat has merit. Not only does it limit your intake of oxidized fats, it decreases the amount of fats circulating in the bloodstream after a meal. Making better dietary choices, such as fewer fried foods, can effectively lower your blood cholesterol level, too. It's also important to decrease your intake of partially hydrogenated fats. These have been shown to unnaturally increase the number of cholesterol-carrying LDLs in the bloodstream—a step that can stimulate the development of cholesterol blockages.

For those already suffering from heart disease or who have a family history of heart problems, both of these steps are essential. But cutting back on fat and cholesterol does only half the job.

Giving your body the nutrients it needs to protect itself is just as essential. Such an approach can make the difference between a continued stalemate and a forward offensive in the war against heart disease.

## To Find Out More

Read *Dr. Dean Ornish's Program for Reversing Heart Disease* (Ballantine, NY 1990), D. Ornish, M.D.; *Fight Fat and Win* (DCI, Minneapolis 1990) by E. Moquette-Magee, M.P.H., R.D.; *Controlling Your Fat Tooth* (Workman Publishing, NY 1991) by J. Piscatella; and *The McDougall Program* (Penguin, NY 1991) by J. McDougall, M.D.

See also: Dietary Fat, The Dangers of Once-Friendly Fats, Beta-carotene: The Nutrient with Something Special, Fiber for Health, and To Pill or Not To Pill.

# Fiber for Health

*Bulk up, folks*

## Fiber Is Our Friend

Dietary fiber is a type of carbohydrate that's found only in plant products such as vegetables, nuts, fruits, and grains. Nutrition research has associated a high-fiber diet with a lower risk of diabetes, diverticulitis, hemorrhoids, ulcerative colitis, certain forms of cancer, and coronary heart disease. Fiber is also commonly used as a remedy for constipation.

That's an imposing set of talents, and it's particularly impressive when you consider that fiber does not contribute any calories, essential vitamins, or minerals to the body. In fact, it's not digested by the body at all! How can a substance we can't even digest be so healthful? The very fact that you can't digest it is what turns out to be its greatest asset.

## Why Isn't Fiber Digested?

If we think of food as nutrients linked together by padlocks, digestion is the process of opening the locks. It is only after the chain is broken into smaller pieces that the body can absorb and use the nutrients. Digestive enzymes are the keys that open the locks. Fiber is unique because the body lacks the right keys to open its locks. This means that instead of being absorbed, fiber becomes part of the bulk that passes through the entire digestive system and eventually is eliminated from the body.

## Not All Fiber is Equal

The word *fiber* is really an umbrella term. As it travels through the body, what a fiber does depends on how it's built. An important distinction is whether the fiber dissolves in water; so there are two types of dietary fiber: insoluble and soluble, and their health benefits differ.

## Insoluble Fiber

The most familiar of the insoluble fibers is wheat bran, but this type is also in vegetables, fruits, and whole grains, such as corn, rye, barley, and brown rice. Insoluble fiber increases the bulk and weight of the stool as well as the rate at which food travels through your digestive system. This makes for potential benefits against cancer. Population studies routinely find that the incidence of colon cancer decreases as the intake of insoluble fiber goes up. That's because fiber can effectively dilute or even bind potential cancer-causing substances and quickly usher them out of the body.

Insoluble fiber can also bind bile salts, a digestive juice produced by the liver that helps with the absorption of dietary fats. Because the liver makes its bile salts from cholesterol, this binding action by insoluble fiber causes more cholesterol to leave the body.

## Soluble Fiber

Soluble fiber is found in oat and rice bran, legumes (beans, lentils, and peas), fruits, and vegetables. Although these fibers dissolve in water, the body cannot absorb them because of their large size. Soluble fiber can't match the ability of insoluble fiber to add bulk. It can, however, improve conditions connected with diabetes because it tends to slow the rate at which the body absorbs sugar. In addition, through a complex series of reactions, soluble fiber has a demonstrated ability to help lower blood cholesterol levels. You'll notice that fruits and vegetables contain both soluble and insoluble fiber. This is further testimony to the wisdom behind including them in the diet.

## How Much Should I Eat?

At present, the typical American diet contains about 12 to 15 grams of dietary fiber per day. Most authorities recommend doubling this to at least 25 to 30 grams.

## Fiber Sources
*(grams)*

| | | | |
|---|---|---|---|
| 1 slice whole wheat bread | 2 | 1 cup raw spinach | 2 |
| ½ cup all-bran cereal | 13 | 1 medium carrot | 2 |
| 1 cup cheerios | 1 | 1 oz. almonds | 3 |
| 1 Tbs. oat bran | 1 | ½ cup dried figs | 9 |
| 1 cup white rice | 1 | ½ cup dried apricots | 5 |
| 1 cup brown rice | 3 | 1 medium apple | 3 |
| 1 med. potato with skin | 5 | 1 banana | 3 |
| 1 med. sweet potato | 3 | 1 cup broccoli | 4 |
| 1 cup red kidney beans | 15 | 1 Tbs. peanut butter | 1 |

## The Skinny on Supplements

For years, people have been taking fiber supplements to relieve periodic constipation. Supplement use became more common as information on fiber's other benefits became known—especially soluble fiber's cholesterol-lowering potential.

It's important to understand, however, that when you add concentrated fiber to the diet, there is a greater chance of side effects such as bloating, cramps, diarrhea, and gas. In addition, loading up on fiber can interfere with the absorption of nutrients. This is a particular problem with supplements such as psyllium, the soluble fiber found in Metamucil (a popular over-the-counter aid intended for the relief of constipation). Medications may also be affected, so touch base with your health professional before adding any fiber supplements to your diet.

To add fiber to your diet, it's best not to rely on supplements. It makes more health sense to gradually shift to a diet based on fresh foods, with plenty of fruits, vegetables, legumes, and whole grains.

## To Learn More

I suggest: *The Fiber Prescription* (Fawcett/Ballantine, NY 1992) by M. Winick, M.D. See also: Eating for a Healthy Heart, The Wonderful World of Digestion, Carbohydrates, and Benevolent Bugs.

# Fiber Facts and Fads

*Oats on the bran stand*

## The Low Down on Oat Bran

By now oat bran has a war-weary media personality. After taking a fast track to food fame as a cholesterol-lowering aid, oat bran experienced a precipitous drop in popularity following media reports that smeared its reputation. The report in question came from a journal study that said oat bran was no better at lowering blood cholesterol than low-fiber wheat flour. Left out, however, was the fact that subjects in this particular study were young and middle-aged women with normal cholesterol levels. By contrast, most of the studies that established oat bran's cholesterol-lowering ability were performed on older men with elevated cholesterol levels.

The stage had been set, however, for this fall from grace. Oat bran had been overmarketed as a magic bullet that could turn virtually anything into cholesterol-busting health food. During its heyday, food manufacturers scrambled to add oat bran to everything under the sun. It could be said at the time that the only thing better than oat bran was more oat bran. Nutritionists seemed to sit on their hands as all this was happening. They seemed grateful that people were finally interested in adding fiber to their diets—even if it meant such bizarre creations as oat bran donuts.

An important lesson to be learned from this affair is the ongoing need for consumers to appreciate the nature of scientific journalism. When a research report makes the transition from journal to headline news, the dropping of key details can greatly influence the public's perception. A journalist with science savvy needs to be somewhere in the loop to make sure everything is handled correctly. With the debunking of oat bran, this didn't happen. The problem started with the announcement during a network newscast that oat bran had little effect; few other details were provided. The next morning, reports in the daily newspapers served only to echo the misinformation.

Oat bran was, and is, a good source of soluble fiber. Scientific studies continue to show that oat bran is a great addition to a healthy diet. If there is any dietary lesson to take from the oat-bran affair, it's that there are no magic bullets in nutrition. The healthfulness of a diet is measured by the foods we eat—not the fiber we add.

## Try Dried Fruit

Dried fruit is a fabulous, often overlooked source of fiber. Figs and dates contain 9 grams of fiber per half-cup serving; prunes contain 7 grams per serving and apricots and raisins contain 5 grams. By comparison, a slice of whole-wheat bread or a half-cup of broccoli contain about 2 grams of dietary fiber.

Besides their fiber content, dried fruit is also an excellent source of B vitamins and minerals. The pick of the group, though, is the fig. Prized since the time of the pyramids, figs are one of the richest nondairy sources of calcium. One half-cup serving of figs contains 144 milligrams of calcium, which on an ounce-by-ounce basis places them higher than milk. Figs are also a good source of iron, vitamin B-6, magnesium, and copper. Apricots are also a definite standout because one serving provides 25 percent of the U.S. RDA for iron and enough beta-carotene to satisfy almost 75 percent of the RDA for vitamin A.

These high-fiber fruits are perfect as a nutritious snack—at home, in a child's lunch box, or stashed in a drawer for a workday nibble. They're also good chopped up in cottage cheese or yogurt, or in cereals or pancake mixes, where they can eliminate the need for added sugar. By rotating among the different fruits, you lend flavor and variety to the morning routine while adding nutritional value to the meal.

Because these are high-fiber foods, it's best not to abruptly add any large quantities to your daily diet; the result could be an overstimulated digestive system. Try starting with a small serving and work up to a comfortable level. Portion control may also be needed with children. My six-year-old son, for example, loves apricots, figs, prunes, and raisins. He'd eat as much as I'd let him have, so I can't give him as many as he wants.

Be wary, however, of the fruit rolls and all those other types of fabricated fruit doodads aimed at youngsters. These pseudofruits use popular children's characters, such as Ghostbusters, Ninja Turtles, and Mario Brothers, as well as dinosaurs, clowns, and jet fighters. The apparent aim is to cajole parents into choosing the products as a convenient way to add fruit to their children's diet. Although these products boast being made with "real fruit," they're primarily a gummy fiberless sugar concoction that pales in comparison to the genuine article.

# Cutting Cancer Risk

*The foods you choose can help you*

## Facing the Reality

It is estimated that three out of four families in this country will experience some form of cancer. As frightening as this sounds, it's important to realize that cancer is a disease over which we have a remarkable degree of control—more than you might realize. A family history of cancer is not a legacy written in stone. You can inherit a greater risk of cancer, but whether you get cancer, depends on an interaction between that risk and a number of environmental and lifestyle factors.

Tobacco remains at the top of cancer risk list, being responsible for almost one-third of all cancer deaths in the U.S. The other major player is diet. Scientists now estimate that at least 50 percent of all cancers can be prevented by changes in diet. What we eat (or fail to eat) will either help or hurt our body's anti-cancer campaign.

## What Is Cancer?

Simply put, cancer stems from a "mistake" in a cell's DNA—the inherited genetic blueprint that tells a cell what to do. Substances that alter genes fall into two categories: *mutagens* cause genetic changes that may or may not lead to cancer; *carcinogens* alter genes in ways known to cause cancer.

The immune system, the body's internal police force, is designed to recognize foreign substances as well as irregular cells. As a result, most aberrant cells are identified and eliminated before any harm is done. Cancer takes root either when the immune system is not up to par, or when the cell is reprogrammed in a way that confounds any attempts at control. But even then, cancer is not a sure thing; precancerous cells can survive only if conditions favor their growth.

46

## What You Eat Does Matter

Key watchwords for any healthy diet are *variety* and *moderation*. Variety helps to broaden your nutritional horizons; moderation lessens the risk from overemphasizing any one food. In the case of diet and cancer, this has particular significance.

Here's one example. A potent carcinogen named aflatoxin is produced by a mold that grows on peanuts. Although food processing companies try to remove all the moldy peanuts before they get used, someone who eats peanut butter every day stands a greater risk of being exposed to this carcinogen than someone who eats it only occasionally. By eating a varied diet, you lessen your chances of overloading on any one carcinogen.

Therefore, there are two fundamentals to an effective anti-cancer diet: Limit your intake of foods associated with a higher incidence of cancer, and increase consumption of those foods that keep the body healthy and bolster its defenses.

## Food to Restrict

As a rule, it's best to limit your intake of foods known to contain higher levels of mutagens or carcinogens. These include salt-cured, smoked, and nitrite-preserved foods, such as hams or sausages. Barbecued foods, particularly those having a charred crust, should also be limited, and fish from suspect waters should be avoided.

Most epidemiological studies identify a high-fat, low-fiber diet as the type most often associated with a high incidence of cancer. The American Cancer Society supports the current guideline of limiting dietary fat to no more than 30 percent of calories. Some studies indicate, however, that even this may be too high, and recommend that fat intake be no more than 25 percent.

It may turn out that the type of fat is the key. In a large population study, scientists found no relationship between total fat intake and incidence of breast cancer. When they looked closer, however, a link was found between partially hydrogenated vegetable oil—a common fat in processed foods—and cancers of the breast and prostate.

## An Anti-cancer Diet?

To help reduce your chances of getting cancer, increasing dietary fiber is an important first step. There's a large body of evidence that associates dietary fiber with a decreased incidence of colon cancer. There's also preliminary evidence that a high fiber intake may protect against breast cancer as well as other cancers.

Whenever possible include those foods that contain antioxidant nutrients. These nutrients have a proven ability to stop or suppress many of the elements known to contribute to the cancer process. These nutrients, and some of their food sources, include the following:

• Beta-carotene: Dark yellow and green vegetables.
• Vitamin C: Citrus, peppers.
• Selenium: Seafood, cereals, meats, whole grains.
• Zinc: Meats, whole grains, seafood.
• Vitamin E: Wheat germ, nuts and seeds, and their oils.
• Vitamin A: Vitamin A-fortified foods, organ meats.
• Omega-3 fats: Fish, such as salmon or halibut, and flax-seed oil.

Cruciferous vegetables, which includes cabbage, Brussels sprouts, cauliflower, kale and broccoli, are also foods to include in your anti-cancer diet. They appear to contain substances that have an additional anti-cancer effect aside from that which comes from their vitamin, mineral or fiber content.

Yogurt too may turn out to be an important anti-cancer weapon. A recent clinical study at the University of California at Davis found that a daily intake of yogurt (with active cultures) had a positive effect on the immune system.

## Diet Isn't Everything

The body does not passively wait for cancer to develop. It has a host of defensive systems set up to prevent cancer from occurring. However, as widespread and effective as the defensive potential might be, if the anti-cancer guns are nutritionally unmanned, the cancer process has a better chance of gaining ground. Finally, although good nutrition can protect us, it cannot make us tobacco, excess sun, or harmful chemicals are going to take their toll, regardless of what we eat.

## To Learn More

I suggest *Cancer and Nutrition* (Avery, Garden City Park, NJ, 1992) by C. Simone, M.D.; *The Complete Book of Cancer Prevention* (Rodale Press, Emmaus, PA 1988); and *Nutrition for the Chemotherapy Patient* (Bull Publishing, Palo Alto, CA 1990) by J.L. Ramstack, Ph.D. See also: Fiber for Health, Beta-carotene: The Nutrient with Something Special, Eating to Bolster Your Immune System, Chronobiology, Barbecued Food: License to Grill?, Seafood Safety, and Benevolent Bugs.

# Fish Oil & Health

*Oil's well that swims well*

## Certain Fats Are Friendly

Many people consider fat to be the consummate dietary villain. One type, however, can be a boon to your health. This fat contains a type of fatty acid called Omega-3 and it's found in seafood and some seed oils.

Here's the lowdown on this latest nutritional twist: About five years ago, a group of reports touted the role of fish in preventing heart disease. Since then benefits have been reported for rheumatoid arthritis, high blood pressure, ulcerative colitis, psoriasis, and complications from diabetes.

All the research has pointed to the oils in fish as the source of these unique properties. More recently, these oils have been used in animal studies to successfully inhibit the cancer process. This growing evidence has improved our understanding of how fats work in the body, and also attests to the importance of fish in a healthy diet.

## The Skinny on Omega-3 Fats

Omega-3 fatty acids are a type of polyunsaturated oil that is manufactured by plants that grow in the sea and a few that grow on land. The fish that eat these sea plants (as well as the fish that eat those fish) accumulate these fatty acids in their bodies. These are mainly the varieties of fish found in cold water. On land, there's a generous supply of omega-3 fatty acids in flax-seed (linseed oil), and smaller amounts in walnut, soybean, and canola oils, and wheat germ.

One safety note: Fresh fish should always smell fresh. The Omega-3 fatty acids are highly reactive and will go rancid when exposed to warm air and give off the unpleasant smell we associate with spoiling fish. At this point the fatty acids (as well as the fish) are no longer fit for consumption.

## Why They're Special

Although the bulk of the fat in our bodies is used as a source and storage form of energy, a small amount is used to form powerful hormone-like compounds with tongue-twisting names like prostaglandins and thromboxanes. There are many different types which all behave differently, but they all help control how the body operates. It turns out that the type of fats we eat help determine which ones get made. When omega-3 fatty acids are in our diet, our bodies manufacture those types of control compounds that have a more healthful effect. Therefore, current recommendations are to eat at least two, 4-ounce servings of fish per week.

## Health Benefits Galore

A heart attack occurs when a blood clot blocks the flow of blood through an artery. Omega-3 fats reduce the stickiness of the blood cells, called platelets, that clump together to form clots. In experiments where fish consumption is increased, blood clots form at a slower rate and the incidence of heart attacks is significantly less.

Omega-3 fats also help moderate high blood pressure. In studies, when patients having chronically elevated blood pressure, called "essential hypertension," switched to a fish-based diet, their blood pressure decreased significantly. Improvement has also been noted in the immune system. In separate controlled studies, symptoms of rheumatoid arthritis and ulcerative colitis improved when volunteers were fed high levels of omega-3 fats in capsule form.

The anti-cancer potential of these oils is also encouraging. It's thought that diets high in fat represent a risk factor for cancer. But the cancer level is low in populations in which the high-fat diet is based on fish. One study involving 26 countries discovered that the incidence of breast cancer decreased as fish consumption rose.

# Where can I Find These Wonder Fats?

## Omega-3 Fatty Acid Content
*(Grams per 4 oz. serving)*

| | | | |
|---|---|---|---|
| Anchovies (canned in oil) | 2.3 | Trout (rainbow) | 0.7 |
| Perch (Atlantic) | 0.3 | Mackerel (Atlantic) | 1.8 |
| Bass (striped) | 0.9 | Tuna (bluefin) | 1.4 |
| Salmon (king, chinook) | 1.7 | Oysters (Pacific) | 1.0 |
| Halibut | 0.5 | Whitefish | 1.6 |
| Sardines (Pacific, canned) | 1.8 | 1 Tbs. food-grade linseed oil | 7.5 |
| Herring (Pacific) | 1.9 | 1 oz. (7 nuts) walnuts | 1.6 |

Because fish from polluted waters can be a source of contamination, it's best to avoid fish caught or raised near industrial plants. Better to stick with varieties from offshore or deep-sea areas, or from lakes and streams known to be free from harmful chemicals. Always strive for variety in the types of fish you select.

Incidently, when preparing fish, it's best to trim away the dark-fleshed area on the underbody as this tends to be the place where contaminants, if any, will be deposited. Trimming the fish in this way does *not* eliminate all omega-3 fatty acids as much of it resides in the meaty portion.

### To Learn More

Three helpful books to check are: *Eat Fish, Live Better,* (Harper & Row, 1989) by Anne M. Fletcher, M.S., R.D.; *The Omega-3 Phenomenon,* (Rawson Associates, 1987) by Donald Rudin M.D. and Clara Felix; and *Fish, The Basics,* (Simon & Schuster, 1990) by Shirley King. The American Seafood Institute has a seafood hotline with experts who can answer your questions about preparation, storage, and nutrition value: 800-328-3474 (M-F, 9am-5pm EST). See also: Seafood Safety, Dietary Fat.

# Eating to Bolster Your Immune System
*May the force be with you*

## We Need Strong Immune Systems

The world is filled with unseen microorganisms, many capable of causing serious illness if allowed to grow in our bodies. The skin is our first line of defense. But often these bugs manage to slip in via a cut or one of the body's openings (nose, mouth, etc.). At that point, the responsibility lies with the immune system to conquer the invaders before they gain the upper hand.

The immune system is the body's internal security force. Not only does it help control how often we get sick, it plays an important role in determining how long we take to recover. What you eat helps determine whether your immune system functions like the A Team or a bunch of bungling amateurs.

The implications of a malfunctioning immune system don't stop at a few infections or colds every year. This vital system is also responsible for identifying and discarding cells that have undergone unplanned mutations—the first small step on the way to cancer.

## Eating for Health

Our understanding of the effect of nutrition on the immune system began over 30 years ago. Then, as now, malnutrition was followed by an increased susceptibility to infectious disease, an indicator of a disabled immune system. Our understanding of the relationship between nutrition and the immune system has grown along with our ability to explain how various nutrients influence immunity.

The nutrients in food provide the raw materials for the manufacture of the immune system's arsenal of weapons. Besides our basic need for protein and calories, the list of immunity-related nutrients has grown to include several vitamins, minerals, and certain fats. The foods listed below includes representatives of the fruits, grains, vegetables, dairy, and meat groups—another strong statement of the value of a varied diet.

The relationship between nutrition and the immune system is of particular importance to hospitalized patients, alcoholics, and the elderly. It's not uncommon for individuals in these groups to have an immune system that's not up to par. If the cause is a deficient diet, the immune system will usually spring back after needed nutrients are again provided.

## Immunity Good Guys

It's known that a diet deficient in any of the following factors lessens the immune system's ability to protect the body:

• Beta-carotene (breaks down into vitamin A): Dark green, deep orange or yellow vegetables, and some fruits.

• Vitamin E: Wheat germ, nuts and seeds such as almonds and peanuts, and whole grains.

· Vitamin $B_6$: Chicken, fish, liver, pork, and eggs. Also brown rice, soybeans, whole wheat, oats, peanuts, and walnuts.

• Vitamin C: Fresh fruits, especially citrus, and vegetables.

• Vitamin A: Foods fortified with vitamin A, organ meat.

· Folic acid: Liver, yeast, leafy vegetables, legumes, and some fruits.

• Zinc: Mainly found in animal products, such as meat, liver, eggs, and seafood (especially oysters). Whole grains also contain lesser amounts.

• Iron: Meats, eggs, vegetables, and cereals, many of which are fortified with iron.

· Selenium: Seafood, liver, and other meats; also found in some grains, depending on the selenium content of the soil in which they're grown.

• Omega-3 fatty acids: Fish oils and flax-seed oil, and to a lesser degree canola, almond, and walnut oil.

## Can You Supercharge Your Immune System?

It would be great if you could supercharge your immune system by taking megadoses of the above nutrients, but its unclear whether the body can work that way. And, with a number of these nutrients there's a fine line between dose and overdose. For example, selenium, vitamin A, zinc, and iron can be toxic at high levels. And with the exception of beta-carotene, all the nutrients listed above can have negative side effects at elevated levels.

Periodically, though, we hear of studies touting the benefits from higher-than-RDA intakes. How much, then, is enough, and at what point does increased intake become an overdose? Unfortunately, at the present time, science doesn't have an answer to these questions. Defining an optimal intake depends on your genetic makeup together with your age, sex, lifestyle, and general state of health.

Have as your primary goal a diet that provides a full recommended dietary allowance of the above nutrients. There's nothing wrong with taking a supplement to ensure an adequate intake of these important dietary factors. Supplements should not, however, be looked upon as a way to turn a poor diet into a healthy one.

## Future Possibilities

Our ever-expanding knowledge of the interaction between nutrition and immunity holds great promise. Perhaps one day we'll be able to use nutrients to fine tune our immunity for specific purposes. Imagine a nutrition regimen specifically tailored to give the immune system a boost against arthritis, cancer, or this year's version of the flu. While the time is not yet here, the pieces of the puzzle are rapidly falling into place.

## To Learn More

Check out *Prevention Magazine's 30-day Immune Power Program* (Rodale Press, Emmaus, PA, 1992) by E. Michaud. See also: To Pill or Not to Pill, Beta-carotene: The Nutrient with Something Special, Garlic, Aging in Good Health, Cutting Cancer Risk, Eating for a Healthy Heart, Nutrition for a Stressful Lifestyle, Fried Food Facts, and Allergies and Other Adverse Reactions.

# Is it the Diet or the Dieter?

*Guidelines for sensible weight loss*

## The Dieting Maze

There are a host of dieting options, from do-it-yourself regimens to over-the-counter diet pills and milk shakes to formal diet programs. While clever gimmicks and persuasive testimonials might lure you—and you even might succeed at dropping a few pounds—ultimate success comes down to this: Is the method a temporary fix, or does it help you keep weight off for good?

Failure at weight loss is so common that many experts say it's the likely result of any attempt to shed unwanted pounds. Studies focusing on long-term follow-up often find that only 5 to 10 percent of dieters manage to keep the weight off.

If you number among those planning to tackle a weight problem, here are a few strategies to help improve your odds for success. A key first step is understanding what you're up against.

## Why Is It So Hard?

We tend to consider a weight-loss diet to be a planned event. But it's important to realize that a diet comes as a total surprise to the body, whose many control systems cannot recognize the difference between a diet and an actual famine. Though we might have an idea how long the diet will last, the body is not in the loop; it assumes that a scarcity of food is the new status quo, and its innate drive for survival is activated. Similar to the way you would cut back on spending if your salary were cut, the body shifts into economy mode. Exactly what happens depends on the severity of the diet. Actions might include a slowing of metabolism, lowering of body temperature, or other cutbacks that leave you feeling short of energy and interested in sleep.

## The Yo-Yo Effect

It's hard enough going through the hunger pangs, headaches,

and exhaustion. But to be told there's a chance you'll end up fatter for the effort is simply intolerable. Yet it happens. People who continually try to lose weight—unsuccessfully—may end up in worse shape than if they hadn't tried in the first place. What gives the body this seemingly cruel streak?

To lose weight, the body has to dip into its energy reserves. This is triggered by lowering our calorie intake and upping our activity level until the body needs more calories than it's ingesting. However, as it starts to draw upon its calorie savings account—the fat deposits—the body gets defensive about losing its energy nest egg.

Similar to how we might hoard our savings after a job layoff, the body becomes more stingy with its energy after we "go off" a diet. The net effect of repeated cycles of feast and famine is a body with a greater tendency to hold on to its fat. Studies have found that during and after weight loss, there's often a decrease in the rate at which calories are burned when the body rests. This decrease in energy use is thought to be an important reason why it's so difficult to maintain weight loss.

### Who Meets With Success?

Although many studies have focused on the type of diet, too little attention has been given to the personality of the dieter. Are there traits shared by people having similar weight-loss experiences? If so, can we use this information to guide people toward programs better suited to their needs?

To begin answering these questions, a joint project was conducted through Kaiser Permanente in Oakland, CA, the Department of Public Health at UC Berkeley, and the Department of Nutrition at UC Davis. The study involved women in three groups: relapsers, who had lost weight and then regained it; maintainers, who lost weight and kept it off, and controls, women who had always maintained a static non-obese weight.

The volunteers were questioned on weight history, dieting history, childhood food experiences, meal and snacking patterns, emotion-related eating, and methods used for handling troubling situations.

## Fascinating Results

Several significant differences were noted. Relapsers were more likely to take appetite suppressants and participate in formal weight-loss programs; they typically skipped breakfast and went on restrictive diets that denied them many of the foods they enjoyed. Most maintainers, on the other hand, did not seek or want help from support groups, diet partners, or health professionals; relapsers would have liked even more assistance. When using the same approach to weight loss, relapsers adapted their lifestyle to the program while maintainers usually tailored the program to fit their lifestyle.

During the weight-loss period, both maintainers and relapsers reported stressful events involving family, jobs, or careers. However, maintainers tended to confront and work on these issues, while relapsers often resorted to avoidance behavior such as eating, sleeping, or drinking more, or simply wishing the problem would go away. Another significant finding was that 90 percent of the maintainers, versus 34 percent of relapsers, engaged in exercise at least three times a week.

## The Right Diet for You

All these findings point to personality as a significant determinant for success in long-term weight reduction. But more important, there's no such thing as a one-size-fits-all plan. While most commercial ventures suggest that their programs will work for anyone, their main accomplishment may be only a short-term loss. As suggested by the Kaiser study, people who seek treatment for a weight problem should be screened and guided into one that suits their personality. Additionally, regardless of what these programs' brochures claim, one day the program ends and you will have to call the shots.

### Becoming a Maintainer

It is possible to become a maintainer. In the Kaiser study, some of the maintainers had at one time been relapsers. But to make the change, relapsers not only had to learn how to lose weight, they had to take part in a program that understood and helped support some basic changes in personal habits. As often happens with new behavior, the road is rough in the beginning. But what you learn as part of your weight-loss regimen can eventually become a part of a normal pattern. For example, no longer would you exercise to lose weight; rather exercise becomes part of a new, healthier lifestyle that you enjoy in and of itself. The key seems to be not focusing solely on the diet. Changes in lifestyle, such as regular physical activity, can provide the energy drain to swing the balance—and this could be nothing more than a daily brisk walk.

### Define Your Goals

Before you begin, take a good long look at yourself and the other members of your family. Do you tend to gain weight without overeating? It's well established that a tendency to retain extra weight runs along family lines. Coming from a large-framed family doesn't mean you have to abandon hope of losing weight, but it can help you set realistic goals.

Next, understand that your motivation must come from within. Attempts to change your weight solely at the behest of others are usually doomed to failure. While you may drop pounds a plenty, your chances for long-term success are only as good as your personal commitment.

Many advertised programs may tout an ability to bring about radical change, but such results are not the norm. Your best approach is a long-term strategy, where changes are subtle and lasting as opposed to drastic and short-lived. And this gradual shift should not emphasize only reducing calories; it must include an activity component. Exercise not only burns calories, it checks the slowdown of the rate at which your body burns calories—a natural side effect of dieting.

## Strategies for Success

• **Meal planning:** Eat 3 meals a day and select definite portions before the meal. If you're still hungry after the main course, fill up on salad, low-calorie vegetables, fruits, and breads.

Meal composition may be equally as important as calories. In looking at weight changes in a group of 303 women over 1- and 2-year periods, scientists found that those who lowered their amount of dietary fat were more successful at weight loss than those who simply decreased their calories.

• **Drink plenty of liquids**: Adding more liquids to your diet, such as low-calorie beverages or soups and about eight glasses of water a day, provides fullness and helps cut down on the number of calories you eat.

• **Focus on 5-a-day**: Try to have at least five servings of fruits and vegetables every day. (A typical serving is a medium piece of fruit, 1 cup of a leafy vegetable, ½ cup of fruit or cooked vegetables, ¼ cup of dried fruit, or 6 ounces of fruit or vegetable juice.)

• **Eat slowly:** The body doesn't provide instant feedback that it has had enough food. Pace your meals to a minimum of 20 to 30 minutes in length. Eating rapidly until you're stuffed usually means you've had too much. If you like to snack, have low-calorie snacks available for those times when you're most likely to reach for a bite.

• **Keep your activity level up:** Introduce new activities, such as riding a bike or taking a walk. Set up a schedule, possibly as a commitment made with friends, in which you ride or walk together at least three times a week. Make walking and taking the stairs a part of your daily routine. Park away from the entrance to work or shops rather than hunting for the closest space.

• **Track your efforts and reward your accomplishments:** Select a way to score your progress, and set up a series of incentive rewards for reaching intermediate goals. Consider enlisting the help and participation of other family members.

Shift to a weekly or even a monthly weight check. Body weight is a sum of fat, muscle, bone, and water, and does not always reflect changes in body fat. Understand that there will be periods during which your scale weight will not change despite continued adherence to your plan. As you begin to lose weight, alter or replace clothes that no longer fit. You'll immediately know if lost pounds begin to reappear.

## Why Not You?

While grim success statistics might seem to justify keeping your dieting aspirations at bay, bear in mind that such results are usually based on follow-up of individuals enrolled in formal programs. And even with this, some people succeed—so why not you? With conviction and good planning, positive results can be achieved. And even if you fall short of your desired goal, the above strategies will definitely result in a healthier you.

## To Learn More

There are several helpful books about weight and weight-loss programs. An excellent review of diet programs can be found in *Diets that Work* (Lowell House, Los Angeles 1992) by D. Scanlon, R.D. Other recommended books include: *The New Fit or Fat* (Houghton Mifflin, Boston 1991) by C. Bailey, *The Callaway Diet: Successful Permanent Weight Control for Starvers, Stuffers and Skimpers* (Bantam, NY 1990) by C.W. Callaway, M.D.

As exercise is a vital component to any regimen, consider: *The Exercise Habit* (Human Kinetics, Champagne, IL 1992) by James Gavin, and *Great Shape: The First Fitness Guide for Large Women* (Bull Publishing, Palo Alto, CA 1992) by Pat Lyons.

After you've reached your target weight, there's *Now That You've Lost It: How to Maintain Your Best Weight* (Bull Publishing, Palo Alto, CA 1992) by Joyce Nash, and *The Weight Maintenance Survival Guide* (American Health Publications, NY 1990) by K. Brownell. See also: Vegetarianism Explored.

# Beta-carotene:
# The Nutrient With Something Special
*Why fruits and vegetables are so good for you*

## Mother Told You to Eat Your Vegetables
If there's ever been a compound to crow about, it's beta-carotene. This carrot-colored compound, found in most yellow and green vegetables, has garnered an excellent reputation among health scientists—and with good reason. It has to do with what's called the "vegetable effect."

Studies looking for links between diet and disease consistently find that the incidence of killer diseases, such as heart disease and certain cancers, goes down as the consumption of vegetables (and fruits) increases. Over the years scientists have been trying to learn what causes the "vegetable effect." Is it something in the vegetables themselves, or just the fact that the more vegetables you eat, the less room you might have for other, less-healthy fare? The presence of beta-carotene in many vegetables may be one of the answers.

## What Does It Do?
The answer appears to be connected with oxygen. Beta-carotene is related to vitamin A; in fact it looks like two pieces of vitamin A stuck together. Whenever there's a need for vitamin A and beta-carotene is present, the body activates an enzyme that changes it into the active vitamin. But when a sufficient amount of vitamin A is present, beta-carotene is available to perform other functions, and this is where the carrot-colored compound really begins to shine. Basically, when enough beta-carotene is present, it serves as an antioxidant.

What does this mean? Obviously, we need oxygen to stay alive. But it turns out that oxygen, in the wrong place at the wrong time, can do serious damage to the body. The problem comes when the oxygen reacts and forms "free radicals"— compounds that damage cells and are believed to be involved in the development of heart disease, cancer, aging, and a host of other ailments. An antioxidant such as beta-carotene can stifle those free-roving bits of oxygen that may be up to no good.

**How Much Should I Have?**

At a *minimum*, have no less than one daily serving of a food that's rich in beta-carotene; but the recommended five servings of fruits and vegetables per day is the best way to ensure that your body is getting an ample amount of this important nutrient. (A typical serving is a medium piece of fruit, 1 cup of a leafy vegetable, ½ cup of fruit or cooked vegetables, ¼ cup of dried fruit, or 6 ounces of a fruit or vegetable juice.)

## Where Do I Find It?

In general, most dark green and yellow vegetables contain beta-carotene. Particularly rich sources include yams, sweet potatoes, butternut squash, carrots, broccoli, kale, spinach, apricots, cabbage, spinach, and cantaloupe. Beta-carotene can also be taken as a food supplement—as a separate pill or part of a multivitamin preparation.

## When You've Had Too Much

Beta-carotene is essentially nontoxic. Perhaps the most noticeable effect from a large amount is that you might actually begin to look like a carrot. This is because in addition to its nutritional qualities, beta-carotene is a strong colorant. It's used as a additive to color food such as cheddar cheese, butter, and margarine—anywhere a natural orange color is desired.

When you eat more beta-carotene than the body needs, the excess is removed naturally. But when intake exceeds the rate at which it can be used or discarded, the body begins to stash the extra beta-carotene wherever it can. If excess builds up, the body takes on an orange tinge. The condition is most noticeable in fair-skinned people, and appears on the palms, soles, and the center of the face. However, carotinemia, as it is called, is harmless, and the coloring will disappear when the intake of beta-carotene is reduced.

**What's on the Horizon?**

Considering its positive qualities, you'd think there would be a specific RDA requirement for beta-carotene—but there isn't. The RDA system for nutrient recommendations was originally established as a guideline against deficiency diseases. To date, beta-carotene is mentioned only because it can supply vitamin A, a function separate from its prowess as an antioxidant.

This, however, is likely to change. Health authorities are in agreement over the need for beta-carotene to stand on its own as a required nutrient. At present, though, scientists don't know how much beta-carotene is necessary to provide the optimum impact on health.

There also are discussions of using beta-carotene in a new line of "designer foods." These formulated foods, in theory, would be supercharged with ingredients, such as beta-carotene, that afford them certain health promoting qualities. At present, however, the best way to get this wonderful substance is through a daily dose of vegetables and fresh fruits.

**To Find Out More**

See: Food Coloring, Eating to Bolster Your Immune System, and Eating for a Healthy Heart.

# Vegetarianism Explored

*Meatless goes mainstream*

## A Healthy Choice

A change to a vegetarian style of eating does not come with a magic wand granting long life and eternal well-being. The potential, though, is enormous. Many dietary fats are just about shoved off the table, and foods rich in fiber and anti-cancer substances grace your plate with newfound regularity. Health statistics for vegetarians include lower rates of heart disease, obesity, obesity-related diabetes, colon cancer, lung cancer, breast cancer, hypertension, osteoporosis, kidney stones, gallstones, and diverticular disease. Though some gains are attributed to the lifestyle that's frequently adopted along with the new eating habits, these findings are certainly impressive.

## Are There Drawbacks?

Vegetarianism has only minor drawbacks. When one decides to give up meat, fish, and dairy, traditional sources of such essential nutrients as calcium, iron, zinc, vitamin $B_{12}$, vitamin D, and riboflavin are lost. Therefore becoming a successful vegetarian means learning which foods are required for a complete diet. These food selections and combinations become very important, especially for children and pregnant or lactating women.

In addition, unless your family and friends are vegetarian, switching to a no-meat menu could affect your social life. Restaurant eating, parties, air travel, and even home food preparation changes. You may not be able to eat a number of the meals you'll be served away from home. But in most cases, all that's required is some advance communication with those involved in meal preparation. Keep in mind, however, that these drawbacks tend to be short-lived and they pale when stacked up against the health benefits you'll experience.

## Not All Vegetarians Are the Same

*Vegan*: Consumes no foods of animal origin.
*Lacto vegetarian*: The only animal products consumed are dairy.
*Ovo vegetarian*: The only animal products eaten are eggs.
*Lacto-ovo vegetarian*: The only animal products eaten are dairy and eggs.
*Pesco vegetarian*: Fish is the only animal product consumed.
*Semi-vegetarian*: Eats meat, fish, or poultry, but only occasionally.

## Why Go Vegetarian?

People decide to become vegetarians for any of a number of reasons. For some, it's a choice based on religious or ethical beliefs. Many make the move after a personal health crisis in the hopes that this style of eating will provide the best chance for recovery and future well-being. Others decide to go vegetarian because they believe an animal-based diet is either unhealthy, simply wrong, or both. Whatever the reason, approximately 12.4 million people in the U.S. claim that they eat a vegetarian-type diet, and their numbers continue to grow.

Before you try a vegetarian diet (or any diet for that matter) it's important to understand the fundamentals of good nutrition. All the essential nutrients can be found in a diet consisting of vegetables, fruits, grains, and nuts, but it's a matter of putting them together in the right combinations.

## Proteins Pose Little Problem

All proteins are made from building blocks called amino acids. The body can manufacture about 13 or the 22 amino acids found in nature. We need to consume protein foods to supply these nine essential amino acids (EAAs). Most foods have some amino acids. Animal proteins are considered "complete" proteins because they contain all nine. Except for soy, vegetable proteins are "incomplete" in that they're missing one or more of the EAAs.

As a vegetarian, however, you can easily meet your daily protein requirement by combining different foods so that sufficient amounts of all the EAAs are present during the day. There are three basic types of vegetable protein: whole grains, such as rice, corn, oats and barley; legumes, such as beans and lentils; and nuts and seeds, such as almonds and peanuts, and sunflower and sesame seeds. By including foods from two or more of these groups, you end up creating a complete protein.

## Vitamin B12: A Special Case

Vitamin B12, needed for the proper functioning of nerve tissue and red blood cells, is found primarily in animal foods. A deficiency leads to a condition called pernicious anemia. Because B12 is produced by bacteria, vegetarians can use specially fermented soy products, such as tempeh or miso, as a dietary source. The alternative is to rely on foods fortified with vitamin B-12 or a food supplement.

## Vegetarian Support Network

There are magazines and local and national organizations that offer help in learning how to eat a vegetarian diet. Their aim in promoting vegetarianism is to educate the public about a way of eating they feel is healthier for the body and for society.

Vegetarianism, however, carries no guarantees. Poor food choices are poor food choices whether one is a vegetarian or a meat eater. Likewise, those consuming beef, fish, and poultry are not de facto barred from receiving a passport to good health. If all the essential nutrients are consumed, a similar formula for a healthy diet and lifestyle can hold for all types of eating.

## A Final Word

The decision to go vegetarian should not be looked upon as giving something up, but rather as a change in approach to eating. In American society being a vegetarian is perceived as difficult. But that's not the body talking; that's our meat-minded culture. We are firmly entrenched in one style of eating and often assume that everyone agrees. Although any move away from the mainstream takes conviction, you don't have to sign a lifetime contract to vegetarianism. The vegetarian experience opens up a whole new world of ingredients, tastes, and methods of preparation that can have positive health benefits whether it's for a few days, a week, or a life-long affair.

## To Learn More

There are a host of magazines and well-written books with information and recipes for the dabbler to the dedicated. I recommend *Vegetarian Times, The Gradual Vegetarian* (Dell, NY 1985) by L. Tracy, *Moosewood Cookbook* (10-Speed, Berkeley, CA 1992) by M. Katzen, *The McDougall Program* (Penguin, NY 1991) ny J. McDougall, M.D., *Recipes from an Ecological Kitchen* (Morrow, NY 1992) by L. Sass, and *Diet for a Small Planet, 20th Anniversary Edition* (Ballantine, NY 1992) by Frances Moore Lappe. You can also contact the Vegetarian Awareness Network: 800-USA-VEGE. See also: The Joys of Juicing, and Keeping Pesticides off Your Plate.

# Boning Up on Calcium

*Saying "no" to osteoporosis*

## No Laughing Matter

Make no bones about it, our skeleton is destined to turn into a fragile shell if we deprive it of the raw materials it needs. The key weight-bearing bones in the body are the hip, upper thigh, and spine. If the mineral content of these bones dips too low, they loose their ability to support the body and can snap or begin to crumble without warning. This condition is called osteoporosis (os-tee-oh pore-OH-sis).

At present osteoporosis is incurable. It's believed to account for well over a million broken bones every year and is indirectly involved in one in five deaths in people over 70. It's estimated that one-third of the post menopausal women in this country suffer from this disease.

The strength and long-term health of the body's precious framework depends to a large degree on our diet. Calcium, the most plentiful mineral in the body, tops the list. Its role in our bones is only one of calcium's responsibilities.

## Prevention Is a Long-Term Proposition

Like an active bank account, the bones of our skeleton, despite their solid feel, are involved in a continuous process of mineral deposits and withdrawals. Childhood, adolescence, and early adulthood—up to about age 30—are the critical times to "bone up" on dietary calcium. It is during these periods that the body has the capacity to save its dietary calcium. The amount of savings, however, depends entirely on the calcium in the diet, and the importance of this cannot be overemphasized.

Once we hit our 30s the body's automatic teller begins to shift gear. Our dietary deposits are no longer able to keep pace with the withdrawals, no matter how much calcium we eat. The third decade of life is the start of a slow but continuous erosion of the skeleton. From that point on, diet helps determine how fast this deterioration occurs.

69

## Calcium Is Not the Only Consideration

Other factors besides a long-term low calcium intake that increase the risk of osteoporosis include being female, passing through menopause before age 45, a lack of weight-bearing physical activity, being underweight, being Caucasian, smoking, excessive alcohol consumption, and having a family history of the disease.

## How Much Should You Take?

### RDA for calcium

| Children and adults | Calcium (milligrams) |
|---|---|
| 1-10 years: | 800 |
| 11-24 years: | 1200 |
| over 25: | 800 |
| Pregnant: | 1200 |
| Lactating: | 1200 |

## Best Food Sources

When dietary sources of calcium are discussed, milk and milk products tend to move center stage. Dairy products represent over 75 percent of the calcium in the American diet. One 8-ounce glass of skim milk contains about 302 milligrams of calcium, that's 25 percent of the RDA for a teenager or young adult. Milk products, however, are not the only source of calcium.

This is important to know because many people either don't care for or can't tolerate dairy products because of either lactose intolerance or an allergy to milk. For lactose intolerance, there are remedies available (see, "The Wonderful World of Digestion" page 30). For a milk allergy, however, you will have to get calcium elsewhere. There are plenty of foods besides dairy that contain calcium. It is found in green leafy vegetables, small fish with edible bones, broccoli, dried fruits, legumes, and nuts. Other options include calcium-fortified foods, such as cereal or orange juice.

## Calcium Sources
### (milligrams)

| | | | |
|---|---|---|---|
| ¼ lb. sardines | 433 | ½ cup garbanzo beans | 150 |
| 1 cup almonds | 316 | ¼ pound tofu | 150 |
| 1 cup arugula | 302 | 5 dried figs | 144 |
| 8 oz. Ca-fort orange juice | 302 | 1 Tbs. blkstrp molasses | 137 |
| 1 cup collard greens | 304 | ½ cup cooked soybeans | 102 |
| ½ cup boiled amaranth | 276 | ½ cup cooked navy beans | 70 |
| 1 cup cooked broccoli | 180 | ½ cup dried apricots | 67 |

## What About Supplements?

Another option is to take calcium in pill form. While this doesn't remedy a poor diet, it will provide the nutrients your body needs. Keep in mind that as with most minerals, calcium has to be in solution to be absorbed. Calcium carbonate, the most common and least expensive, is found in antacids such as Tums. This form, however, is the least soluble of the calcium salts. It requires an acid environment to dissolve and should be taken with meals or with a glass of orange or tomato juice.

Calcium citrate, calcium gluconate, and calcium lactate are more soluble, but they also cost considerably more. These compounds have less calcium per unit weight, so the pill size is larger than a comparable-strength calcium carbonate supplement.

One economical alternative is to purchase calcium carbonate powder by the pound (your local pharmacy or health food store should be able to order it for you). It is stable indefinitely at room temperature. Sprinkle about an eighth of a teaspoon of this white, tasteless powder on your food a few times a day; tomato-based sauces or other acid foods are ideal. Don't overdo it, though, or your food could taste gritty. One pound should last over a year.

Other foods in a meal can affect how the body uses its dietary calcium. Calcium absorption is decreased in high-protein or high-fat meals.

## Other Calcium Benefits

Keep in mind that besides its celebrated role in our bones, calcium is also the key element in our teeth. An insufficient intake of calcium during the formative years can lead to weakened tooth enamel and greater susceptibility to decay. Calcium also plays a role in muscle contraction, control of blood pressure, blood coagulation, and the immune system. As you can see, ignoring calcium is not wise. Like the skeleton it affects, it can come back to haunt you. When we are thirsty our body tells us to drink; when hungry, we look for food. But there are no warning signs for inadequate calcium. Your first symptom might be a broken bone, and by then it could be too late.

## To Learn More

See also: Allergies & Other Adverse Reactions, and Vitamins and Minerals.

# Nutrition for a Stressful Lifestyle

*You want it* when?

### Eating and Stress Don't Mix

Whether it comes from the demands of family, a troubled relationship, a high-pressure job, or no job at all, stress is an all-too-common fact of life. And although good nutrition can help the body withstand day-to-day pressures, food and stress, it turns out, make a very poor combination.

### The Body Under Stress

A classic example of a stress reaction is the fight-or-flight response that occurs when the body senses physical danger. Adrenaline, one of the body's "stress" hormones, announces its presence by producing that heart-pounding sensation familiar to anyone who has experienced a good scare.

When this happens, your blood pressure begins to rise. Blood flow to the skin and the digestive system is reduced, and a greater supply is directed toward the large muscle groups. Muscle fuels—stored fats, amino acids and quick-energy carbohydrates—enter the bloodstream. In case of injury, platelets, the blood components that help stop bleeding, increase in number. Hearing sharpens, pupils dilate to increase the field of vision, breathing deepens to provide more oxygen, perspiration increases to keep the body cool, and, finally, muscles tense in preparation for action. With all this going on, the last thing the body needs is a meal. That's why eating under stress often causes heartburn, bloating, indigestion, and nausea.

### Good Nutrition Can Help

Sensible food choices can help buffer the effects of stress, for nutrients not only affect how well the body handles stress, they help determine how fast the body recovers. It's known, for example, that stress can increase the need for such nutrients as vitamin C, the B vitamins, magnesium, and zinc.

For most folks, these increased requirements can be met by a healthy diet that supplies the recommended dietary allowances (RDAs). But for individuals under severe stress, such as physical injury or surgery, there may be a need for supplements. In these cases it's best to consult a health professional, such as a trained nutritionist or a physician with nutrition savvy, for recommendations tailored to your specific needs.

## Eat Wisely Under Stress

During stressful periods you don't want food sitting in your stomach for long periods of time. So avoid large meals or foods laden with fats, such as hot dogs, cheeseburgers, French fries, and chips. Instead, stick to smaller meals containing plenty of complex carbohydrates, such as fresh vegetables, fruits, and grains. They help sustain energy, are typically high in important nutrients, and don't load you down.

Limit your intake of caffeine before periods of anticipated stress and after times that tensions have been high. Cut back on salt, particularly if you have high blood pressure. And although alcohol might be a tempting remedy for chronic stress, the potential for abuse is well known. If taken in lieu of a healthy diet, alcohol drains the body of needed nutrients and hastens one's demise.

## Exercise, Exercise

Because the stress response brings muscle fuels to the bloodstream, exercise is an important part of any stress-relief formula. Any exercise routine, such as going for a brisk walk or forsaking the elevator for the stairs, can help release tensions and return you to a calmer state.

If you're at the dining-room table and stress makes an unexpected appearance, stop eating. If possible, try to excuse yourself for a brief period. If you can't get away, use the act of eating to help put the skids on your tension. First, concentrate on taking a few, very slow deep breaths before you continue your meal. Then, as you place foods in your mouth, focus on the different tastes and the physical act of chewing and swallowing.

## Chronic Stress Can Be Deadly

Danger exists for individuals under chronic stress who either have a poor diet or are at high risk for cardiovascular disease. The increased level of circulating fats from the stress response means there will be an increase in the blood cholesterol level as well. When you also consider the increased level of clot-producing blood platelets and the higher blood pressure, it's easy to see why stress is associated with a higher incidence of strokes and heart disease. Stress can also blunt the effectiveness of the immune system, the body's protector against infection and disease. Colds, for example, are more common after periods of stress.

## How Else Can Nutrition Help?

If the stresses in your life are unavoidable, it's especially important to start your day with a healthy breakfast. A morning meal of protein, carbohydrates, and some fat can help stabilize your blood-sugar level and make your body better equipped to handle upcoming challenges. To be sure, people under stress should learn to handle their reactions as well as their diet. But nutrition is an important tool, and food selection is one factor you can control.

# Good Nutrition in a "What's for Dessert?" World

*Tips for guiding your children to good food*

## Strategies For Young Eaters

If you are the parent of young children and you're concerned about their diet, you're not alone. Four out of five parents have the same concerns. It's easy to get frantic about what children eat as you see them get excited over macaroni and cheese, but turn up their noses at anything on the menu that would lend some balance to their diet.

Well, don't fret. Simple strategies can help you stimulate your child's appreciation for nutritious food and can, at the same time, let you feel more in command as you strive to improve their diet. The key areas to concentrate on are menu planning, meal preparation, and coping with unpredictable mealtime behavior.

## What's On The Menu?

The first thing you need do is to look at eating from a child's perspective. Think about what children go through as they sit at the table every day and are told, in effect, "This is what you're eating for dinner." Imagine how you would react if every time you sat in a restaurant, the waiter handed you a dish without letting you order.

So one way to get your children more interested in eating well is to involve them in menu planning. Discuss food options and ask for input. If there is more than one child, have them take turns. If possible, take them along on shopping trips. Asking your children to select favorite vegetables or fruits, and then enlisting their help as you pick them out at the market may increase the odds that they'll eat them.

## Surviving the Store

At the grocery store your children will be at the receiving end of a tremendous effort devoted to influencing their minds (and consequently your behavior). They will see cartoon character promotions, special kid designs on packages, and kid's-eye-level placement of certain foods. These all tend to go hand in hand with the highly-produced advertisements that are clustered around children's television shows.

It's best not to have them confront these temptations on an empty stomach, so before you go shopping, consider letting your kids help you put together a snack for the trip, and plan how you'll react if they try to toss high-fat treats or over-sweetened cereals in the shopping cart. Depending on your past experiences, it may be helpful to go over basic ground rules before you enter the store.

## What about Kiddie TV-Dinners?

Highly-processed children's meals are better than no food at all, or a meal full of snack foods, but they're not the substance on which long-term healthful eating habits are established. There's no problem if they are used on occasion because of time constraints or as an indulgence to a child's persistent requests. If, however, you find such meals to be the routine rather than the exception, it may be time for a reexamination of priorities.

One problem with such meals is that it's the promotion, not the food quality that sells the product. As children accompany parents up and down the aisles, the packages can represent an island of familiarity to young eyes. When noticed, the friendly-looking cartoon character kindles the desire to ask Mommy or Daddy to take it home. The flip side of this story may have a beleaguered parent picking up the dinner for its undeniable convenience or its potential to quell mealtime difficulties: "See honey, here's a dinner just for you."

Keep in mind that studies have found that the incidence of adolescent obesity increases 2 percent for every additional hour of daily television. While one might think this finding is due to a lack of physical activity, there would be no surprise if there were a correlation between obesity, the number of commercials a child views, and the resulting food choices they make.

## Help In The Kitchen

Once home, think of ways that your children might help with meal preparation. Whether it's making a lunchtime sandwich, helping measure ingredients, or simply arranging food on a serving plate, being involved before the meal can increase satisfaction with what's to come.

## Table Politics

It's appropriate to discuss the importance of a good diet. But the use of coercion or the dangling of rewards label the food as something not worth considering on its own merits. It also sets up future confrontations by letting children know there's a possible reward if they hold out long enough.

When children balk at eating all that's served, it's best to let them pass on those foods in which they show no interest. But avoid offering to custom-cook a meal whenever the prepared menu is rejected. Try to have some bread or fruit on the table so they can pick at these while they watch you enjoy your meal.

## Balance not always an Imperative

Remember that if you perceive food refusals or other behavioral quirks as a challenge to your authority, mealtime will degenerate into a power struggle. Remind yourself that missing an occasional meal, failing to eat from all the food groups on a daily basis, or never touching the spinach or broccoli are not signs of impending malnutrition. The body has amazing powers to conserve needed nutrients and make the most of them when they finally appear.

Don't sweat the periodic lapses. There's no way to predict how tastes develop. Food fetishes and phobias are facts of a child's life that tend to ebb and flow over time. For a few months, they may hate carrots, only to later insist that carrots are their favorite vegetable. Talk to other parents. What your children's peers enjoy can influence what your kids choose to eat.

In the end, aim to instill a sense of appreciation for all that's involved in bringing food to the table in a supportive family setting. Add a nudge toward a healthy food selection, plus the example you set, and you're on track for promoting good eating habits.

## To Go Further

There are several excellent books that can provide basic nutrition information along with more detailed strategies and advice. Three I recommend are: *How to Get Your Kid to Eat... But Not Too Much* (Bull Publishing, 1987) by Ellyn Satter, R.D.; *Parents' Guide to Feeding Your Kids Right* (CTW Family Living Series, Prentice Hall Press, 1989) by Karen Moloney; and *Food and Your Child* (Time-Life Books, 1988).

# Aging in Good Health

*Will good nutrition keep you young?*

## The Fountain of Youth?

Does good nutrition wield special powers to combat the aging process? Aging doesn't happen suddenly, in that you're young one day and old the next. Rather, it is a cumulative process that proceeds at different rates in different people. But diet and other lifestyle factors *can* play a central role in defining how that process will be expressed in your life.

This is a timely topic considering that the baby-boom generation is now entering its fifth decade, and by the year 2020, over half the people in the U.S. will have joined the over-50 crowd. The definition of what it means to be older, however, continues to undergo radical changes. Larger segments of the population are living longer, doing more, and enjoying better health then ever before.

## What Happens As We Age?

Besides the obvious visible signs, the body's metabolism goes through radical change as it gets older. An older body requires fewer calories because it needs less dietary energy. In addition, the body may digest and absorb needed nutrients less efficiently. The ability to feel thirst may also diminish, resulting in an inadequate water intake. It's also common for older people to experience such diet-related problems as difficulty in chewing and a decreased sense of smell and taste.

Other problems, such as reduced vision, loss of mobility, loneliness, depression, and income limitations, may affect an individual's ability to partake of and enjoy the eating experience. Often, despondency over the loss of a partner affects the very desire to have a meal. All of these can lead to dramatic changes in what, how, and when people eat.

## Eating to Stay Young

Many studies have documented the importance of staying well nourished as you age. One study, for example, showed that even among older people in good health, those whose diets contained more of the essential nutrients performed better on memory and learning tests. Good long-term eating habits also help out when you're ill. The payoff includes faster wound healing, fewer surgical complications, and shorter hospital stays.

One widely held theory of aging explains how the compounds called free-radicals cause damage to the cells of the body. Free-radical damage has been associated with heart disease, cataracts, and certain types of cancer as well as other diseases of old age. Research has shown that a few nutrients, including vitamin E, vitamin C, beta-carotene, selenium, and zinc, have the ability to combat free-radical damage.

## Practical Strategies

The best basic dietary advice remains to eat a wide variety of healthy foods. But eating the same foods day after day is unwise because it limits exposure to the different nutrients. Here are some other nutritional guidelines:

• Focus on fresh vegetables and fruits, low-fat dairy products, lean meats, nuts and seeds, legumes, and whole grains.

• When cooking, keep nonfat dry-milk powder nearby and sprinkle it in your food; it's a great source of protein, calcium, and vitamin D.

• Take advantage of the salad bars at supermarkets and restaurants; it's a great way to put together a nutritious meal without waste.

• Make a point to drink at least six to eight glasses of water, or water-based beverages daily.

• If, for any reason, you cannot or will not eat a healthy diet, consider taking a vitamin/mineral supplement. While it's always preferable to get these nutrients from food, this may not be possible. The bottom line: better to get the nutrients from a supplement than not at all.

• If you decide you need a supplement, check with your physician beforehand about the effects it might have on any existing health conditions or prescription medications. Ask if you might benefit from additional amounts of certain vitamins or minerals. When shopping for a supplement, look for an inexpensive one-a-day type that contains minerals as well as vitamins. Take it with a meal to ensure better absorption.

• Stay away from anti-aging gurus who promise longevity via their products and services, usually at a hefty price. Health fraud is big business, and older Americans make up about 40 percent of all victims. Don't become a statistic by joining this group which wastes approximately $2 billion every year on fake anti-aging remedies.

## Age-Related Weight Gain

The body's tendency to gain weight with age stems from a pre-programmed slowdown in its basal metabolic rate (BMR). The BMR is the body's minimum energy requirement—that amount of energy (expressed in calories) needed to maintain vital bodily functions, such as heart rate, breathing, and body temperature. Calories needed to satisfy the BMR represent a hefty two-thirds of the body's daily energy requirement.

The BMR begins to rise at birth and reaches its peak during childhood. After that, it decreases at a rate of about 2 to 4 percent per decade. The rate of decrease is affected by changes in the amount of muscle in the body. This is because muscle is an "active" energy-burning tissue, whereas body fat is an "inactive" energy-storage depot. Therefore, as activity decreases with age (a typical pattern), the decline of the BMR accelerates.

Repeated dieting can also decrease the BMR. Because a small amount of muscle tissue is lost during rapid weight loss, each episode of weight loss and regain leaves the body with a higher percentage of fat tissue. Cutting back on food is not the best, and certainly not the only, way to slow age-related weight gain. If not done with care, continual cutbacks could leave your diet lacking the full complement of essential nutrients.

Physical exercise turns out to be a more potent weapon; not only does the activity burn calories, it helps put the skids on the rate at which the BMR slows down and helps keep your bones strong. Activities such as a daily brisk walk or any other weight bearing exercise may be all that's needed. By combining exercise with a shift away from fatty foods toward those higher in carbohydrates and fiber, you'll be better able to keep your energy needs high and cut that creeping weight down to size.

**To Go Deeper**

*Prescription for Longevity* (Dutton, NY 1992) by J. Scala, Ph.D., R.D.; *Biomarkers* (Simon & Schuster 1991) W. Evans PhD.; and *The Nutrition Game, the Right Moves if You're Over 50,* (Bristol Publishing, San Leandro, CA 1990) by E. Langholz, M.S., R.D. are three good resources. See also: Beta-carotene: The Nutrient with Something Special, Eating to Bolster Your Immune System, and To Pill or Not to Pill.

# To Pill or Not to Pill

*Should you be taking supplements?*

## Nutrition Insurance

Since the days when potions were marketed by sideshow con artists, people have always been attracted to pills and powders that promise an extra boost. Given this, it's not surprising that many Americans look to supplements as a way to ensure a form of nutrition insurance. But do we need such insurance, or are the only beneficiaries the companies that sell the pills?

### Getting the Nutrients We Need

The nutritional adequacy of the American diet has been a topic of debate since the first measurements of food consumption. The recommended dietary allowance (RDA) is defined as the level of intake that will satisfy the nutrient needs of practically all healthy persons. Most Americans, however, do not meet all the RDAs for vitamins and minerals on a daily basis. This in itself is not that serious of a problem. The RDAs are not rigid requirements that must be met every day, but rather goals to be met over time. There's little danger from missing a nutrient on a particular day so long as your intake over a 5 to 10 day period is at the RDA level.

But what if we consistently fail to eat properly? Although we may never experience a full blown deficiency disease, our chronically deficient diet is likely to have some negative effect on our health. If this is the case, isn't getting nutrients from a pill better than not getting them at all?

## The Surgeon General Says No

Yes seems a reasonable answer, but you won't find the surgeon general echoing this sentiment. A conservative health establishment maintains a consistently thumbs-down attitude about vitamin and mineral supplements. They're considered unscientific, potentially dangerous, and a waste of money. According to a consortium of medical and nutritional societies, supplement use can be justified only for a small number of groups, such as people on very low-calorie diets, those unable to absorb nutrients from their food, women with heavy menstrual bleeding, and women who are pregnant or lactating. There's never been a category for people who simply do not eat well.

## Promising Research

In recent years, food supplements have moved beyond their fill-in-the-gaps image. Evidence is mounting that extra amounts of some nutrients can be effective against common ailments and several age-related illnesses. For example, there's growing evidence that antioxidant vitamins--beta-carotene and vitamins E and C—are beneficial against heart disease, certain cancers, rheumatoid arthritis, and cataracts. In addition, calcium, besides slowing the onset of osteoporosis, has shown some ability to lower high blood pressure and prevent colon cancer. Niacin has been used alone and in combination with other medications against elevated blood cholesterol, fiber against colon cancer, and omega-3 fats (fish oils) against heart disease. Despite these scientific findings, there's no official acknowledgment that supplements have any value.

## Why the Anti-pill Stance?

One apparent problem with giving a nod to supplements is the concern that people could take the endorsement out of context. While a daily supplement can raise the intake of nutrients to recommended levels or beyond, an overdependence on pills could change the way we think about food. It would be tragic if a "junk food plus supplements" diet began to look as good as one based on fresh, whole foods because it doesn't even come close. Additionally, although there's significant knowledge about specific nutrients, science has barely scratched the surface of how they interact in food. Therefore taking isolated nutrients in pills cannot equal consuming them in their natural state in food.

If you're interested in improving your eating habits, the first step is rarely found in a bottle of supplements. But so long as it's clearly understood that a vitamin/mineral pill cannot transform a poor diet into a healthy one, the decision to use a supplement can be an entirely reasonable one.

## Planning Your Strategy

Before shopping for a supplement, you should know what you're looking for. Otherwise you risk being cut adrift in a sea of inflated claims and misinformation. Reading about the nutrients your body needs can help you better understand which, if any, you might be missing. With more information you may decide that a simple strategy, such as 5 servings a day of fruits or vegetables, is all that's needed to boost the nutrients in your diet.

If you feel that supplements would be of value, a basic multi-vitamin/mineral pill is a good place to start. Look for pills that contain 100 to 300 percent of the recommended dietary allowances. As freshness can affect vitamin potency, opt for brands that include expiration dates. When you visit your physician, always be up-front about your use of supplements, because they can interfere with prescription medication, especially those with higher-than-RDA levels.

Where diet is involved, food must always come first. But for folks constantly concerned with the adequacy of their diet, taking a supplement for nutrition insurance is not necessarily a bad policy.

### To Go Further

Consider reading *The Essential Guide to Vitamins and Minerals* (Harper Perennial, NY 1992) by E. Somer, M.A. R.D., and *The Doctors' Vitamin and Mineral Encyclopedia* (Fireside, New York 1991) by S. Hendler, MD, Ph.D. See also: Recommended Dietary Allowances, Fish Oil and Health, and Beta-carotene: The Nutrient with Something Special.

# Iron: The Mineral with Mettle

*Don't suffer from iron poor blood*

## We All Need Iron

The body uses iron to make hemoglobin, an oxygen-carrying compound in blood, as well as myoglobin, a compound that handles oxygen in the muscles. When there's not enough iron, the levels of hemoglobin and myoglobin decrease and with them goes the body's ability to produce energy. Anemia (*an*=without, *emia* =blood) is the most widespread deficiency disease in the world. It is marked by fatigue, headaches, dizziness, and a general "run down" feeling—symptoms often mistaken as normal side effects of a stressful lifestyle. The most common anemia type is an iron-deficiency that can be caused by:
• a lack of iron in the diet,
• inefficient absorption of iron in the diet, or
• a loss of blood.

## Anemia Risk

We see iron-deficiency anemia most often in groups where there's an increased iron need: children to four years of age, teens during periods of rapid growth, women throughout the menstrual years and especially during pregnancy and lactation, frequent blood donors, endurance athletes, and anyone experiencing a significant loss of blood. Anemia can also result in people with disorders of the digestive system that affect the body's ability to absorb nutrients.

### Getting Enough Iron Isn't Necessarily Easy

Iron in food comes in two groups: *heme* iron, the type absorbed most efficiently, is present in red meats, poultry, fish, and eggs; *nonheme* iron sources include cereals and breads made with iron-enriched grains, nuts, seeds, legumes, dried fruits, and some dark green leafy green vegetables. The Daily Value is 18 milligrams per day.

## Iron Sources
*(milligrams)*

| | | | |
|---|---|---|---|
| 1 cup cooked spinach | 5 | 1 Tbs. blackstrap molasses | 3 |
| ½ cup dried apricots | 8 | ¼ lb. lean ground beef | 3 |
| ½ cup red kidney beans | 3 | 3 oz. cooked liver | 6 |
| ½ cup raisins | 2 | 1 cup Cheerios cereal | 4 |
| 1 oz. almonds | 1 | ½ cup raw oysters | 8 |

From this list, it's clear that iron is present in a variety of foods. Why then the continued prevalence of iron-deficiency anemia? One reason is that only a small percentage of dietary iron gets absorbed. In addition, there are naturally occurring chemicals in several foods, such as tea, coffee, whole grains, and some vegetables, that make iron unavailable to the body.

## An Iron Strategy

If you have an iron deficiency, the first step is to include more iron-rich foods. Try having iron-rich meals along with high-acid fruits, such as oranges, or fruit juices high in vitamin C, because they enhance iron absorption.

There's some preliminary evidence that dietary calcium might inhibit the body's ability to absorb iron. So to play it safe, try to have at least one "iron" meal without coffee, tea, or calcium-containing foods or beverages, such as milk, cheese, and other dairy products. Those who are low in iron and are also taking calcium supplements should refrain from taking the calcium along with iron-containing foods.

During pregnancy and lactation, there's special emphasis on eating a healthy diet. Many women also take prenatal supplements with their meals as a form of nutrition "insurance." There's a loophole in the policy, though, because most supplements combine calcium and iron in the same pill. If your supplement contains both minerals, discuss with your physician the possibility of taking a separate iron supplement between meals or at bedtime.

## Iron From Cookware

Periodic use of cast-iron pans is an excellent way to add iron to the diet. When acid foods, such as spaghetti sauce, are prepared in cast iron, a small amount of iron dissolves into the food. The actual amount of iron drawn into food depends on the condition of the cookware; a cast-iron pan that's frequently seasoned with oil tends to give off less iron, although some iron will be released.

## Can You Get Too Much?

Yes, but it's not easy. The body happens to be quite good at regulating its iron level. There is a protein needed for iron absorption that's not available when the body's iron stores are full. Therefore, except for those folks who have a rare genetic iron-storage disease called hemochromatosis, it's highly unlikely that anyone could eat enough iron-containing foods to cause a toxic overdose. You could overdose on iron supplements, however, but only if you routinely ingested in excess of 100 milligrams of iron per day. It also might be possible if your daily diet included a hefty serving of high-acid foods, such as tomatoes, prepared in cast-iron cookware.

There's been speculation that too much iron could lead to heart attacks, but such a connection does not appear to be solid. We're familiar with the tendency of iron to rust, which results from its ability to react with oxygen. Although bodies don't get rusty per se, free iron could grab onto oxygen, then force it on nearby substances, such as fats or cholesterol. (It is these oxidized fats and cholesterol that are thought to be the real villains in heart disease.) But iron is rarely on its own in the body. Rather, it is tied up in such compounds as hemoglobin, the substance that makes red blood cells "red" and carries oxygen from the lungs directly to the cells. In addition, a well-nourished body should have a daily supply of antioxidant nutrients: vitamins C, E, A, and beta-carotene. It's the responsibility of these nutrients to prevent the type of errant oxidation for which iron is being accused.

## To Learn More

See also: Vitamins & Minerals, To Pill or Not to Pill, Beta-carotene: The Nutrient with Something Special.

# Foods & Moods

*What and when we eat seems to affect brain functioning*

## Eating to Feel Good

The nutrients in our diet can influence whether we are alert, depressed, or ready to doze. Although the connections between what we eat and our levels of alertness aren't fully understood, it's fascinating to think that diet might help or hinder the way the brain works. The idea of a link between diet and behavior came from studies on nutritional deficiencies. One of the first connections had to do with niacin, a water-soluble vitamin.

In the early 1900s, as many as half the patients in hospitals for the insane in the southern United States were victims of a disease called pellagra (pe-LAY-gruh). Symptoms included skin rash, intestinal problems, and mental confusion that eventually led to insanity. At the time, diets among the poor living in the Southeast consisted primarily of cornmeal, salt pork, and molasses. This diet was deficient in protein and niacin as well as many other vitamins. In 1937, scientists discovered that pellagra was caused by a niacin deficiency. When a large dose of niacin was given to the pellagra victims, their insanity, as well as their other symptoms, disappeared like magic.

We now have a better understanding of the major deficiency diseases and their effect on behavior. Today, interest in this area has shifted toward looking at ways our diet might affect the way healthy individuals feel and perform.

## How Eating Habits Affect Performance

It's been reported that skipping meals, especially breakfast, can have a negative effect on the way students perform in the classroom and on tests. Having too much to eat can also decrease alertness. One Scottish study showed that a large meal, such as the size often eaten during Thanksgiving, decreased performance on a complex task to about the same degree as going without sleep for a night. Additionally, although simple sugars are sources of quick energy, studies of adults show that high-carbohydrate meals often lead to sleepiness, decreased attention span, and impaired concentration.

## Avoiding the Energy Roller Coaster

Although no diet can counteract the tedium of repetitive tasks, what you eat can help determine whether you're awake on the job or ready to fall asleep. We know, for example, that large meals and those high in sugar or fat encourage drowsiness.

The tired feeling comes on in three stages. First, as you're eating, the pattern of blood flow begins to shift away from the muscles and toward the digestive tract in preparation to receive the nutrients from the food. Next, as sugar from the meal enters the bloodstream, insulin is released by the pancreas. In reaction to these events, the brain, via its homemade tranquilizers, tells the body to sit back and relax.

The reason behind this is that the body is unable to do a good job on digestion and on muscular work at the same time. The warning to not engage in vigorous swimming soon after a meal is based on this principle. But while such involuntary relaxation might be welcomed after a long day of work, it can be a real nuisance at 10 AM or 2 PM. Often, however, we encourage this by what we eat.

The day begins with a coffee-and-pastry breakfast. The caffeine plus the rapidly absorbed sugar provides an immediate energy surge. But as insulin is released, energy dwindles into the doldrums, and in a couple of hours you're ready to lay your head down on the desk. Then, low and behold, it's time for a coffee break; time for the snack machine and another jolt of java and it's up again for the next ride on the energy roller coaster.

If this cycle sounds too familiar, shift to smaller meals of complex carbohydrates and protein. For breakfast this could be a whole-grain, unsweetened cereal with low-fat or skim milk. If a sweetener is needed, opt for fruit over table sugar. Fructose, the carbohydrate found in most fruits, is not absorbed as quickly as sucrose and it doesn't have the same insulin-stimulating effect. By this same logic, fruits and raw vegetables, such as apples, oranges and carrots, make excellent selections for the coffee break. Small, protein-based meals may actually encourage alertness and better performance. It's believed that the protein encourages the brain to produce its own form of chemical stimulant.

## Sugar and Hyperactivity in Children

Many parents believe that sugar leads to hyperactive behavior in their children. To date, however, scientists have been unable to affirm any connection between sugar intake and hyperactivity.

In typical studies, children classified as "sugar responders" received either a sugared or an artificially sweetened beverage. Their behavior then was rated by their parents (or scientists) who were unaware of which treatment was being administered. Most studies have been unable to find an effect. In 1987, the Sugar Task Force of the U.S. Food and Drug Administration concluded that sugar was not linked to behavioral changes in children.

Despite such assurances, every now and then a study adds fuel to the debate. Typical of these was a Yale University study that gave adults and children sugared beverages on an empty stomach. The scientists then looked at blood sugar and levels of adrenaline—the "fight or flight" hormone that's released when we are frightened or when blood-sugar levels fall too low.

Three to four hours after taking the drink, the blood-sugar level in both adults and children had dropped. However, the adrenaline level in the children had increased to twice that of the adults. Unfortunately, the scientists took no measure of the children's behavior. But the finding of an increased release of adrenaline certainly gives credence to parents' claims of hyperactive behavior in children after they consume a high-sugar meal. (Keep in mind also that the above responses to carbohydrates were found with simple sugars, such as glucose, corn syrup, honey, or table sugar. These carbohydrates are rapidly absorbed and cause the blood-sugar level to rise—key elements in the ability to affect behavior.)

## To Investigate Further

See also The Wonderful World of Digestion, Carbohydrates, and Nutrition for a Stressful Lifestyle.

# Garlic

*As good as ten mothers?*

## The Stinking Rose

Count Dracula and his fellow vampires dread only three things: the light of the sun, the sign of the cross, and garlic. That's heady company for garlic, a flavorful herb affectionately known as "the stinking rose." But garlic, a member of the lily family and a relative of the onion and scallion, is now showing its mettle beyond the widely respected ability to cure a bland meal. Although garlic has been touted for having curative properties since the days of the pyramids, we are now only beginning to understand the science behind the potential health applications of this herb.

## Not to be Sniffed At

Garlic has been credited with combating heart disease, stimulating the immune system, attacking bacteria, viruses, and funguses, and increasing the body's ability to resist cancer-causing agents.

The power of garlic against infection has been known for centuries. Ancient Greek and Egyptian writings mention garlic as an effective remedy against a variety of ailments. In World Wars I and II, the British, German, and Russian governments put garlic extracts on bandages to help disinfect wounds. More recently, scientists have identified compounds in garlic that can lower blood cholesterol and triglycerides (the main way fat is carried in the blood). Garlic can also reduce the tendency for blood to clot, and one substance in cooked garlic lowers blood pressure.

Garlic's anti-cancer abilities includes inhibiting the formation of cancer-causing nitrosamines. It has also been known to prevent some forms of cell damage, which could be connected with cancer. Although more research needs to be done to confirm this impressive list of health benefits, these factors may help explain the decreased incidence of heart disease observed in populations in which garlic is consumed on a regular basis.

## Garlic Research

Both the American Institute for Cancer Research and the National Cancer Institute are exploring garlic's potential, funding research projects that look at ways its ingredients might be used to fight cancer.

Population studies in China and Italy show a relationship between a high intake of garlic and lower rates for cancers of the digestive tract. In other experiments, mice fed a garlic ingredient had significantly lower numbers of tumors after exposure to potent cancer-causing substances. And in a pilot study with AIDS patients, an aged garlic preparation significantly enhanced factors known to play a role in the body's defenses against viruses and tumors.

## Garlic Breath

Although garlic's health benefits are impressive, not all foods are improved by its unique flavor. In addition, many people do not appreciate the telltale odor that frequently emanates from an eater of garlic. The characteristic odor is created as the components of garlic are disbursed throughout the body. When they travel to the lungs, these compounds give rise to "garlic breath," and when they reach the skin, the olfactory offender becomes noticeable in perspiration. This explains why brushing one's teeth or even taking breath mints does little to suppress garlic odor.

## Can I Eat Too Much?

A few individuals may experience stomach distress if they eat too much garlic. For most people, though, the only side effect is the lingering odor. Eating fresh garlic by itself may increase the likelihood of problems. In one experiment, volunteers taking doses of garlic juice reported burning of the mouth, esophagus, and stomach, lightheadedness, nausea, and sweating.

## What If I Don't Like the Taste?

There is a wide assortment of garlic supplements now available in health food stores. The capsules, which often contain garlic oil extract, do not prevent odor; all they do is delay its presence until the garlic goes through the body. But there are supplements based on a deodorized, aged garlic extract that appear to offer similar health benefits as whole-clove garlic.

## The Bottom Line

Should these findings convince you to add more garlic to your diet? Unfortunately, there's no guidance about how much is needed to achieve positive health effects. In addition, there's little information on possible side effects from long-term garlic supplementation. With the mounting evidence of its health-promoting qualities, however, you may seek to increase your intake of this odoriferous herb.

Feel free to have as much garlic as you find palatable, but don't expect it to be a magical cure-all. While the research results are fascinating, garlic cannot absolve the sins of an unbalanced diet and an unhealthy lifestyle. So while the science behind garlic's qualities unfolds, flavoring food with this herb remains the best and unquestionably most "tasteful" way to add garlic to your diet.

# Benevolent Bugs

*Bringing culture to your intestines*

## Friendly Bacteria

Despite their reputation for causing infection and ill health, not all bacteria are problematic. In fact, there is a vast colony of "friendly" bacteria that live in the lower portion of the digestive system. Called the intestinal flora, these bacteria play an important role in our general health. But in the large intestines (or colon) where the bacteria live, it's not all a one-sided affair. Alongside the friendly bacteria are other, not-so-friendly bugs seeking to gain the upper hand. Foods such as yogurt contain the types of benevolent bugs that can help strengthen the friendly flora and make it a stronger ally.

## What a Little Flora Can Do

The lineup of potential benefits from healthy intestinal flora is nothing short of impressive. Research now associates these friendly bacteria with:

• Protection against colon cancer and other diseases in the intestines.

• Protection against vaginal yeast infections.

• Stimulation of the immune system.

• Enhanced absorption of the protein, vitamins, and minerals in milk.

• A reduction of the symptoms of lactose intolerance.

## Yogurt: A Healthy Food With a Rich Past

The history of bacteria in dairy products dates from the Bible. In those days, well before refrigeration, any attempt to store milk led to sour milk. At some point, it was discovered there were different types of sour milk and that only some made people ill.

With little understanding of how or why, people found that by taking a small amount from a "good" batch of sour milk and causing a similar souring in a new batch of fresh milk, they could store the milk for longer periods of time. In this way, the "culturing" of milk became an early form of food processing and preservation.

The notion that cultured dairy products might be healthful was popularized in 1906 when Elie Metchnikoff, a Russian biologist working at the Pasteur Institute in Paris, proposed that health and longevity were linked to the type of bacteria living in the intestines. In his 1906 book, *The Prolongation of Life,* Metchnikoff attributed the health and long lives of Balkan tribes to the bacteria used to make the yogurt that was a staple of their diet.

## Can Flora Become Unhealthy?

The key to any health benefits from intestinal flora is keeping the balance of power on the side of the benevolent bugs. This is not always an easy task, as there are thousands of strains of bacteria—both friendly and unfriendly—as well as several different yeast organisms.

In recent years science has begun to study the factors that influence the bacteria in the intestinal flora. Researchers have discovered that although the flora is usually quite stable, it can be affected by what you eat and any medications you might take. Whenever there's a rapid change in the flora, you can expect to experience temporary discomfort such as cramps, diarrhea, bloating, or gas.

## Change Upsets Flora

The diet of the flora consists of undigested food. Hence the makeup of the flora is affected by any radical changes in our diet, such as the addition or removal of large amounts of fiber. Digestive upset, which often accompanies such changes, can be minimized if the changes are gradual. Physical or emotional stress can also change the conditions of the lower intestines where the flora live. Some researchers speculate that the effect of stress on the intestinal flora might predispose the body to the diarrhea often experienced by travelers.

Of all these factors, however, nothing affects the flora more than antibiotics. When taken to eliminate illness-causing bacteria, antibiotics destroy friend and foe alike which permits yeast organisms, normally kept in check by the friendly flora, to grow in greater numbers. This is one reason why yeast infections often flare up during and after the taking of antibiotics.

## Keeping the Good Guys in Control

One way to maintain a healthy flora is to keep sources of friendly bacteria, like yogurt or acidophilus milk, in your diet. Yogurt, although made from milk, is well tolerated by people with lactose intolerance—the reduced ability to digest the lactose in milk. This is because yogurt bacteria produce their own lactose-digesting enzyme.

To provide any of the additional health benefits, though, your source of friendly bacteria must contain a live, or active, culture. As the activity of friendly bacteria can decrease with age, it's best to eat yogurt that's as fresh as possible. In addition, some yogurt products are heat-treated, which kills off the bad as well as the good bacteria. (If a product is heat-treated, it has to say so on the label.)

Some yogurts added *L. acidophilus* or *L. bifidus* bacteria. These types have special value because, unlike the standard yogurt bacteria (*S. thermophilous* and *L. bulgaricus*), *L. acidophilus* and *L. bifidus* bacteria can establish themselves as long-term residents in the intestinal flora. Along the same line, milk drinkers should consider switching to low-fat milk with added *L. acidophilus*. For a few pennies more, you get all the potential benefits from this bacteria in every glass—and there's no difference in taste.

## The Scoop on Frozen Yogurt

Frozen yogurt is made from a specially formulated premix. Similar to cup yogurt, the premix is made from milk that has been cultured by a strain of friendly bacteria. Unlike yogurt in the cup, however, the culturing process is halted before the characteristic tartness can develop. The mix is then pasteurized—a step that kills potentially harmful bacteria along with the friendly bacteria used to culture the milk.

Honey Hill Farms and Columbo, two large manufacturers of frozen yogurt premix, both add a new batch of friendly bacteria after pasteurization. Because of this, their frozen yogurt can contribute to the health of flora. So if you're a frozen yogurt fan, it pays to find a brand that adds new culture after pasteurization.

Depending on the fat content of the yogurt, the premix will contain any of a variety of stabilizers, such as carrageen, guar gum, and carob bean gum. These are naturally occurring substances that help reduce the formation of coarse ice crystals and, along with constant stirring by the yogurt dispensing machine, help maintain the dessert's characteristically smooth texture.

When compared with a flavored cup yogurt, most frozen yogurt contains comparable amounts of protein, carbohydrates, and calcium. Of course, this assumes that you don't pile on the sugary, high-fat crumbled candy bars, broken cookies, or sprinkles typically offered at the soft-serve yogurt counter.

## Non-dairy Sources

Most natural and health food stores sell *L. acidophilus* and *L. bifidus* as a food supplement. These capsules, when taken as directed on a regular basis, can be an excellent non-dairy source of the friendly flora. As with yogurt, though, freshness is important, so make sure you use it up before the expiration date.

## Related Topics

See also: The Wonderful World of Digestion and Allergies and Other Adverse Reactions.

# The Joys of Juicing

*Can we drink our ills away?*

## A New Health Craze

Promoters of juicing sing the praises of freshly-made fruit and vegetable juices. They shout and tout how, with a few glasses a day, you can drink your troubles away. There's no question that juicing has been catching on. As evidence of its popularity of *The Juiceman's Power of Juicing,* by Jay Kordich (William Morrow, 1992) sat atop bestseller lists for ten weeks and has about 400,000 copies in print. Once found only in health and natural food stores, juicers can now be found at most department stores. Such machines however, cost anywhere from $45 to over $200. And although drinking fresh juice is a tasteful and healthy practice, it's questionable whether it can accomplish all that its promoters claim.

## Fad Fueled by TV

Much of juicing's popularity is due to an onslaught of "infomercials," those half-hour commercials that run on the cable networks. Juicing has many stars on this circuit, including Kordich, who sells his juicer, the Juiceman II, and fitness icon Jack LaLanne hawking his machine, the Juice Tiger. In these "shows," Kordich and LaLanne make a variety of fruit and vegetable juices to the preprogrammed glee of the host and audience. Although contrived, the shows are informative. It's helpful to see how different fruits and vegetables can work in combination. But as with the juicers themselves, it's important to know the difference between substance and pulp.

## Dubious Claims

There's no reason to believe that you can "juice" away all your health problems. So it's unfortunate that the infomercials and many books on juicing feature juice prescriptions for a wide range of ailments, everything from arthritis and cancer to migraine headaches and cellulite.

How can proponents make such claims? A health claim like, "This juice I'm selling will cure your arthritis" would definitely be illegal. But with juicing advice in books and on TV, the law is unclear. The legal loophole is that the author is speaking only in general terms about food being prepared via juicing and that he's selling the machine not the juice.

The lack of a scientific basis for the wide range of juice prescriptions also gives rise to conflicting advice. While one author endorses pineapple juice for arthritis, another pushes broccoli, kale, and spinach, and yet another recommends bean sprouts, carrots, and cucumbers. All these ingredients have positive nutritional attributes, but as a cure for arthritis? That's questionable.

## Juicing Does Have Its Good Points

It's unfortunate that the focus on curing specific diseases overshadows the true values of juicing. In the United States, for example, the average consumption of soft drinks per person is upwards of 46 gallons a year. Our bodies would obviously be better off if we got our refreshment from fresh vegetable or fruit juices instead. Not only do juices have wonderful flavors, they contain valuable nutrients not available in soda pop. For example, a 6-ounce glass of fresh carrot juice contains only 73 calories and is loaded with beta-carotene and other nutrients. Fresh apple, pineapple, or melon juices yield flavor and aromas unmatched by any other beverage.

## Not a Replacement for Food

The beneficial effects from eating more fruits and vegetables are not disputed. And it's a lot easier to drink a pound of carrots than to eat one. But because juice doesn't have fiber, the object is to have juice in addition to, not instead of, fresh fruits and vegetables. And, although proponents of juicing might swear you get all but the fiber, it's unclear what proportion of the nutrients are left behind with the pulp. It's also unknown whether the juicing process itself destroys some of the nutrients.

## Choosing a Juicer

There are three basic types of juicers. Extractors, the most popular kind, grind the food with a high-speed spinning dish that traps the pulp. They often have an ejector that deposits the pulp in a convenient bin. Masticator-type juicers chew up the food at a slower speed and make juice by mechanically pressing the ground-up produce against a screen. Finally, there are specialized blender/juicers that grind the entire fruit or vegetable. This is the only type of juicer that doesn't remove the pulp and, as a result, juices from these machines retain the food's fiber. The tradeoff, however, is that the output can end up a thick sludge rather than juice.

You'll find the greatest price variation among the juice extractors, the different price tags—from about $45 to over $200--reflecting the power and noise level of the motor, pulp capacity, and cleaning ease. The masticator and blender/juicers tend to be in the $200+ range. There's no "best" method—it's all a matter of taste (and pocketbook).

## Advice for the Juicer-to-Be

• Make sure you like the taste of fresh juice before you spend money on a juicer. Find a juice bar in your area or arrange for a demonstration so that you can sample a variety of freshly made juices.

• When shopping for a juicer, find a model that's easy to clean. If cleaning is a bother, the machine is likely to sit unused.

• The key to fresh juice is "fresh," so only make enough for immediate consumption. If larger amounts are needed, place the excess in a covered container and refrigerate.

• To avoid any possible digestive problems such as an upset stomach, don't overdo it at first. Introduce new fruits and vegetables slowly.

## To Investigate Further

Look at *Juice it Up* (101 Productions/Cole Group, Santa Rosa, CA 1991) by P. Gentry. See also: Fiber for Health and Fiber Facts & Fads.

# Eating By the Clock

*Working with the body's natural rhythm*

## The Body Loves Routine

No matter what your political persuasion, your body tends to be quite conservative. It thrives when routine events, such as eating and sleeping, take place at about the same time every day. This reality helps explain hunger pangs, jet lag, and even a ritual daily visit to the bathroom. More than mere habit, the pattern of these occurrences are tied to a "biological clock" that ticks within the body.

The field is called chronobiology (*chrono*=time, *bio*=life). It's roots are in the early 1700s, when botanists discovered that plant behavior followed a daily cycle. In recent years, scientists have discovered the presence of biological rhythms in the human body. As we continue to learn more, it may prove that awareness of these patterns could serve us in the prevention and treatment of many ailments.

## Rhythms Are Everywhere

Such health factors as heart rate, blood pressure, body temperature, and urine excretion are all seemingly tied to a master clock. For each function, there tends to be distinct rhythms with peaks and lulls of activity throughout the day. Those that cycle every 24 hours are called circadian rhythms (*circa*=about, *dian*=day), but there are cycles that occur at weekly, monthly, and yearly intervals as well.

For example, if you're trying to lower your high blood pressure through diet, exercise, or medication, the time of day at which you take your blood-pressure measurements can influence your conclusions about which is or is not working. In this case, it might be best to have multiple before-and-after measurements taken at the same time of day.

## When You Eat Seems to Matter

One finding from chronobiological research is that a calorie is not the same when consumed at different times of the day. Studies were conducted in which volunteers ate one meal a day at either breakfast or dinner. In both cases, the body adapted to the new feeding schedule and the volunteers reported hunger pangs before their scheduled meal. Of particular interest was the finding that dietary calories acted differently in each group. Those who had their meal at dinnertime tended to gain weight; those eating at breakfast did not. What this means is that a calorie goes farther when consumed near the end of the day. Advice for dieters might be to pay special attention to evening eating.

## Meal Timing for Problem Eaters

The idea of looking at *when* in addition to *what* you eat is intriguing. A focus on timing could help people who find it difficult to eat large meals. This might include the elderly or those with disorders of the digestive system. Others that could benefit include individuals with limited food budgets; athletes in training seeking to foster muscle growth; and dieters continually baffled by their inability to lose weight. Research into chronobiology may even help solve part of the puzzle of the high-fat/low-heart-disease French diet, where the main meal is lunch.

It may also be worthwhile to review some old research. Significant effects may have been overlooked simply because of bad timing. For example, a reaction that normally occurs at dinner might not show up if the test is conducted early in the day.

## Reducing Jet Lag

Whenever you fly over multiple time zones there's a noticeable difference between clock time and body time. Depending on distance traveled, it can take several days for the circadian rhythms in your body to re-adapt to the new time. In the interval you feel the general discomfort known as jet lag. What and when you eat before, during, and after the trip may help reduce the lag. A few days before a trip, those flying east should eat and go to sleep earlier than usual, whereas those with a western destination should eat later and attempt to stay up a few extra hours. When flying, avoid heavy meals, have plenty of fluids, and avoid alcoholic beverages. Upon arrival, have high-protein meals in the morning and high-carbohydrate meals before those times you want to rest. If you're a coffee drinker, starting on the day before departure, drink your coffee according to the clock time at your destination.

## Promising Cancer Progress

One of the new frontiers of chronobiology involves nutrition and cancer therapy. Ross Laboratories of Columbus, Ohio, recently held a conference on the Role of Nutrients in Cancer Treatment. The conferees discussed how healthy cells tend to have a daily rhythm of growth and rest. By contrast, cancer cells are always growing.

Chemotherapy, the use of cancer-fighting drugs, works by stopping chemical reactions that are necessary for life. The dose is adjusted so that the fastest-growing cells—in this case cancer cells—bear the brunt of the effect. Using chronobiology, it was discovered that side effects from chemotherapy could be minimized when the patients receive these powerful drugs while their normal cells were at rest. Likewise, these principles can be applied to mealtimes; a cancer patient could eat only when the healthy body cells are hungry, thus avoiding giving unnecessary sustenance to the cancer.

## Other Possibilities

There's little question that research efforts in the field of chronobiology may unlock many of the body's mysteries. Where science once tended to gloss over the time factor, an awareness of chronobiology has provided a lens to observe natural rhythms and the significant effects they have on human health.

# Pumping Up Your Diet

*Good food fosters good athletic performance*

## A Burgeoning Field

In recent years, nutrition for athletes has grown into a sophisticated branch of science, complete with research journals and sports laboratories around the world. It's a far cry from the days when a thick steak on the football training table marked the limit of nutritional awareness. (One Eastern European track coach went so far as to serve reindeer meat in the hopes that it would make his runners go faster.) Today we continue to learn how nutrients affect performance, whether it's a daily walk, riding a bicycle, pumping iron at the local gym, or running down the football field.

## How Do Athletic Needs Differ?

The nutritional needs of an athlete, or any physically active individual, can be broken into two categories: supplying raw materials for building muscles and providing the energy for the muscles to perform. It's now believed that intensive muscle building or endurance events can as much as double the body's protein requirement. (Note: there is no evidence, however, that those engaging in routine workouts or aerobics have any need for increased protein.)

Regardless of your level of exertion, few people have to add protein to their menu. The current high consumption of protein foods like meat, fish, poultry, dairy products, legumes, nuts, and seeds in most of our diets is already more than adequate to meet most demands, and an excessive intake of protein has no magical power to build more muscles.

## Too Much Protein is Not Good

Like anyone else, when an athlete takes in more protein than his or her body needs, the excess is changed into energy, and that usually means fat. For an athlete in training, though, this can cause problems, as the process of converting protein to energy places a load on the kidneys, the organ responsible for removing the protein waste from the body. The excess protein can also cause a loss of dietary calcium.

Despite this information, the use of protein-powder supplements, complete with promises of dramatic results and alluring pictures of bulging muscles, is prevalent in most gyms. But remember, it's the exercise, not the excess protein, that builds the muscles.

## The Best Energy Food

Although fat is the most concentrated form of dietary energy, athletes should rely on complex carbohydrates as their main energy food. In the body, carbohydrates are the only fuel that can provide instant energy. The liver and muscles store a small amount of a carbohydrate, called glycogen, which serves as a source of energy whenever there's an extra demand.

Food sources of complex carbohydrates include whole grains, vegetables, fruits, breads, and pasta. They are preferred to simple sugars like glucose or sucrose because they take longer to digest, giving a steadier energy supply. Eating a variety of complex carbohydrates also helps provide a good intake of dietary fiber.

## The Saturated Fat Trap

Because of their greater need for calories, many athletes chow down on fat-laden fast foods. While this may satisfy energy needs, it does little to help athletic conditioning or performance and could set them up for health problems later in life. The main source of fat in athletes' diet should be that already present in protein foods they're consuming: lean meats, fish, and low-fat dairy products. Nuts and seeds make good snacks because besides being low in saturated fat they help provide essential fatty acids and are a good source of fiber.

## What About Vitamins and Minerals?

Vitamins and minerals also play a key role in the energy-producing reactions in the body, and as such, are vital for maximum performance. Research has shown that intense exercise will slightly increase demand for some of these nutrients.

For example, the body's supply of iron—a lack of which is the most common nutritional deficiency in the U.S.—is further drained by the demands of endurance exercise. The best food sources of iron include red meat, dark green leafy vegetables, and iron-fortified cereals.

Calcium intake, needed for bone growth and muscle contraction, is also traditionally low in the American diet. Athletes who don't eat dairy products may be low in this mineral unless they take steps to include non-dairy sources of calcium. Whatever your preference, keep in mind that aside from dairy products, calcium can be found in greens such as arugula, collards, and kale, as well as almonds, figs, chickpeas, and tofu. There are reports of bone thinning as well as osteoporosis in the serious female athlete; this condition, however, is thought to be linked to a decreased estrogen production and resulting irregular menstrual flow that's sometimes found in the female athlete.

## Don't Forget the Water

Water is an integral part of any discussion of nutrition and athletics. As the rate of breathing picks up during physical work, more water is lost through the lungs. A significant amount of water is also used to cool the body during exertion. In addition, water helps shuttle the waste products from energy production out of the body in the urine. Dehydration, even when mild, can impair performance and cause the body to overheat. Because one's awareness of thirst can be impaired during exercise, it's best to make drinking water a part of any exercise routine.

## Good Food Is the Key

For athletes and other health-conscious individuals food remains the best and most readily absorbed source of all nutrients. Those who opt for a balanced and varied selection of protein and complex carbohydrates from all the food groups will have little difficulty meeting their nutritional needs.

## Recommended Reading

Here's an excellent all-around book on high-performance nutrition by a scientist and former triathlete: *Power Foods* (Rodale, Emmaus, PA 1991) by Liz Applegate, Ph.D. *Nancy Clark's Sports Nutrition Guidebook* (Leisure Press, Champaign, IL 1990) by Nancy Clark, M.S., R.D. is also good.

# Potential Problems with What We Eat

# When Tainted Food Gets the Best of You

*Foodborne illness strikes one and all*

## We've All Had It

Most of us have experienced food poisoning. A mild case usually results in a queasy stomach, intestinal upset, and a general sick feeling. Often what people think to be a case of the 24-hour flu is, in reality, the after effects of a tainted meal. But the symptoms can be much more severe. Indeed, bacterial food poisoning is likely to cause 6 million illnesses and more than 9,000 deaths this year. Rather than showing signs of going away, the problem is only getting worse.

## Who's to Blame?

The villains are the bacteria and viruses that contaminate food. It's not unusual for fresh food, especially animal products, to contain some of these microorganisms. The problem arises when a quantity of these bugs manages to hitch a ride into your body on a serving of food. The most common cause of foodborne illness is the mishandling of food after purchase. Whether at home or in a restaurant or other food-service facility, unsafe methods of storage and preparation increase the odds that problem-causing bugs will end up on your plate.

## A Bacterial Rogues Gallery

**Salmonella:** Usually found in poultry products, eggs, unpasteurized milk, and meats such as beef and pork. Salmonella is often found in an animal's intestinal tract, and food can be contaminated during slaughter and preparation for sale.

**Staphylococcus:** Can be a problem with any food. Staph bacteria is normally present on our skin and inside our nose and throat. Food handlers can "infect" foods if, during an illness, they were to sneeze or cough on food or handle it with unwashed hands.

**Clostridium botulinum:** Usually a problem with improperly canned or preserved foods. This bacteria is found everywhere and is usually present in the soil. The spores of these bugs produce the deadly toxin that causes botulism. Food-preservation techniques, such as canning, must include a heat treatment that lasts long enough to kill the botulism spores.

**Campylobacter jejuni:** Unpasteurized milk, meats such as beef and pork, poultry, and fish are likely hosts. Like salmonella, this bacteria is usually present in the intestines, and contamination is usually the result of poor hygiene during preparation for sale.

**Listeria monocytogenes:** Found in contaminated milk products, this stubborn bacteria continues to grow at refrigerator temperatures and can survive heat treatments such as pasteurization. Contamination is believed to be from animals, soil, and sewage.

## Bitten by the Bug

In most cases, symptoms of food poisoning include nausea, moderate to severe intestinal distress, fever, and a bloody stool. These symptoms can begin as early as a couple of hours after the meal (staphylococcal poisoning), or as late as a couple of days (campylobacter and botulism). Botulism differs from other food poisonings in that the toxin also affects the nervous system. In addition to intestinal distress, symptoms can include blurred vision, headaches and difficulty speaking, swallowing, and breathing. This disease can be fatal, especially in the very young and the very old.

## What About Eggs?

The FDA estimates that Salmonella bacteria is found in one in every 10,000 fresh eggs and recommends that you avoid eating raw eggs and any foods containing raw eggs. Eggs are considered safe from salmonella only when the yolk and white are cooked firm. Many food-service organizations and restaurants are now switching to pasteurized eggs to avoid this problem. At first it was thought that eggs were contaminated with salmonella after being laid, possibly through a crack in the shell. It was later discovered, however, that the bacteria was present before the shell was even formed.

Fresh eggs should be kept in their original container under refrigeration in a cold part of the refrigerator—not in the door. If uncooked, eggs can be safely kept for a few weeks. Hard-boiled eggs under refrigeration can be kept up to one week. In either case, though, quality declines somewhat with time. Obviously the odds are against a single egg being contaminated, but for individuals most vulnerable to the ravages of food poisoning, taking all precautions would be prudent.

## Who's Most Vulnerable?

The severity of the poisoning is tied to the strength of the immune system, the body's defense against invading bacteria. In healthy individuals, most bouts of food poisoning pass quickly. But for those with an impaired immune system, such a malady can be life threatening.

Those who tend to suffer the most are the very young, due to an undeveloped immune system, and the very old, in whom inadequate nutrition, poor blood circulation, or other health problems inhibits the proper functioning of the immune system. In both of these groups, a smaller amount of acid is produced in the stomach, which allows larger amounts of bacteria to survive digestion in the stomach.

Diabetics are also at higher risk for foodborne illness because their tendency toward higher blood-sugar levels makes their systems more conducive for the growth of bacteria.

Cancer patients, those with advanced liver disease, individuals who are HIV positive, and transplant patients on immune-suppressant drugs all have a seriously disabled immune system that is unable to fight off foodborne bacteria. The group at greatest risk, however, is the one in which the very fabric of immunity is gone—those with full-blown AIDS. For them, even the slightest exposure can be disastrous.

As at-risk individuals are often under the care of others, it's vital that caregivers have the proper training and education to prepare and serve foods safely.

**To Go Further**

• For those with friends or family in extended-care facilities, the USDA has developed a videotape and training materials for food handlers. Titled "Food Safety Is No Mystery," it's targeted at those with limited education. The tape cost's $20.50 and can be ordered through Modern Talking Pictures Service, 800-237-4599.

• The USDA also offers a booklet and videotape titled "Eating Defensively: Food Safety Advice for Persons with AIDS." Write to the AIDS Information Clearinghouse, P.O. Box 6003, Rockville, MD 20850. The booklet is free; the videotape is $8.95.

See also: Getting the Bugs Before They Get You.

# Getting the Bugs Before They Get You

*Becoming an anti-foodborne activist*

## Hot or Cold Is Best

As ornery as these bugs can be, temperature remains their Achilles' heel. In general, bacteria tend to grow between 40° and 160° F. When chilled, bacterial growth tends to slow, and when heated to 160° most are baked out of existence. The bacteria that causes botulism are stopped by acid, so high-acid foods such as tomatoes, citrus, and pickled foods tend to be safe. These bacteria are also thwarted by nitrite preservatives, which is why sodium nitrite is added to all cured meat products.

## Temperature Control

• Refrigerators should be set no higher than 40° F, and freezers should be set at 0° F.

• Frozen foods should be defrosted in the microwave or the refrigerator, not on the counter (and don't let juices drip on other foods).

• Marinate foods in the refrigerator.

• Fresh meats, poultry, or fish that will not be consumed for several days should be frozen immediately after purchase.

• Put leftovers in the refrigerator as soon as possible; to be safe, wait no more than 2 hours after the meal.

## Cleanliness

Even if food is properly cooled or cooked, you still can be get food poisoning from careless handling. This usually happens when cooked food comes in contact with hands, utensils, counter tops or other surfaces that have not been cleaned since contact with uncooked food. Here's how to reduce the risk:

• Wash your hands before handling food. Also wash hands, utensils, and dishes after handling uncooked food.

• When grilling, use a clean plate to carry the cooked food, not the same one that held the raw meat.

• Sponges and towels can also harbor bacteria, so be careful when using these on surfaces that will be in contact with cooked food.
• Those with cuts or sores on their hands should wear gloves when preparing food.

## Are Wooden Cutting Boards Safe?

The safety of a wood surface depends on the food being cut and how often and in what manner you clean the board. Wood is not the best material on which to prepare all food. Although they're attractive, wood cutting boards can absorb liquids, and food particles can easily become imbedded. When this happens, the board is a potential breeding ground for bacteria. If wood is your surface of choice, however, there are steps you can take to help make it a safe cutting surface.

To control the absorption of fluids, the wood surface first must be seasoned with oil. Don't use vegetable oil, however; edible oils such as corn, soy, olive, and canola will turn rancid and affect food. Instead, use a nonedible oil such as mineral oil. There s also a product called block oil, made especially for seasoning wood butcher blocks.

After each use—especially with meats—the cutting board must be carefully cleaned. At the very least, this means using very hot water plus detergent. To ensure that the surface is germ-free, use a mild disinfectant, such as a bleach/water solution (the USDA recommends a solution of 1 tsp. bleach per quart of water). Then rinse well.

If there is only one cutting surface available and it's wood the potential for problems is greater. It's best to have a separate board for cutting meat; a good choice is hard plastic that can be easily cleaned or put in the dishwasher. Always keep in mind that food is only as clean as the dirtiest surface it touches. By separating meat from nonmeat cutting surfaces, and adopting a good board-cleaning routine, you reduce the possibility of cross-contamination between foods.

## The Lowdown on Containers

A container serves as an effective barrier between the food and the air. A simple but important safety practice is to be sure to close the top or seal the bag immediately after use. Buying in smaller portions is another option; this prevents food waste, but the tradeoff is increased expense, more trips to the market, and more empty packages. Consider buying in bulk and then splitting larger packages—one half for daily use while the remainder sits tightly sealed in the refrigerator or freezer.

A container must remain in good condition to be safely reused. The key points are cleanliness and a tight seal. Containers of fatty foods, such as spreadable cheeses, can be difficult to clean if the rim or any irregular surface can trap food particles. If you plan to reuse containers, be sure to scrub them well by hand between uses—dishwasher cleaning is unreliable because it often doesn't remove dried-on debris. If you can't clean the container absolutely, don't reuse it. Over time, many containers crack or deteriorate to the point that they no longer provide a good seal and should be discarded.

## A Final Word

Bacteria are everywhere—on our skin, our clothes, in dirt, on countertops and all perishable food. The types of bacteria that cause foodborne illness aren't necessarily the ones that spoil food, so just because food looks good is no guarantee that it's safe. If these two sections on foodborne illness have made you wary, that's good; food poisoning is a problem that, by and large, is under our control. It will only go away when we make it.

## For More Information

• Contact the USDA food safety hotline, 800-535-4555. Although primarily an information source for the proper handling of meat and poultry, it will help with other food-safety matters. Ask for the booklet, "Is Someone You Know at Risk for Foodborne Illness?" Hotline hours are weekdays, between 10 AM and 4 PM EST.

• To get a free pamphlet explaining the general principles of foodborne illness, request "A Quick Consumer Guide to Safe Food Handling," by writing Safe Food, Consumer Information Center, 574-X, Pueblo, CO 81009.

Here's a couple of books with more food-safety information: *What's Left to Eat* (McGraw Hill, NY 1992) by Sue Gebo, M.P.H., R.D.; *Fighting Back: How to Protect Yourself against the "Food Bug" and Report Food Poisoning Hazards* (M&C Publishing, 8121 Manchester Blvd, #594F, Los Angeles, CA 90293, 1992) by M. Doom, R.E.H.S. See also: When Tainted Food Gets the Best of You.

# Seafood Safety

*Has that fish led a clean life?*

## Is It Safe to Eat?

Concerns continue to be voiced about the safety of eating fish. This is unfortunate because fish is high in protein, a good source of B vitamins, and relatively low in fat. Nutritional value, however, is not the problem. At issue are potential hazards from chemical and bacterial contamination.

The safety of fresh fish depends on two elements: the environment in which the fish was raised and whether the fish was properly handled and refrigerated after the catch. These are valid concerns, but with a little information you can minimize your risk and enjoy your fish for the wholesome meal it provides.

## A Fish Reflects its Diet

In polluted water, contaminants enter the food chain with the lowest sea creatures, such as algae or plankton. These contaminants work their way up the food chain as the tainted organisms are eaten by small fish who then become a food source for a list of increasingly larger predators. The amount of contaminants in any fish depends on how long (if at all) they have lived in polluted waters, and on the pollutants (if any) in the organisms they've eaten.

Freshwater fish are natural inhabitants of bays, rivers, lakes, and ponds, many of which might have questionable water quality. Therefore it is wise to ask where the fish was caught and to avoid fish of unknown origin. Deep sea varieties generally don't pose a hazard if they've spent their life out at sea. Again, ask where the fish came from. In theory, commercial fishing is done at least 20 miles offshore—away from most sources of pollution. But those who engage in sport fishing should be knowledgeable about the waters in which they fish. The joys of landing a big one are easily outweighed by any potential health hazards from an unsafe meal.

## Farm-Raised Fish

Some fish have definitely led a clean life. These are fish raised on specialized farms in a controlled environment—usually a spring-fed pond—where they dine on a well-balanced, vegetable-based fish chow. This ensures uniform, high quality. Most fish farms are routinely checked by state inspectors. Americans buy about 10 million pounds of farm-raised fish every year. Types of fish most commonly raised on farms are trout, catfish, salmon, and crayfish.

The nutritional value of a farm-raised fish is similar to that of its free-range cousin. One exception, however, might be the oils in the fish. Ocean fish, such as salmon, dine on smaller fish, insects, and plants. These foods are sources of omega-3 fatty acids, the health-promoting oils for which salmon and other varieties of high-fat fish are known. As the salmon consumes its ocean diet, these beneficial oils become a part of its body composition. Fish raised on farms, however, dine on a controlled diet that contains little of the omega-3 fats; hence the farm-raised fish will provide significantly less of these fats.

## After the Catch

If not handled and stored properly, a fish out of water becomes a breeding ground for unwanted bacteria. Ice can effectively inhibit bacterial growth, but it must be used properly. On the way to the store and while awaiting sale, whole fish must be kept on a bed of ice. If the fish are stacked on top of each other in a refrigerated display case, there should be enough layers of ice to ensure that all the fish are sufficiently cooled. Cut-up fish, such as fillets and steaks, should be kept in single layers on lined trays over ice to ensure that the flesh or juices don't come in direct contact with the ice.

## The Scoop on Surimi

Surimi is a generic name for a type of processed seafood, widely available in Japan, that has recently been introduced in the U.S. It's made up of less expensive varieties of fish, such as pollock, that are boned, rinsed, and minced until nothing more than a bland and colorless mass. It's then formed, flavored, and colored to resemble more expensive fish varieties, such as crab, lobster, scallops or shrimp.

Surimi contains a number of non-fish ingredients, such as sugar, carbohydrate-based binding agents, and flavorings (which may or may not include glutamate). It's low in fat like standard shellfish but, because of the added carbohydrates, contains about one-third less protein.

It may be difficult to tell the difference between a surimi-based seafood salad and one containing the genuine article, especially if the salad includes many other ingredients. Because of this, you should always check the label or ask the deli attendant to verify that you're getting what you want.

**Choosing the Best Fish**

When buying fish, the burden falls upon you to find the right store. A good one gets its fish from reputable sources and has the trained employees and proper equipment to handle it safely. Here are some general guidelines:
• Fresh fish should always smell fresh.
• When buying whole fish, the eyes should be clear, not cloudy.
• There should be a sheen on the gills.
• If you press on the flesh with your finger, it should spring back.
• Fish should remain cold from the store to your home; ask for ice if it's a long trip.
• Discard questionable fish—especially if you detect any off odors or flavors.
• Handle fish like any uncooked meat, making sure you wash hands, utensils, and serving dishes to avoid cross-contamination between raw and cooked food.
• Before cooking, trim off fatty areas and dark meat under the skin; these are the areas where contaminants tend to accumulate.
• Cook fish thoroughly—until the flesh becomes opaque and flakes easily with a fork.
• Eat a variety of seafood—don't always eat the same type of fish.

## To Go Deeper
See also: Fish Oil & Health.

# The Dangers of Once-Friendly Fats

*Margarine headed for a meltdown*

## More Harm Than Good?

Changing from animal to vegetable fat in processed foods will reduce one's dietary intake of saturated fat as well as a minor source of dietary cholesterol. This is why over the past 30 years so many people have been instructed by their doctors to switch from butter to margarine. There's recent evidence, however, that such a shift causes more health problems than it could ever hope to solve because of the way fats are prepared for use in margarine and other processed food.

## The Hard Facts

The concern centers on hydrogenation, a widely-used industrial process. At room temperature, oils (less saturated) are liquid, and fats (more saturated) are solid. The hydrogenation process, also called hardening, can change an unsaturated oil into a solid block of saturated fat—but it usually doesn't go that far. More often, the unsaturated vegetable oil, such as soy, corn, or canola, is "partially" hydrogenated into a semisolid fat, such as margarine or shortening.

Food manufacturers make extensive use of partially hydrogenated oils, with good reason. Through this process a liquid vegetable oil can be hardened into various consistencies for commercial use. A partially hydrogenated oil can be made spreadable and is more shelf stable. The degree of saturation, or hardness, depends on the intended use.

So what's the problem? During the hydrogenation process, an unusual breed of unsaturated fats called *trans* fatty acids (TFAs) are produced. Until recently, there wasn't any widespread concern about TFAs. Because they are unsaturated fats, the majority of scientific opinion was that they posed no health risk. Now, however, TFAs are looking more and more like real troublemakers.

## TFAs and Heart Disease

In 1990 a major study in the *New England Journal of Medicine* suggested that TFAs may represent a greater risk than the saturated fats they were designed to replace. The study found that TFAs not only increased blood cholesterol, they also raised the LDL (least desirable or bad cholesterol) and lowered the HDL (highly desirable or good cholesterol).

The study was criticized because the level of TFAs in the experiment was thought to be higher than that present in the typical diet. Since then, however, published research has shown that the amount of TFAs in the American diet is higher than was previously thought, comparable to that used in the study. In 1992, another TFA study was published in the *Journal of Lipid Research*, this time using only half the amount of TFAs in the previous study; similar negative effects were found.

Scientists are beginning to understand how TFAs do their damage. At a meeting of the American Oil Chemists Society in 1992, a paper detailed how TFAs can turn the beneficial HDLs into risk-promoting LDLs. This "missing link" further supports the evidence in the earlier studies. And at the 1992 annual meeting of the Society for Epidemiologic Research, scientists from Harvard reported that of a group of 85,000 women followed since 1980, those consuming the highest amount of TFAs had the greatest risk of developing heart disease.

## Links to Cancer and Other Health Problems

Another report, from the Harvard School of Public Health presented at the 1992 National Data Base Conference, connected TFAs with the incidence of heart disease and cancer. It was suggested that food manufacturers find a means to reduce TFAs in the food supply. And as if this weren't enough, there has been preliminary evidence, from both animal and human studies, that TFAs may impair the immune system and have a negative effect on fetal and infant growth. The gist of all this research indicates that partially hydrogenated fats, and the TFAs they contain, represent a greater health risk than the saturated fats they replaced—so steer clear.

## Implications for Industry and Agriculture

These findings are shaping up to be a major problem because partially hydrogenated fats are found throughout the food supply. As research continues to verify that partial hydrogenation adds an unnecessary health risk, the food industry could be facing consumer avoidance of the affected products.

Agriculture also has much at stake. Some of the country's largest cash crops, such as soybeans and corn, are used to form hydrogenated-oil products. If these findings have the expected impact on consumer demand, there will need to be a change in the amount of these vegetables grown for this purpose. At present plant breeders are developing new lines of crops to contain the types of fat that will make hydrogenation unnecessary. This development, though, could be years away.

## A TFA Sampler

Here's a list of some common foods made with partially hydrogenated fat, and the grams of TFAs they contain. As you read it, you can understand the difficulty in swallowing the previous estimates that the average TFA intake in this country was under 8 grams per day. Where do you think you stand?

### Trans Fatty Acid (TFA) Content
*(grams)*

| | |
|---|---|
| 1 Tbs. butter (for comparison) | 0.5 |
| 1 Tbs. vegetable shortening | 2.7 |
| 1 Tbs. margarine | 3.5 |
| 12 soda crackers* | 5.2 |
| 1 plain donut* | 5.5 |
| 1 serving fried fish* | 5.7 |
| 3½ oz. tortilla chips* | 7.7 |
| 1 serving fried chicken* | 7.8 |
| 4 oz. gourmet muffin* | 8.2 |
| 1 large order French fries* | 9.2 |
| 3½ oz. serving potato chips* | 10.4 |
| 12 Oreo-type cookies | 16.9 |
| 12 pecan sandies-type cookies | 26.5 |

*when made with hydrogenated vegetable shortening

## Avoiding TFAs

The best way to avoid TFAs is to control your fat consumption. Your TFA intake will be small when you eat a minimum of high-fat processed foods and stick to those with low or no hydrogenated fat. Because most snack foods tend to be high in fat, these are the first ones to watch. Your use of shortening and spreadable vegetable fats should also be kept to a minimum. When using a spreadable fat, consider butter, or make your own "soft" spread by mixing butter with a liquid, monounsaturated oil such as canola, olive, or almond oil. If you are going to use margarine, choose a liquid or tub margarine—one that lists partially hydrogenated fat no higher than third on the ingredient statement. Ironically, canola-based margarines tend to have the highest TFA content.

## For Further Information

See also: Dietary Fat and Eating for a Healthy Heart.

# Getting the Lead Out

*It's bad—and it's everywhere*

## Not a Pretty Picture

Lead is toxic whether formed into a bullet or used to make paint. But bullets and paint are not the only sources of this metal. For most people, food and drink are the main ways that lead gets into the body. And what's more, there are other nutrients in the diet that help determine how toxic lead will be.

## Portrait of a Villain

Because lead is found everywhere, it's not unusual for our bodies to contain small amounts. Normally, we can eliminate it, albeit slowly. The potential for health problems occurs when the intake of lead exceeds the body's ability to handle it. It's then that lead builds up and becomes dangerous.

This is because after lead enters the body, the red blood cells carry it to most of the tissues. Indeed some of lead's negative health effects come from its interference with the manufacture of hemoglobin, the oxygen-carrying substance in the red blood cells. Lead can also enter the brain, and it freely passes through the placenta to a developing fetus. The list of lead's negative health effects includes harm to the kidneys, nervous system, high blood pressure, growth retardation, and a permanent impairment of mental abilities.

The degree of damage depends on the amount of lead. Because these toxic effects are most evident during periods of rapid growth, exposure to lead is most dangerous during pregnancy, infancy, and childhood.

## Diet Is a Potent Ally

Often overlooked in discussions about lead are the health effects of other nutrients in the diet. Two nutrients—calcium and iron—play an integral role in how much lead the body absorbs.

Dietary calcium entered the picture when studies found that

animals raised on a low-calcium diet absorbed more lead than those on a high-calcium regimen. The current belief is that lead is absorbed through the same pathway as calcium. This means that a recommended intake of dietary calcium will reduce the opportunity for lead to enter the body.

Iron is another nutrient known to affect the toxicity of lead. About 20 years ago scientists discovered that a diet low in iron increases the amount of dietary lead the body will absorb. Someone suffering from iron deficiency has a significantly higher risk of lead poisoning. The lead/iron connection has public-health implications: Inner-city populations having the highest incidence of iron-deficiency anemia are also those that have the greatest exposure to lead.

## Get the Lead Out

• Older or imported ceramic bowls, plates or dishes may contain lead in their paints or glazes. Unless cleared for lead, avoid using them with food, especially high-acid food such as tomatoes or citrus.

• Leaded crystal is loaded with lead. Short-term, mealtime use may be acceptable, but research has shown that significant amounts of lead ends up in foods and liquids stored in leaded glass.

• The soft foil caps on wine bottles are often made from lead. A crystalline lead deposit can form where the top of the cork meets the bottle—especially if there's any sign of wine seepage. To remove the deposit, use a damp cloth to wipe off the rim and neck of the wine bottle after you remove the cork. Also be sure to wipe off the cork before you reinsert it into the bottle.

• Food manufacturers in many Third World countries continue to use lead solder for canned foods because it's inexpensive. Until this policy changes, consider imported canned foods a potential source of dietary lead. There's a particular danger with acidic foods, such as citrus juices, tomato products, or pickling brine (vinegar). Unfortunately, there is no reliable way to spot lead versus nonlead seams in cans.

• Many inks used on food wrappers contain lead. There's little danger so long as you keep the ink side away from food, or rinse food that has been in contact with the ink.

• Fish, especially shellfish, from lead-contaminated waters can contain hazardous amounts of lead. Avoid fish caught near industrial plants. Stick with varieties from offshore or deep-sea areas, or from lakes and streams known to be free from lead and other pollutants. Always strive for variety in the fish you select. When preparing fish, trim away the dark-fleshed area on the underbody, as this is where contaminants, if any, tend to accumulate.

• Your tap water can be a major source of dietary lead. If the water pipes in your house (or the municipal supply pipes) are made from lead or contain lead solder, water flowing through the pipes will also contain lead. Different amounts will be present depending on the age of the pipes, the type of water, and how long the water has been sitting. Soft water leeches more lead than hard, high-alkaline water, because in hard water, pipes can develop a layer of mineral salts over time, partially insulating the running water from the lead. Your faucets, even those recently made, can also be a source, as they're often made with a lead-containing alloy.

To limit your exposure, avoid using hot tap water with food. If your tap has been idle for several hours, run the water for a couple of minutes or until you feel the temperature turn cold, suggesting that fresh water is now in the pipes. (Be sure to collect this run-off for non-food uses.)

## Lead Testing

You can purchase lead test kits for use at home from HybriVet Systems (800-262-5323) or Frandon Enterprises (800-359-9000). Decide which is suited to the type of material you intend to test. The National Lead Information Center (800-532-3394) (English/Spanish), is set up to answer your questions, send you information on lead poisoning and prevention, and provide a contact in your state for more information.

To test for lead in water, contact the National Testing Laboratory (800-458-3330) or contact the EPA water-safety hotline (800-426-4791) for a list of certified laboratories in your area.

# Fried Food Facts

*There's no sense frying to please you*

## A Love Affair With Fat

America's consumption of fried foods continues to grow. This comes as no surprise to anyone who notice the plethora of fast-food restaurants that saturates the nation's landscape. Despite health warnings to lower the level of fat in the diet, fat-laden fried foods continue to be a popular fixture in the American diet. It's estimated that more than 400 million pounds of commercial frying oil are used every year. The French fry still reigns as the most popular item in the restaurant industry. And in a sad reflection of American values, fried-food restaurants have become symbols of westernization in developing countries. To understand why fried foods are bad, you first need to know how they are cooked.

## How Do Oils Fry Foods?

Frying oil, similar to the hot air in an oven, is nothing more than a heat-transfer medium. The main difference between the oven and the deep-fryer is that cooking oil interacts with the food and lends a unique taste and texture. When food is lowered into hot oil, cooking vapors are produced. Although the vapors are mainly steam from the water on the surface of the food, traces of the cooking oil are also present.

## Oily Dangers

While fat content is the red flag most often associated with fried foods, little attention is paid to other potential dangers from these foods: the vapors given off while food is fried, and the possible hazard from eating food that has been fried in overused oil.

Unlike heated air in an oven, cooking oil begins to break down as soon as it's used. The rate of breakdown increases as the frying temperature rises. Breakdown accelerates when the oil is used repeatedly, if it's subjected to excessive or long frying times, and when food debris collects in the hot oil.

As the oil breaks down, a mixture of nasty byproducts begins to form, including vitamin destroyers, stomach irritants, enzyme inhibitors, mutagens, and lipid oxidation products. You can inhale in these compounds when you breathe in the cooking fumes over the hot oil. They also can enter your body as part of the fried-fat calories in the food you eat. Although this sounds menacing, if frying oil is used properly, only small amounts will form, which don't represent a significant hazard. If, however, the oil is continuously overheated or kept in service too long, toxic levels can easily accumulate.

In a study of 1,400 Chinese women, scientists at the Shanghai Cancer Institute reported that cooking practices might help explain the high incidence of lung cancer in nonsmoking Chinese women. The study showed an association between lung cancer and cooking-oil vapors. The risk of cancer increased with the number of meals cooked by deep-fat or stir-frying. The cancer risk also tended to increase along with the women's reports of eye irritation. (Eye irritation often results from exposure to the smokiness that accompanies deep-fat or stir frying.) The researchers also found that those women having the highest intake of foods rich in beta-carotene, such as dark green leafy vegetables, had the lowest risk of cancer.

### Has the Oil's Gone Bad?

Unfortunately there are no government regulations to ensure that frying oils are used correctly. The safety of any fried food, whether French fries or vegetable tempura, depends on the quality-control practices of the individual restaurant. Some change their frying oil according to set intervals, whereas others make use of more precise tests to indicate when oil should be discarded. The danger comes from those establishments that won't change their oil until it's ready to get up and crawl out of the fryer.

## Flagging a Dangerous Meal

Foods fried in overused or otherwise mistreated oil can often be recognized: they absorb more fat, tend to carry an off taste, and the batter coating from foods such as fish filets and onion rings tends to fall off. French fries from overused oil might have a spotted surface and a thickened, hard, oily crust. Cake donuts, certainly not a nutritional gem at their normal 25 to 30 percent fat by weight, can contain greater than 60 percent fat by weight when fried in abused oil.

Restaurant chains that continuously fry foods are more likely to have fixed guidelines for the use and discard of cooking oils. Consumers should be wary of restaurants in which frying oil is used infrequently, as there's a greater chance that oil sits at high temperatures for extended periods.

## To Counteract a Love of Grease

If you have a periodic craving for fried foods, make sure your diet always includes at least 5 daily servings of fresh fruits and vegetables to supply the dietary antioxidants to help your body cope with the inevitable presence of frying's nasty byproducts.

## Related Topics

See also: Eating for a Healthy Heart, Cutting Cancer Risk, Beta-carotene: The Nutrient With Something Special.

# Caffeine: Trouble Brewing?

*Grounds for concern are measured in cups*

### Give Me My Coffee!

Some of the most health-conscious people drink coffee. Many of us who make special efforts to prepare healthy meals with fresh ingredients, wouldn't consider starting the day without coffee. In spite of periodic warnings that the caffeine in coffee might not be healthy, most of us are quite willing to ignore its failings and keep the faith with our morning brew. This loyalty is likely due to a combination of acquired taste, personal habit, and the addictive buzz the drink doles out. But how much are we drinking coffee for the taste, and how much because we dislike the way we feel when we miss our daily dose of caffeine?

Ours is not the first society to be enamored with caffeine. Anthropologists say that people have been using it in one form or another since the Stone Age.

### What Does it Do?

To no one's surprise, caffeine stimulates the brain. Its other effects include an increase in heart rate, an increase in acid release by the stomach, quicker transport of food through the digestive system, and a relaxation of the smooth muscles, such as those found in the lungs. Caffeine is also a diuretic, which means it increases the volume of urine produced by the body.

### How Caffeine Works

Once in the body, caffeine goes just about everywhere. In a woman, this may mean it makes its way to a developing fetus or into breast milk. Because caffeine is a foreign substance, the body starts eliminating caffeine as soon as it appears.

The "half-life" of caffeine varies. Those who break down caffeine fastest are smokers and, strangely enough, children. It takes them about three hours to eliminate half the caffeine in their body. The half-life for the average nonsmoking adult is five to seven hours. For women taking birth-control pills, the rate increases to 13 hours. The half-life in pregnant women is 18 to 20 hours, but returns to normal levels within a month after delivery. A newborn does not have any real ability to metabolize caffeine until he or she is several days old. Any caffeine received through mothers' milk during this period has a half-life of about three to four days. These are important points to consider for pregnant and nursing women.

## Is It Safe?

Caffeine has a mixed safety record. Although it's on the FDA's GRAS (Generally Regarded as Safe) List, caffeine has quite a dark side. Over the years, it has had an on-again, off-again connection to ulcers, heartburn, cardiovascular disease, fibrocystic breast disease, cancer, birth defects, and behavioral problems stemming from its stimulant quality.

Just being associated with such diseases might be enough to give one's coffee a bitter taste. Despite this, however, many refuse to give up their coffee—or at least switch to decaf. Some explanation may lie with the fact that the evidence is inconclusive. One study reports that caffeine is a problem, only to be followed by another saying it really isn't. One could take any of the above health problems and find support for either side.

## It's Definitely Addictive

What *is* widely accepted is that the body easily becomes addicted to caffeine. Depending on the daily intake, an abrupt withdrawal of caffeine will usually lead to withdrawal symptoms ranging from a simple headache to nausea, drowsiness, depression, and reduced attention span. These tend to be short-lived, however, and most can be avoided by cutting back on caffeine gradually.

You may experience withdrawal effects even if you drink as little as two cups a day. In a study published in the *New England Journal of Medicine*, half of the 62 coffee drinkers experienced moderate to severe headaches, and about one in 10 reported depression and anxiety. The symptoms were connected to caffeine, because those who stopped drinking coffee but received caffeine capsules didn't report the same problems.

## The Bottom Line

Except for the side effects from sudden withdrawal, there are no well-established problems associated with caffeine in moderate amounts, which translates to no more than a few cups a day. This is, of course, based on the assumption that you are an "average," healthy, nonpregnant, non-nursing adult.

The key to coffee's continuing popularity is apparently not tied to convincing people that it's good for them. Rather, it lies in feeling comfortable with the notion that it's not so bad if you don't drink too much. That line is thought to hover around 300 milligrams a day—but this varies from individual to individual. Signs you've had too much include increased headaches, muscular tremors, palpitations, nervousness, and irritability.

## Where Caffeine Lurks
### Caffeine Content
*(milligrams)*

| | |
|---|---|
| 6 oz. cup brewed coffee | 100 |
| 1 rounded tsp. instant coffee | 57 |
| 12 oz. cola or Dr. Pepper | 40-50 |
| 6 oz. cup tea (brewed 5 minutes) | 46 |
| 1 oz. semisweet chocolate | 13 |
| 6 oz. cup cocoa | 5 |
| 8 oz. chocolate milk | 5 |
| 6 oz. cup decaffeinated coffee | 2 |
| 1 tablet Vivarin | 200 |
| 1 tablet NO-DOZ | 100 |
| 1 tablet Excedrine | 64 |
| 1 tablet Midol | 32 |

## For More Information

Read *America's Favorite Drug* (Odonian Press, Berkeley, 1992) by Bonnie Edwards, R.N.

# Spare the Salt

*Your body will thank you*

### Don't Reach for the Shaker

A salt shaker is usually nearby whenever food is served, and next to sugar, we add more salt to our food than any other condiment. But there is a widely-held belief that too much salt leads to high blood pressure. Although this connection between salt and high blood pressure may be true only for a minority of individuals, there are good reasons to moderate our use of salt.

### Need for Salt Is Minor

Salt, which usually refers to table salt, is a chemical compound called sodium chloride. Both sodium and chloride are essential for life. Our health, however, can be maintained with as little as one-tenth of a teaspoon of salt per day. By contrast, an American's average daily intake is 10 to 35 times that amount.

Where does all that salt in our diet come from? It turns out that 10 percent is naturally present in food; 15 percent is added during cooking and at the table, while a whopping 75 percent comes from processed foods.

### Why So Much in Processed Food?

Food manufacturers find salt attractive for several reasons. Besides its role as a flavor enhancer, salt retards the growth of a variety of microorganisms. In fact, in the days before refrigeration, salting was the only practical way to keep meats and fish from spoiling.

Salt also plays a role in food texture. Processed meats such as bologna, frankfurters, and luncheon meats contain high levels of salt because it helps form and maintain the gel-like consistency. Salt is also abundant in tomato-based products, such as spaghetti and pizza sauce or tomato juice, and it is used widely in cheese and prepared soups.

## Salt in the Body

For nerve impulses and muscle contractions to take place, the body's salt/water balance has to be kept within fixed limits. Because of this, our body carefully regulates the amount of salt in its fluids and tissues.

If we ingest too much salt, the body immediately attempts to water down the excess salt, a step that's required before it can be eliminated through the kidneys. To do this, water gets pulled from inside our tissues into the bloodstream. This triggers a sense of thirst to provide more needed water. Between the control of thirst and the function of the kidneys, the concentration of salt in the body vary no more than 1 percent.

## The Link With High Blood Pressure

Perhaps the main concern about excess salt is due to its association with hypertension, or high blood pressure. Hypertension currently affects 1 out of 4 Americans. It's called the silent killer because there are no warning signs until problems such as heart disease, stroke, or kidney disease have already developed. The only real way to detect hypertension is to have your blood pressure checked.

The connection between salt and hypertension was suggested after several population studies compared salt intake with blood pressure. Scientists found that hypertension was rare in societies with a low-salt diet, while in societies with a high-salt diet, hypertension was more common. This finding, along with those from several animal studies, led to a public-health policy to lower salt in our diet.

There is some logic to this association. After all it was known that the body responded to a high salt intake by diluting the salt and thereby increasing the volume of fluid in the blood. Perhaps this increased blood volume was the cause of the higher blood pressure observed in the studies.

## Is Salt At Fault?

Scientists now question whether salt is the key. The population groups that had a low salt intake and a low incidence of high blood pressure also had active lifestyles and ate a vegetarian diet. In addition, further studies have found that other factors may be more effective than salt at controlling blood pressure. For example, high blood pressure usually takes a nosedive whenever excess weight or alcohol consumption is reduced.

When a person with hypertension goes on a low-salt diet, only 1 out of 4 experiences any decrease in blood pressure. For the remaining 3, the low-salt diet, by itself, just doesn't do it. This means that in the general population, only one out of 16 is a salt-sensitive hypertensive. A review article in the *American Journal of Hypertension* concluded, "There is no justification for the recommendation that salt intake be restricted in the general population to avert blood pressure rise."

## To Salt or Not?

Unfortunately, science has not yet come up with a way to predict who gets hypertension. At present it's known that there is a strong genetic component and that African-Americans are more likely to develop high blood pressure than European-Americans. Therefore, the key is to routinely have your blood pressure checked, particularly if you are black, obese, have a high alcohol consumption, or tend to be inactive.

Incidently, it's been reported that blood pressure varies throughout the day. There's even a condition called "white coat hypertension," in which blood pressure tends to rise in the presence of a health professional. Because the likelihood of a false positive (or negative) is greatest with only one measurement, it's considered best to rely on multiple measurements to confirm any diagnosis of high blood pressure.

If you are at high risk, or are uncertain about your blood pressure, keep your use of salt use to a minimum. Avoid reaching for the salt before you taste your food. Saltiness is one of our basic tastes, and salt can help bring out the flavor in food. The key, however, is to enjoy the natural flavor of food, not that which sits in the salt shaker.

## Where Salt Hides Out

The dietary guidelines of the Food and Nutrition Board state you should limit your sodium intake to no more than 2,400 mg sodium per day. Here are some common "salty" foods along with the level of sodium they contain.

### Salt Content
*(milligrams of sodium)*

| | |
|---|---|
| 2 slices bacon | 202 |
| ½ cup cheddar cheese | 350 |
| 4 oz. potato chips | 532 |
| 1 hot dog (without bun) | 638 |
| ½ cup sauerkraut | 780 |
| 1 cup tomato juice | 882 |
| 1 medium dill pickle | 928 |
| ½ cup grated parmesan cheese | 931 |
| 1 cup dry-roasted salted peanuts | 986 |
| 1 cup refried beans (canned) | 1,073 |
| 1 cup chicken noodle soup (canned) | 1,106 |
| 1 cup spaghetti sauce (from can) | 1,236 |
| 1 cup potato salad | 1,323 |
| 1 tsp. salt | 2,300 |

# Sugar: The Sweet Truth

*Don't let sugar get the best of your diet*

## Sweet and Innocent?

Sugar seems harmless sitting in a jar on the table. Yet something about those sweet white granules has branded it as dangerous. The sweetener has been called everything from harmless empty calories to white poison. One consumer group has gone so far as to call sugar an unsafe food additive. What's the real story?

## What, Exactly, Is Sugar?

Technically, sugar can refer to any simple carbohydrate. But to most of us, sugar refers to sucrose, the granulated sweetener used in cooking and at the table. Sucrose consists of two single carbohydrates named glucose and fructose. Glucose is the body's most important carbohydrate and is referred to as blood sugar. The other half, fructose, is also referred to as fruit sugar because it's the main sugar found in fruits.

Although proteins, fat, and complex carbohydrates have to undergo digestion, this is not the case for sucrose. All sucrose has to do is mosey up to the wall of the small intestine and it immediately gets absorbed. After absorption the glucose and fructose are split, and both are dumped into the bloodstream.

## We Don't Really Need Sugar

Glucose is the part of sucrose that is of interest to the body, because glucose is a primary source of energy. It is the only fuel used by the red blood cells and is the preferred fuel of the brain. A small amount of glucose is made into glycogen, a special glucose reserve found in muscles and the liver. From this you can see why maintaining the blood glucose level is important.

But despite this, the body does not need sugar or sucrose. *Any* digestible carbohydrate, such as bread, pasta, rice, etc., is either made from, or can be converted to, glucose. In a pinch, even protein can be broken down and made into glucose. With such a variety of potential sources, the body can get along fine without any sugar in the diet.

## Link to Disease

When intake of sugar exceeds the body's immediate needs, the excess is changed into triglycerides, a storable form of fat energy. The larger the dose of sugar that hits our system at one time, the greater the quantity of triglycerides that will be formed. Once made, these fats have to be shuttled through the bloodstream to the body's fat-storage areas. They travel in lipoproteins— special "fat" carriers that contain cholesterol. Although studies have failed to make a connection between sugar consumption and heart disease, a high-sugar diet is unwise for those at high risk for heart disease.

The relationship with diabetes is more obvious. Insulin, produced by the pancreas, is the hormone that keeps the blood-sugar level from getting too high. A rise in blood sugar, such as after a typical meal or a sugary snack, triggers the release of insulin. This is the signal for glucose to be removed from the blood and either used for energy, converted into muscle glycogen, or turned into fat, the body's energy storage form. Diabetes occurs when, for any of a number of reasons, there's insufficient insulin to do the job. Diabetics, as a result, have to keep their sugar consumption to an absolute minimum; and people at high risk for developing diabetes should limit their sucrose intake.

## Sugar and Obesity

Obesity has also been occasionally linked to the overconsumption of sugar. While some people may point to the ease with which people binge on sweet snacks, it's questionable to think of sugar as a cause of obesity. Overconsumption is not unique to sugar. By weight, sugar has less than half the calories of a fatty snack. A review of the scientific literature does not reveal any special influence sugar has on the development of obesity.

## It Does Rot Your Teeth

The millions of bacteria that normally live in our mouth have a special fondness for sugar. As they digest it, they release acids that slowly dissolve the teeth. The degree of the problem is as much a reflection of sugar as it is one's brushing and flossing habits. The villains in this area are not limited to sucrose, but include sweets like fruit rolls or honey—any food in which the carbohydrate remains in contact with the teeth for an extended length of time. Dried fruits and sugared snacks between meals are especially at fault.

## Sugar by Any Other Name Tastes as Sweet

The most common sugar, the granulated type you put in your coffee, appears on labels as "sucrose" or simply "sugar." It's made from two simple sugars, one part glucose and one part fructose. Aside from being combined in sucrose, these two simple sugars are often found alone. Glucose is also called dextrose. Fructose, or fruit sugar, which is the sweetest (1.4 times sweeter than glucose) may appear on labels as "levulose."

Two other commonly used sugars are lactose, or milk sugar, and corn syrup, a sticky liquid that's primarily glucose. There's also "high-fructose corn syrup," a sweetener in which most of the sugar has been changed to fructose. The list of caloric sweeteners in foods also includes: barley malt, brown sugar, honey, invert sugar, mannitol, sorghum maple syrup, cane sugar, grape sugar, maltose, and sorbitol.

Some of the confusion over sugar labeling will decrease with the new food labeling legislation that takes effect in 1993. Labels will clearly state the total sugar content, *and all types of sugar will be listed together*.

## Facing the Reality

We eat more sugar than any other condiment—an estimated average of 70 pounds per year without adding a sprinkle. That's because there's so much sugar in processed foods. This not only reflects our love affair with the white stuff, but also the different ways food manufacturers use sugar other than as a sweetener. For example, sugar is used to help inhibit the growth of microbes or a food for yeast in dough-based products.

The bottom line is that a diet high in sugar is not healthy. But sugar is neither a poison nor an unsafe food additive. The problems associated with sugar are likely the result of overconsumption—and the fact that those excess sugar calories tend to displace other foods offering a greater variety of nutrients.

If you yearn for something sweet, fruit is the best way to go. Not only is fruit sugar not as concentrated, by itself it's a type of sugar the body can process without causing a glucose overload.

## Related Issues

See also Foods & Moods for a discussion of sugar and hyperactivity in children.

# Barbecued Food: License to Grill?

*Where there's smoke . . .*

## Flame Broiled Can Be Hazardous to Your Health

Whether it's chicken, corn, zucchini, or roasted peppers, preparing food on the barbecue makes for a delicious and convenient change of pace. From a safety standpoint, however, barbecuing makes food more dangerous to eat. Does that mean barbecued food should be condemned as unsafe? Unfortunately, there's not a simple yes or no answer.

## What's the Problem?

To better understand the concerns about barbecuing, it helps to know about the two types of substances that can form when foods are prepared with the level of high heat typically used in grilling. The first, called *mutagens*, can cause changes in the cell's genetic material. In some cases mutations are harmless, but in others they can potentially lead to cancer and birth defects. Unfortunately it's impossible to know what any particular mutagen will do. The degree of harm is based on which cells in the body are affected and how seriously the genetic material is altered. The second substance, called *carcinogens*, also make changes to a cell's genetic material, but they differ from mutagens in that their changes have a *demonstrated* ability to cause cancer.

When you use hot coals, lava rock, mesquite or a gas flame to cook protein foods (beef, pork, lamb, chicken, or fish) or carbohydrate foods (vegetables or fruits), mutagens form as the food is charred. And if fat drippings hit the heat source during cooking, a potent carcinogen named benzopyrene is formed. This carcinogen can then be carried up in the smoke and deposited on the food. Notice that this tells us what *can* occur during barbecuing without stating the chances that it actually *will*.

## How Great is the Danger?

To answer this, we need to know about the *relative* risk of barbecuing, which is calculated by viewing one hazard in relation to others. Those who study health statistics have determined that an individual increases his or her odds of death by one in a million through any of the following actions:

• Traveling 300 miles by car.
• Eating 40 tablespoons of peanut butter.
• Rock climbing for 1.5 minutes.
• Bicycle riding for 10 minutes.
• Having one chest X-ray taken in a reputable hospital.
• Canoeing for 6 minutes.
• Spending 20 minutes being a man aged 60 or older.
• Eating 100 charcoal-broiled steaks.

Bicyclists, taxi drivers, canoers, rock climbers, and especially males over 60 would feel that the risks involved in these activities are tolerable. Despite this, however, we cannot deny that the risks exist. In the same way, it is true that if you char your foods, potentially harmful substances will be formed; and if you eat char-broiled foods, theses substances will enter your body.

Let's liken the risk to crossing the street. There's no question that there's a risk of being hit by a car every time we cross the street? But one does not walk against the light in heavy traffic, nor do sane people step into a crosswalk as a vehicle speeds toward them. Precautions are needed. Assuredly, the more time spent crossing the street, the greater one's hazard. The point here is not to dismiss the risk of eating barbecued foods in a cavalier manner, but rather to suggest moderation and caution.

It's important to never lose sight of the big picture. If you worry about eating barbecued food while sitting outside in the sun unprotected by sunscreen, or while smoking, eating a fatty diet, are inactive, or drinking alcohol in excess, your priorities need examining. These factors represent a much greater risk than the chicken on the grill.

## Reducing the Risk

You can decrease the chance of mutagens and carcinogens

forming by following these barbecuing tips:

• Don't place food directly over the charcoal. This prevents the usual smoke-up when drippings fall on the hot coals.

• Limit basting while grilling. This only adds to the smoke that carries the carcinogens.

• Plan ahead, extend cooking times, and keep temperatures more moderate by controlling air flow. The lower the heat, the less smoke and charring.

• If cooking chicken, leave the skin on for grilling, then remove it before you eat. This not only removes the charred part, but gets rid of saturated fat too.

• Consider precooking your foods in a conventional or microwave oven. This limits the time spent on the grill without having major effects on flavor.

## What Else You Eat May Make a Difference

• Fiber adds bulk and has the potential to lessen your exposure to whatever mutagens might be present. Also, vegetables such as broccoli, cauliflower, and brussels sprouts belong to the crucifer family, which contains known anticarcinogenic substances. These foods may decrease the potential long-term effects that dietary mutagens and carcinogens may have.

• Fruits and vegetables provide sources of vitamins A and C, two nutrients with proven anti-cancer properties.

## Related Topics

See also: Eating to Bolster Your Immune System and Beta-carotene: The Nutrient With Something Special.

# Toxins Courtesy of Mother Nature

*Natural doesn't mean harmless*

## The Surprising Truth About "Natural" Food

Do you realize that if the safety standards used on food additives were applied to whole, natural foods, a large portion of our food supply would be banned as too dangerous? Nature, you see, equips plants with the ability to produce an arsenal of chemical weapons to ward off insects, bacteria, fungi, and animal predators. If taken in sufficient quantities, these natural toxins can cause illness, cancer, or even death. But so long as we eat smart and don't overdo it, our bodies can cope with these substances.

## Common Examples

• Potatoes, when exposed to sunlight or allowed to sprout, produce solanine, a bitter-tasting toxin that affects the nervous system. Solanine is most concentrated in the sprout, but it's also present in potatoes having a greenish tint to the skin. To keep potatoes safer longer, store them in a cool dark place. Carefully remove all sprouts and green portions before cooking. And discard any potatoes that taste bitter.

• Cyanide, a deadly poison, is naturally present inside the seeds of apples and the pits of apricots, peaches, cherries, and other fruits. There's no danger if you don't chew on the pit, because the cyanide isn't released unless the pit is crushed. Lima beans and other legumes once contained cyanide compounds, but through selective breeding, commercial varieties were developed that no longer have this trait.

• Cabbage, mustard greens, cauliflower, and brussels sprouts, contain goitrogens, compounds that prevent iodine from being used by the thyroid gland. Without iodine the thyroid cannot function normally and the condition called goiter results. Goitrogens are not a concern unless the above foods are a major part of your daily menu. Eating iodized salt or ocean fish are good ways to ensure an adequate intake of iodine.

• Shellfish such as oysters, clams, and mussels, are poisonous at certain times of the year when they are invaded by a toxic algae during the event called the red tide. While they don't damage the shellfish, these microorganisms produce a paralyzing nerve toxin, for which there's no known antidote.

• Honey, despite its wholesome image, can contain minute amounts of the deadly botulism toxin. While the level is too low to threaten adults, children under the age of three should not be given this sweetener.

• Spinach and rhubarb contain oxalates, another toxic compound. One serving of rhubarb leaves (note that people usually serve the stalks, not the leaves) contains 1/5 the toxic dose of oxalates for humans. Spinach leaves and rhubarb stalks contain lesser amounts.

## Governmental Protection is Limited

The law governing food contains a paragraph called the Delaney Clause, which states that no substance known to cause cancer at any dose shall be *added* to foods. For example, safrole, an essential oil found in sassafras bark, nutmeg, and star anise, was once part of the flavoring in root beer. After evidence was published that safrole could cause liver cancer in animals, this flavorful oil was banned as a food additive. But because the Delaney clause applies only to substances *added* to foods, it has no power to regulate carcinogens that occur naturally. As such, there's no warning label for the small amount of safrole naturally occurring in nutmeg and star anise.

## Toxins in Peanut Butter

One natural toxin that's been in the news a lot is aflatoxin, a potent cancer-causing toxin produced by a mold that grows on peanuts and grains. Aflatoxin represents a particular health risk for children and pregnant and lactating women, but it can also affect others who might consume contaminated peanut butter.

According to *Consumer Reports*, most major brands of peanut butter have low levels of aflatoxin, while those sold under store labels or produced by on-site peanut-grinding machines (located in many health food stores) have much higher levels.

Grind-it-yourself machines might give the aura of freshness, but they are a quality-control nightmare. You rarely know how long the peanuts have been sitting around collecting mold. When you throw in a dash of humidity and warm temperatures, the possibility for mold multiplies. And if that weren't enough, contact with warm room air can cause fats in the peanuts to go rancid.

With these machines, the most dangerous peanut butter is that first glop that comes out, which has sat on the grinding surface for who knows how long, exposed to room air, moisture, and the heat from the motor. If you prefer on-site grinding, find a store that has an active machine. Before you start, check that the machine is kept clean, then take a close look at the peanut stock to make sure there are no black, off-color peanuts waiting to be ground.

## Coping With Natural Toxins

As the saying goes, "It's the dose that makes the poison." Natural toxins have the potential to cause problems when eaten in large quantities, but most are harmless when consumed in amounts found in a normal diet. The body, you see, is equipped to handle small quantities of many toxins rather than large amounts of a few. One potato, therefore, poses little risk, but the combined solanine from 150 potatoes is enough to kill a 110-pound person.

Your best defense against natural toxins is to eat a variety of foods. With variety, not only do you limit your exposure, you provide the nutrients the body requires to maintain its defenses. And as the name suggests, natural toxins are part of nature; they are not to be feared so much as respected. If you labored to clear your diet of all fresh foods containing natural toxins, it's likely you'd be left with an empty plate.

## Attention, Peanut Butter Fans

If you're looking to eat healthier, you might want to consider switching to almond butter. Like most other nuts, almonds are high in fat. Almonds' fats, however, are primarily monounsaturated, the type shown to contribute least to the risk of heart disease. Almond oil, it turns out, is quite similar to olive oil. In fact, a study in the *American Journal of Clinical Nutrition* found that the cholesterol-lowering effects of an almond-based diet was comparable to one using olive oil. Other advantages of almonds are that they're high in vitamin E, fiber, and are one of the best non-dairy sources of calcium and magnesium. All these are qualities you won't find in peanuts.

# Allergies and Other Adverse Reactions

*When what you eat doesn't agree with you*

### Just Because You Feel Bad Doesn't Make it an Allergy

In 100 A.D. Lucretius said, "One man's meat is another man's poison." I doubt if he was referring to food allergies, but the words certainly apply. There are many different types of adverse reactions to food, but they're not all allergies.

A true food allergy occurs when the body's immune system believes that a normally harmless food is an invader out to cause harm. The immune system dutifully rises to the challenge and goes into battle with this supposed adversary. The fallout from the skirmish can be symptoms ranging from sneezing, runny nose, asthma, skin rashes, nausea, diarrhea, swelling, and headache, to a life-threatening drop in blood pressure.

### What Causes Such Reactions?

The first step is called sensitization. It usually occurs when part of a food is somehow absorbed before it's completely digested. There is a greater risk of this happening during the first six months of life, before the digestive system is fully mature.

Soon after it enters the body, the food fragment runs into the immune system, the body's security police. Because this particle is where it doesn't belong, the immune system carries out its mission to attack and eliminate all trespassers. Then, to prepare for any future encounters, the immune system sets up a long-term defense plan. At this point the body is said to have been sensitized. If this food is ingested again, the immune system responds, again, this time producing allergy symptoms.

### Frequent Culprits

Although people can be allergic to anything, the most common food allergies involve nuts, eggs, milk, and soy. It's thought that the particular protein structures in these foods may have a peculiar ability to slip through the intestinal wall. If the food you're allergic to is used throughout the food supply, avoiding a reaction can be quite difficult. For example, corn syrup is a popular sweetener in processed foods. Being allergic to corn would also mean avoiding any food that contained a corn byproduct.

## How Is an Adverse Reaction Different?

An adverse reaction refers to any time you react to a food in an undesirable way. All allergies are adverse reactions, but not all adverse reactions are allergies. Adverse reactions are often mislabeled allergies. Two in particular—lactose intolerance and reactions to food additives—are good examples.

## Lactose Intolerance

Many people report stomachaches, bloating, gas, or diarrhea after drinking milk. This is *not* necessarily a milk allergy. More likely if reflects a reduced ability to digest the carbohydrate lactose found in milk. While uncommon in children, about 70 percent of the world's population develops lactose intolerance upon entering adulthood.

One solution to lactose intolerance is to avoid all milk products. But often, people with lactose intolerance are able to consume dairy products as part of a meal containing some fat, which helps by slowing the release of the problem-causing lactose from the stomach. Many folks are also able to eat cheese because it contains lactose in smaller amounts. Yogurt is another option; the bacteria in the yogurt culture make their own enzyme that digests the lactose for you. One final solution is to treat milk with lactase drops or take lactase pills along with milk. Your supermarket dairy section may even stock one of the brands of milk that contains pre-digested lactose.

## Food Additives and Preservatives

People sensitive to preservatives, the flavor enhancer monosodium glutamate (MSG), food coloring, and sulfites in wine or dried fruits may experience reactions resembling those of an allergy. These are not considered food allergies, however, because they don't involve the immune system. That's no consolation for those who suffer from these types of adverse reactions, because the only practical remedy is to switch to foods that don't contain these additives.

## Uncovering the Culprit

Figuring out whether a food allergy or an adverse reaction exists, and then pinpointing the culprit, can be extremely difficult. Not only are the symptoms typical of common illnesses, but the same food allergy causing a runny nose in one person could cause a life-threatening reaction in another.

Conditions under which you eat the suspect food may also play a role. Stress, infection, or nutrient deficiencies, because they have an effect on the immune system, might make you susceptible to a food allergy reaction that might not normally take place. The mystery is further complicated in that some reactions can have a delayed onset of hours or even days!

If you have allergy symptoms that you believe are food related, it's helpful to keep a food diary. By recording all your meals and then comparing this with your allergic reactions, you may see some pattern. Always seek qualified assistance if you or a member of your family want to investigate a possible food allergy. Physicians who are board certified through the American College of Allergy and Immunology are recommended. Approach with caution any practitioners who feature quick-fix methods that sound too good to be true.

## To Learn More

To receive a customized dietary program designed around your food allergies and sensitivities, contact International Food Allergy Association, 302 N. Oak Park Ave., Oak Park, IL 60302 (708) 386-9090. Getting a good book on food allergies could also prove valuable. I recommend *Food Allergy: A Primer for People* (Vantage Press, 1988) by Dr. Alan S. Bock, and *All About Food Allergy* (George F. Stickley Company, 1984) by Fay M. Dong, Ph.D.

# Keeping Pesticides off Your Plate

*Is organic the answer?*

### Who Gets the Crop, Farmer or Insect?

Agriculture is an age-old struggle between growers and the insect world—both intent on reaping the harvest for their own ends. With the advent of "modern" farming techniques, farmers were able to tilt the odds in their favor through the use of chemical pesticides. This, however, has given rise to a new controversy.

Over the past decade, there's been a raging debate over the safety of and need for synthetic pesticides. The public periodically hears stories about a food supply system that is overdependent on synthetic chemicals, that mainstream agriculture is hooked on pesticides. And consumers continue to voice concern over the possibility of unseen, unwanted residues on their food. For the most part, our food supply is safe. But the implications of pesticide use goes far beyond the food on our table.

## Unseen Costs

In terms of variety and abundance, Americans number among the best fed in the world. Yet this status comes with a tremendous price tag in natural and human resources. U.S. agriculture uses almost 45 billion pounds of synthetic fertilizers and 845 million pounds of pesticides each year. These are manufactured primarily from petroleum, which helps explain why farming uses more oil than any other single industry.

Additionally, while public concern about pesticides typically focuses on potential dangers from eating the food, what about the workers who apply these often cancer-causing chemicals? And what of our environment, which becomes the final resting place for all chemicals?

The U.S. Environmental Protection Agency has found pesticides in the groundwater of over 30 states. Fertilizers also find their way into the water supply. In some areas so much nitrogen has been applied to the soil that runoff has made the groundwater unsafe for children to drink.

## Love Affair with Looks

America's obsession with perfect-looking produce is one of the key factors behind the continued demand for pesticides. The National Academy of Sciences, in a report titled "Alternative Agriculture," detailed how the food industry encourages the use of pesticides solely to maintain high cosmetic standards. Separate surveys conducted on citrus fruits by Public Voice and the American Farm Bureau Federation found that, in some cases, over half the pesticides used are for purely cosmetic reasons, such as to prevent minor external blemishes that had nothing to do with the taste or wholesomeness of the fruit.

## The Great Apple Uproar

In 1989 the U.S. went through the Alar/apple scare. This uproar, which followed the announcement of potential dangers from a chemical residue in apples, was a vivid demonstration of consumer muscle. Alar, a suspected carcinogen, was used to make red apples redder and the apple harvest more productive. At the height of the commotion, one national news report showed a mother in a supermarket, expressing fears of letting her child drink apple juice. Newspapers carried the story of another parent who had called local police to stop a school bus so the "offending" juice could be removed from her child's lunch box.

News reports also carried statements from FDA officials and university scientists attempting to assure the public that the danger from pesticide residues was almost nonexistent and was being overblown by the media. A later analysis by scientists tended to affirm this view. What consumers believed at the time, however, was another story. Parental fears about the unknown, unseen dangers overwhelmed any discussion of safety.

## How Real Are Pesticide Dangers?

Many health experts place the hazards from pesticides well behind other dangers in our food supply, such as bacterial contamination and naturally-occurring toxins. They say that the major risks in our food supply are placed there by nature, not technology. However, numerous unanswered questions remain. For example, there is no practical way of measuring how, or if, an amount of residue deemed safe today might affect your health down the road. We also have no way of judging the effects of residues in combination with each other, or what happens when pesticide exposure occurs in conjunction with other health problems. That may be why, despite assurances, survey after survey reveals that American consumers continue to be wary.

## Other Choices Available

There are excellent alternatives to the continued use of pesticides. One involves organic agriculture. Organically grown crops, which generally cost more to produce than most conventional foods, are raised without synthetic chemicals, such as pesticides, fertilizers, animal feed additives, or growth regulators.

Consider the contrasting ways these two approaches would deal with insect pests, a common problem faced by growers. The conventional approach would be to kill the insects by spraying chemical pesticides on the crop. By contrast, the organic approach would be to introduce a harmless insect, such as a ladybug or a lacewing, that's a natural predator to the bothersome bug. In both cases the crop would be saved, but with organics there would be no dangerous chemicals or potential residues involved in the process.

There is another method called integrated pest management (IPM), a compromise between conventional and organic agriculture. This approach makes use of non-chemical techniques whenever possible; however, synthetic chemicals remain a part of the farmer's arsenal that can be called upon if the situation demanded it.

## Can These Work?

Opponents of organic methods argue that without chemical pesticides American farmers could no longer feed the nation, and the cost of food would skyrocket. Such claims, however, do not appear to be accurate. In a three-volume publication on pest management in agriculture, a Cornell researcher reviewed crop yields and pesticide use on hundreds of farms. He reported that farmers could cut pesticide use by as much as half with no impact on crop yields and less than a 1-percent increase in prices.

## In the End
There's little question that it's better to eat conventionally grown produce than not to eat fruits and vegetables at all. Our produce market is not a hazardous place where we need fear every bite. Yet this does not justify blind support for the use of unnecessary synthetic pesticides. We should eat as though our life depended on it. But, at the same time, we need to be aware of the environmental impact of our food choices.

## Steps to Protect Yourself and Your Family
• Wash your vegetables.
• Peel the produce whenever there's a wax coating.
• Buy produce grown locally or regionally.
• Eat fruits and vegetables in season. Those grown in other countries are not necessarily held up to the same level of scrutiny.
• Shop at farmers' markets whenever possible.
• Have a variety of foods.
• Consider buying certified organic fruits and vegetables or those produced on a farm that use IPM.
• If organically grown or IPM products are not available, speak with the produce manager to see if they can be carried.

## To Learn More
Here's an excellent, thought-provoking book on the challenges facing the future of agriculture: *Chicken Little, Tomato Sauce & Agriculture* (Bootstrap Press, NY, 1991) by Joan Dye Gussow, Ph.D. See also: Biotechnology Heads to Market.

# Becoming a
# Savvy Shopper

# Old Label/New Label

*Decoding what the package says*

## Trying to Do it Right is Hard

You're at the market and you reach for the same brand you always buy. But rather than blindly tossing the package into your cart, you pause. There are now a group of look-alike products on the shelf. One's on sale, another says it's lower in fat than your regular brand, one brags that it's "light and healthy," and yet another states that it can prevent cancer. Determined to buy the best product, you begin studying the information on the different packages. Not only are you confused about how to compare one with another, but you think about the long list of items on your shopping list and wonder whether you're going to make it home for supper!

## A Cluttered Past

The marketing of food through commercials and printed advertisements, and on package labels has led to a confusing melange of hype. It's a phenomenon that parallels advancements in nutrition science. As more people became interested in the connection between diet and health, food companies began using labels and advertisements to make and market "healthful" products. A key event occurred in 1984 when Kellogg's advertised that their All-Bran cereal was useful in the prevention of cancer. Previously, such claims hadn't been permitted by the FDA. The difference, in this case, was that the Kellogg's ads had received the endorsement of the National Cancer Institute, another government organization.

The food industry waited to see whether FDA would order Kellogg's to change their ads, but as time passed it became obvious that nothing was going to happen. Other companies followed Kellogg's lead and a flood of health claims and messages worked their way into the marketplace—each trying to outdo the other in proclaiming the healthfulness of their product.

The result was such a hodgepodge of messages and inflated claims that in March 1990, Secretary of Health and Human Services Dr. Louis Sullivan, decried the food label as a "Tower of Babel" in desperate need of reform.

## NLEA to the Rescue

A new law, called the Nutrition Label and Education Act (NLEA), was passed that year, and a set of label regulations were published in January 1993. These regulations were designed to bring some order and consistency to the way foods are labeled. The new labels have begun appearing at the market, but aren't required on all food until May 1994.

## On Every Package: Old System

At present, every package must list the name of the product, the name and address of the company who manufactured, packed, or distributes the product, and the amount of the product contained in the package. Most packages must also have an ingredient list. The ingredients are listed with the most prevalent item (by weight) followed by the remaining items in order of descending weight, but the actual weights of the items are not displayed. (There is no requirement for an ingredient list in those foods that have an FDA standardized recipe, such as ketchup, mayonnaise, peanut butter, and ice cream.)

Under the old system, the nutrition label gives you basic information on serving size, servings per container, and grams per serving of protein, carbohydrate, and fat. The lower portion of the label states the percent of the United States Recommended Dietary Allowance (U.S.RDA) per serving for protein, vitamins A, C, thiamin, riboflavin, niacin, calcium, and iron. (Note: The U.S.RDA is not the same as the Recommended Dietary Allowances [RDA], but they are closely related.) If a nutrition panel is present, the ingredients listing will appear somewhere on that panel.

## On Every Package: New System

Under the new law, food packages will contain all the information required under the old system with a few additions. All foods, including those with standardized recipes, must display ingredient lists as well as nutrition panels. The information on the nutrition panel has been expanded to help you place one serving of that food in the context of your total daily diet.

## What's New? Daily Value

The new label also compares the amount of nutrients in one serving of food with the total fat, carbohydrate, fiber, protein, vitamins, and minerals that should be present in an average daily diet. It's based on a new dietary standard called the Daily Value (DV). DVs are an updated and expanded version of the U.S. Recommended Daily Allowances, or "U.S.RDA," the allowance for vitamins, minerals, and protein that has been used on packaged foods since 1973.

Daily Values for fat, saturated fat, carbohydrate, fiber, and protein are based on the number of calories you eat during the day, while DVs for cholesterol, sodium, and potassium are fixed amounts.

## Daily Values

Fat: 30 percent of daily calories
Saturated Fat: 10 percent of daily calories
Carbohydrate: 60 percent of daily calories
Fiber: 11.5 grams per 1,000 calories
Protein: 10 percent of daily calories
Cholesterol: 300 mg per day
Sodium: 2,400 mg per day

## Table of Daily Values

The bottom half of the new label lists the amounts of fat, saturated fat, cholesterol, sodium, total carbohydrate, and fiber that should be present in an average 2,000 calorie and 2,500 calorie diet so that you can calculate how this item would nutritionally fit into your diet. At the very bottom there's a notation that fat contains 9 calories per gram and protein or carbohydrate contain 4 calories per gram.

# The New Food Label

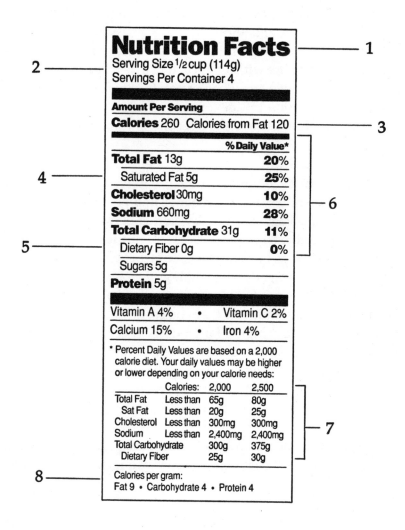

**Nutrition Facts** ———— 1

2 ————

Serving Size 1/2 cup (114g)
Servings Per Container 4

**Amount Per Serving**

**Calories** 260  Calories from Fat 120 ———— 3

| | % Daily Value* |
|---|---|
| **Total Fat** 13g | **20%** |
| Saturated Fat 5g | **25%** |
| **Cholesterol** 30mg | **10%** |
| **Sodium** 660mg | **28%** |
| **Total Carbohydrate** 31g | **11%** |
| Dietary Fiber 0g | **0%** |
| Sugars 5g | |
| **Protein** 5g | |

4 ————
5 ————
6 ————

| Vitamin A 4% | • | Vitamin C 2% |
|---|---|---|
| Calcium 15% | • | Iron 4% |

* Percent Daily Values are based on a 2,000 calorie diet. Your daily values may be higher or lower depending on your calorie needs:

| | Calories: | 2,000 | 2,500 |
|---|---|---|---|
| Total Fat | Less than | 65g | 80g |
| Sat Fat | Less than | 20g | 25g |
| Cholesterol | Less than | 300mg | 300mg |
| Sodium | Less than | 2,400mg | 2,400mg |
| Total Carbohydrate | | 300g | 375g |
| Dietary Fiber | | 25g | 30g |

7 ————

Calories per gram:
Fat 9 • Carbohydrate 4 • Protein 4

8 ————

**1.** This title signals the new format. **2.** Serving sizes are given in both household and metric measures and are consistent from one brand to another. **3.** New requirement. **4.** New requirement. **5.** New requirement. **6.** New requirement: These percentages help you see how the food fits into an average daily diet. **7.** New requirement: This shows average Daily Values at two calorie levels. You may need to adjust the numbers up or down to fit your calorie intake. **8.** New requirement.

When reading this information, keep in mind that a 2,000 calorie diet may be excessive for smaller women and children, and a 2,500 calorie diet would provide insufficient calories for larger individuals and those that are physically active. The purpose of these numbers is to let you see how one serving of the food would compare with a typical day's diet. For example, say you're reaching for a small bag of potato chips and see that one serving will give you 15% of your Daily Value for fat; you might think twice before going on to a second or third serving.

## Helping You Shop

Before you decide on a product, you should examine the name, ingredient list, nutrition panel, and preparation instructions on the package. If your decision is between two similar products, examine their ingredients and nutritional panels side by side to see which one offers more of what you seek. Does one have less fat? Is one made with whole grains? Is sugar the number one ingredient or is it further down on the list? Is one fortified with vitamins and minerals that you seek?

You can identify higher fat foods by checking whether one serving contains no more than 3 grams of fat for every 100 calories. When this is the case the food has less than 27 percent of its calories from fat.

And finally, before you toss the desired brand into your cart, check the package for any defects such as water stains, leaks, or bulges that may indicate mishandling or tampering. You should also check for a freshness date to assure you're getting a product that can be used before it expires.

## The Label Can Only Do So Much

Although food labels can give you useful information, they are not the best tool to educate yourself about health and nutrition. The real strength of the label is to help you decide between items. You still need to understand the relationship between food and health. This basic knowledge will help you to form a nutrition agenda and shopping strategy. And in this context, the label can help you decide which products are best.

# Glossary of Terms used on Food Labels

## Fat

*Fat-Free:* Less than ½ g. (gram) of fat per serving (or per 50 g. of food).

*Low Fat:* 3 g. of fat, or less, per serving (or per 50 g. of food).

*Low in Saturated Fat:* 1 g. of saturated fat, or less, per serving (no more than 15 percent of the calories are saturated fat).

__ *Percent Fat Free:* Contains the stated percent of non-fat ingredients. This term is allowed only in low-fat or fat-free foods.

*Low Cholesterol:* Less than 20 mg. (milligrams) per serving (or per 50 g. of food).

*Cholesterol Free:* Less than 2 mg. of cholesterol and no more than 2 mg. of saturated fat per serving.

*Lean:* Less than 10 g. fat, less than 4 g. saturated fat, and less than 95 mg. cholesterol per 100 g. (3½ ounces). (Used on meat, fish, poultry, and game.)

*Extra Lean:* Less than 5 g. fat, less than 2 g. saturated fat, and less than 95 mg. cholesterol per 100 g. (Used on meat, fish, poultry, and game.)

## Calories

*Reduced Calories:* A product altered to contain 25 percent fewer calories than the comparable food without reduced calories. (Cannot be used if the other food already meets the requirement for a "low calorie" claim.)

*Calorie Free:* Fewer than 5 calories per serving.

*Low Calorie:* 40 calories or less per serving (and per 50 g. of food).

*Light:* Contains  fewer calories or ½ the fat of the usual food. (If the usual food gets more half its calories from fat, the reduction must be ½ the fat.)

## Sodium

*Sodium Free:* Less than 5 mg. per serving.

*Low Sodium:* Less than 140 mg. per serving and per 50 g. of food.

*Very Low Sodium:* Less than 35 mg. per serving and per 50 g. of food.

*Reduced Sodium:* Contains no more ¼ the sodium of the comparable food.

*Light:* Light can be used if the sodium content of a low-calorie, low-fat food has been reduced by half.

## Sugar
*Sugar Free:* Less than ½ g. per serving.

## General Terms
*Free:* An amount small enough to have no likely effect on the body.

*[Nutrient] Free:* Food contains an insignificant amount of the nutrient.

*Low:* Low enough so that you can have it many times during the day without exceeding dietary guidelines.

*Less or Reduced:* Contains at least 25 percent less of the named substance than the comparable food.

*More:* Contains at least 10 percent more of the named nutrient than the comparable food.

*High In:* One serving must contain at least 20 percent of the daily requirement.

*A Source of:* One serving must provide 10 to 19 percent of the daily requirement.

*Healthy:* Must be low in fat and low in saturated fat.

*Fresh:* Must be raw, not frozen, processed, or preserved in any way (irradiation at low levels is allowed). Other uses, such as "fresh milk" or "freshly baked bread" are still permitted.

*Fresh Frozen:* Quickly frozen while still fresh (blanching before freezing is permitted).

*Light:* Can be used to describe properties such as taste, texture, and color, but the label must explain the intent, such as "light brown sugar."

*More:* One serving contains at least 10 percent more of the Daily Value than the food it's being compared to.

*Implied Value:* A product cannot claim to be made with an ingredient unless it has enough to be considered a good source of that ingredient. For example, "made with oat bran" can only appear on products that would be considered a good source of fiber.

## Synonyms
*Free:* without, no, zero
*Less:* fewer
*Light:* lite
*Low:* little, few, low source of
*Fresh Frozen:* freshly frozen, frozen fresh

## Health Claims
The FDA is now permitting a number of health claims on labels stating the role of particular foods in reducing the risk of certain diseases. In order to make these claims, the food has to meet certain criteria. In addition, the language of the claim must always use words like "may" or "might" when discussing the connection between food and disease, and the label must also state that other factors play a role in the disease.

At present there are eight different health claims that will be permitted on the label. The claims and requirements are as follows:

*Calcium and Osteoporosis:* One serving contains at least 200 mg. of calcium, which is 20 percent of the Daily Value. The calcium content must exceed the food's phosphorous content, and the calcium must be in a torm that is readily absorbed by the body.
*Fat and Cancer:* The food must meet the requirements of a "low fat" food. If a meat, fish or poultry product, it must meet the requirement for "extra lean."
*Saturated Fat, Cholesterol, and Coronary Heart Disease:* The food must meet the requirements for "low saturated fat" and "low cholesterol." The fat content must fall under the "low fat," classification, and if a meat, fish or poultry product, it must meet the requirement for "extra lean."
*Fiber-containing Grains, Fruits, and Vegetables, and Cancer:* Food must meet the requirements for "low fat" and be a "good source"

of dietary fiber.

*Fruits, Vegetables, and Grains Products that Contain Fiber, and Risk of Coronary Heart Disease:* Food must meet the requirements for "low saturated fat," "low cholesterol," and "low fat," and must contain at least 0.6 g. fiber per serving.

*Sodium and Hypertension:* Food must meet the requirement for "low sodium."

*Fruits and Vegetables, and Cancer:* Food must meet the requirement for "low fat," and must be a "good source" of at least one of the following: dietary fiber, vitamin A, or vitamin C.

# Preservatives:
# The Good, the Bad & the Ugly

*A fresh perspective*

## Preservatives to the Rescue

If your diet was made up entirely of farm-fresh foods, you'd have little need for food preservation beyond that supplied by a refrigerator. Most of us, however, aren't that fortunate. We have to rely on food suppliers who must cope with the reality that food contains nutritive substances that are just as attractive to microorganisms as they are to us. Whenever there's a need for a shelf life, some form of food preservation is necessary. Usually, that means adding something to the food to stave off the particular type of breakdown that's most likely to occur.

Preservatives come in two basic groups: Antimicrobial preservatives stop the growth of bacteria, molds, fungi, and yeast that can destroy food; antioxidant preservatives prevent rancidity, off-flavors, and discoloration caused by the natural chemical reaction of oxidation.

## Are They Safe?

As a group, preservatives get mixed reviews. Some are essentially harmless in the minute quantities used, particularly those based on natural substances.

Vitamin E (tocopherol) is used in nature to preserve plant seed oils, and vitamin C (ascorbic acid) is used to keep fruits and vegetables fresh. Both are natural antioxidants. Fruits such as cranberries, raisins, prunes, or citrus all contain naturally occurring acids that make effective antimicrobial agents. When used in foods, these compounds have last names like citrate, propionate, benzoate, sorbate, and lactate.

As an example, one such compound often found in breads, calcium propionate, retards the formation of mold. Food manufacturers can add calcium propionate directly, or use raisin juice, which contains propionic acid, the organic acid on which calcium propionate is based. In either case, these compounds and others like them are harmless at the levels used.

## Some Have Less Glowing Records

Noteworthy among those with an inconsistent safety record are sulfites, synthetic antioxidants, and nitrites. Although sulfites are effective antioxidants, the FDA estimates that as many as 100,000 people in the United States react to sulfite preservatives with symptoms like headache, hives, or shortness of breath. Recently, the FDA banned the use of sulfites on fresh fruits and vegetables (except potatoes), but they are still used in beer and wine. If present, though, it must be indicated on the label.

Synthetic antioxidants commonly found in foods include BHA (butylated hydroxyanisole), BHT (butylated hydroxytoluene), TBHQ (tertiary butyl-hydroquinone) and propyl gallate. These preservatives are commonly used because they are less expensive and more efficient than naturally occurring antioxidants like vitamin E. They have been cleared for safety through animal tests, but they are synthetics, and there's still a question of long-term safety and possible build up in the body.

## What About Nitrites?

Nitrites are added to sausages, bacon, and other cured meats because they inhibit Clostridium botulinum, the bacteria responsible for botulism poisoning. In food or in the body, nitrites can be converted into nitrosamines, compounds known to cause cancer in animals. Nitrites and nitrates (which the body can convert to nitrites) are naturally present in several vegetables, including turnip greens, beets, celery, rhubarb, spinach, radish, parsley, and lettuce. Nitrites are also found in beer and cheese

The risk from nitrites in meats, however, is different because the nitrite together with protein and a high cooking temperature make an ideal environment for nitrosamine formation. This means that the nitrosamine could already be formed when you eat such food as bacon or sausage.

The same reaction can take place in your stomach whenever you eat a nitrate-containing vegetable and a protein-food at the same meal. But the presence of other nutrients, such as vitamins C or E, help limit nitrosamine formation. Once again, with cured meat products all the ingredients needed to form nitrosamines are in the same package, and the nitrosamines can already be formed before you eat.

In choosing between the possible dangers of botulism and nitrosamines, a government panel picked nitrite preservatives as the lesser of the two dangers. It was suggested, though, that consumption of nitrite-containing cured foods be limited. So if you're going to eat cured or smoked meats, the use of nitrite preservatives is a risk you must be prepared to accept. Although most smoked and cured meats contain sodium or potassium nitrite, you can find nitrite-free meat products either as locally made, short shelf-life products, or in the freezer case where the low temperature effectively inhibits bacterial growth. (To be safe, however, these products should remain frozen until prepared.) Another option is to look for a product that contains sodium ascorbate (a salt of vitamin C), sodium erythorbate, or vitamin E, as these antioxidants also inhibit nitrosamine formation.

## Preservatives Do Have a Place

Finally, realize that not all preservatives are cause for concern--especially ones based on naturally occurring substances. What's the value of preservative-free foods if half the product gets discarded, or worse, if you end up eating food that has already begun to spoil?

## To Investigate Further

See also: Toxins Courtesy of Mother Nature and Barbecuing: License to Grill.

# Natural Misunderstanding 🍋

*Natural isn't necessarily better*

## What You See is Not Necessarily What You Get

From scanning food advertisements, it looks as though foods are promoted for what they don't have more than for what they do: "no cholesterol," "no preservatives," "no additives." Considering our love affair with such negative attributes, it's ironic that a word as popular and positive-sounding as "natural" has no real meaning in food.

## What, Exactly, Is Natural?

An official definition would have to come from the three governmental agencies that oversee the food industry, the most important one being the FDA. With the exception of meat and poultry products, which are regulated by the USDA, the FDA is the agency charged with protecting our nation's food supply. Among other things, the FDA regulates the information appearing on food package labels. To date the FDA has defined all the descriptive terms that will appear on the new food label—all, that is, except "natural." The Federal Trade Commission (FTC) is the government organization that oversees food advertising in the printed and electronic media. In 1980, the FTC said that to be advertised as "natural," a food cannot contain any artificial or synthetic ingredients. In addition, a "natural" food can be no more than minimally processed. Although they've yet to iron down exactly what "minimal processing" means, the FTC, at least, has some semblance of a working definition.

The USDA also has a definition for "natural" that's in effect for all meat and poultry products. They say that a "natural" food can have no artificial flavors or colors, preservatives, or other synthetic ingredients.

## Natural Is Popular

Although the word *natural* remains undefined by the FDA,

consumers apparently covet the idea for their food. In a *Parade* magazine survey, 79 percent of those asked used "natural" as part of their definition of a healthy food. Given this level of interest, it's not surprising that manufacturers go out of their way to put "natural" on their label. But without labeling regulations, manufacturers are free to take liberties with the term—and many do.

## Natural Deceptions

Fruit juices are good examples of "natural" deceptions. Food manufacturers take a fruit juice with a naturally high concentration of sugar, such as grape juice, and "artificially" strip it of all nutrient value but the sweetness. This stripped white grape juice, which is little more than sugar, is then used to sweeten foods sold as "all natural" 100 percent fruit juice. Naturally, this "all natural" shuffle adds to the price of the product.

Consumers assume they are getting all fruit juice, but often they're getting only a dose of sugar. Indeed, most commercial fruit juices sold as "natural" have grape juice listed near the top of the ingredient list—usually ahead of the juice whose name appears on the product label.

## Is It Natural if It Comes From Nature?

Regardless how processed an ingredient might be, if it originates as a naturally occurring or living material, either mineral, plant or animal, the ingredient can be called "natural." For example, some foods use corn sweetener, which is made by treating cornstarch with an enzyme that breaks down the corn's complex carbohydrate into individual sugar units. Because the sweetener began as corn, it's considered a "natural" sweetener.

Additionally, "all natural" doesn't mean additive-free. There are "natural" colors, flavors, and preservatives. But some of these ingredients would certainly challenge our "natural" sensibilities. For example, a widely-used red coloring (carmine) comes from chemicals extracted from ground-up insect parts. But since the bugs are found in nature, carmine is a natural color.

Simplesse is a fat substitute made from milk and egg proteins. This product is marketed as "all natural" because it started out as food. It doesn't seem to matter what form of processing is used, so long as what starts out has a natural pedigree. There will even be room for biotechnology under this very large umbrella. As new food crops are developed through genetic engineering, if sold after only minimum processing, they also will be "natural" foods.

## Be Naturally Savvy

How unfortunate that "natural" is so misused and misunderstood. The consumer appears to like the idea of "natural" in the mistaken belief that this is a guarantee of wholesomeness. There are plenty of "natural" toxins that attest to this fact.

Until it is properly defined, its presence on a label is nothing short of deceptive. As things stand now, there is no reason to believe that a processed food labeled "natural" is any more or less healthful than a similar product that does not use this word.

## To Go Further

See also: Toxins Courtesy of Mother Nature, Test Tube Tastes, and Food Coloring.

# Test Tube Tastes

*Shooting down artificial fears*

**Fooling our Taste Buds**

The tastes we associate with fresh, whole food come from distinct combinations of naturally occurring chemicals. The business of copying these flavors to add to processed foods involves a high-tech science complete with chemists and secret formulas—all designed to fool your palate into thinking you've gotten hold of the real thing.

**Engineering a Flavor**

Before a flavor can be copied, the chemists first need to identify the compounds that comprise the flavor in the genuine article. If the copy is to be an artificial flavor, all the chemists need to do is use synthetic versions of the natural flavor compounds and reconstruct the taste piece by piece. Where nature might use hundreds of chemicals in a particular flavor, the artificial copy may use only a small number—just enough to give the food a basic version of its intended taste.

If the copy is to be a "natural" flavor, the task is more complicated: the chemist has to combine different naturally occurring substances that, together, add up to the same flavor impression as the target taste.

**Why All This Work?**

Why can't food manufacturers make natural flavors with extracts from the actual food itself, such as using real strawberries to flavor strawberry Jello or strawberry ice cream? Although this direct approach might seem preferable, it's impractical on a large scale. As flavors go, the natural ones are typically weak in intensity. Many are unstable and break down during processing or storage. In addition, natural flavors may interact with other ingredients or even with the packaging material.

There's also a question of uniformity. While fresh foods grown by nature vary in flavor, processed foods must answer to a higher authority: the consumer. Biting into a fresh orange that tastes bitter won't stop you from eating oranges, but that same bitter taste in a processed food made with "natural orange flavor" might lead you to cross it off your shopping list for good. It's clear that the customer expects the taste of a processed food to be as uniform as its package.

Even if scientists could control the vagaries of a pure flavor, the supply couldn't meet the demand. If, for example, manufacturers used real strawberries to make strawberry Jello, the world supply of the fruit would be exhausted in a matter of days. Therefore, to meet the demand for natural flavors, chemists have to search for flavorful natural ingredients that work well in processed foods. They then catalog the different taste characteristics of each ingredient. When chemists are asked to copy a particular food flavor, they go to their catalog of natural ingredients and come up with a blend of flavors that mimics the genuine article.

## Is Natural Better?

These days, there's a strong desire by food marketers to have "natural" or "no artificial anything" on their label. It's questionable, though, what you, the consumer, gain from this.

Going back to our strawberry example, how much strawberry, would you think is actually present in a food made with "natural strawberry flavor, with other natural flavors?" The answer may surprise you. Although there's probably a pinch of flavor from the actual fruit, it's likely that the bulk of the strawberry taste comes from other ingredients, such as *bois de rose*, a natural oil from the tropical rosewood tree.

Government regulations require at least some of the actual strawberry to call a food strawberry-flavored. It's unclear, though, exactly how much strawberry is needed, or whether anyone pays attention to the flavor formula so long as it tastes like strawberries. And by definition, the only requirement to call a flavor "natural" is that all the components come from natural sources. In the example, therefore, strawberries don't have to be a part of the flavor formula.

## Which Tastes Better?

Ironically, one's sense of taste is not always the best way to identify a natural flavor. One product flavored with a higher percentage of real strawberries might actually taste inferior to another that had a better formula in its so-called "other natural flavors." Then, too, the natural flavors might not taste as good as the artificial flavors.

Check some labels next time you're at the store. Combinations of exotic ingredients—indicated on a package label by the innocent-looking words "natural flavors" or "with other natural flavors"—have become commonplace in processed foods. But with today's level of scientific expertise we can no longer assume that a product is more wholesome just because it uses natural flavors, or that it's inferior just because the flavoring is artificial.

Rather than relying on flavors from exotic substances, like oil from the tropical rosewood tree, artificial flavors can be made with synthetic versions of the exact flavor components found in the original fruit. This means that a natural flavor does not offer any taste or safety advantages over its synthetic counterpart and, likewise, because a food is synthetically flavored is no reason to fear its safety.

In the end, a good advertising campaign might persuade a consumer to try a product, but repeat business and ultimate success in the marketplace will depend on how it tastes. In today's marketplace, the only way to avoid the issue of flavoring additives is to stick with fresh foods.

## To Go Further

See also: "Natural" Misunderstanding and Preservatives: The Good, the Bad & the Ugly.

# Food Coloring

## What price beauty?

### Suckers for Good Looks

Nature has a genuine kinship with color. One need only scan the variety of offerings in any produce department to fully appreciate this fact. Color is one of nature's most important forms of communication and we have come to rely on it as an integral part of our evaluation of food. The presence (or absence) of specific colors is seen as an indicator of wholesomeness or ripeness, and as a hint of flavors and textures. We do, in fact, eat first with our eyes.

### When the Color's Wrong

It's not unusual for people to have a hard time with food when the colors are wrong. One study demonstrated that volunteers couldn't correctly identify strawberry flavoring when it was tinted green. And in a classic work on how colors can affect us, a group of people in the early 1970s was fed a meal of steak, peas, and French fries—but under lighting that concealed their appearance. At the conclusion of the meal, the room lights were raised to reveal blue steak, red peas, and green French fries. Despite assurances that the food was wholesome and that the coloring was only the result of added tinting, a number of volunteers became ill.

### Fuels and Fulfills Expectations

Colors have been used in foods for hundreds of years. It's gotten to the point where we expect color perfection and use this as a standard on which to judge a food's level of quality. It is this reliance, together with the marketing of perfect-looking food, that has made adding colors to processed foods necessary in the eyes of manufacturers.

Color manipulation, however, is not limited to processed foods. Oranges, for example, may sometimes be *colored* orange to hide the natural blotches of mottled green that are sometimes present when the fruit is ripe.

## A Checkered Past

Once it was commonplace for food coloring to be used unscrupulously to hide the defects of spoiled merchandise. For example, small amounts of copper sulfate, now a known poison, were added to bring pickles to a brighter shade of green, and lead-containing dyes were used in the past to give candies their bright colors. It took the passage of the Federal Pure Food and Drug Act in 1906 to outlaw such practices.

## Are They Unhealthy?

Over the years many colors have come and gone. A notable case involved the 1976 ban of FD&C Red No. 2, also called red dye No. 2, a widely used food and cosmetic coloring. This color, as with many banned before it, was found to cause cancer in laboratory animals. This ban—which among other things yanked the red candies out of the M & M bag—focused public attention on the possible dangers from artificial colors, and likely was a key event in the industry shift toward the use of natural colors. (Incidently, red M & Ms being sold today rely on a different dye, FD&C Red No. 40.)

## "Natural" Colors

When we add coloring to food, it's not a "natural" event. But to make this most artificial of processes seem more natural, food manufacturers are turning to colors from natural sources. Although the name might suggest differently, natural colors are rarely natural to the food in which they're used. Rather, they are color-rich chemicals that come from animal, vegetable, or mineral sources.

Natural red food color, for instance, can be extracted from beets or it can come from carmine, a crimson pigment from the shell of a Central American insect. Both considered "natural" red colors, they're used in everything from fruit drinks to candy to strawberry ice cream.

## Reading the Label

Label terminology for natural colors can be quite confusing. If a natural color is not "natural" to the food in which it's added—as in the use of a beet powder to tint strawberry yogurt—the food cannot claim to be naturally colored. But since the beet coloring is "natural" in itself, the yogurt could claim to have no artificial colors.

Whenever artificial colors are used they must be indicated on the label. Currently the only color that must be mentioned by name is FD&C Yellow No. 5, also called tartrazine. The FDA ordered this special mention after scientific research projected that as many as 100,000 people in the U.S., including many aspirin-sensitive individuals, could have allergic reactions to the coloring.

The FD&C in the name of an artificial color refers to the Food, Drug and Cosmetic Act, the 1938 legislation that gave federal authority to the regulation of the dyes used in foods, drugs, and cosmetics. The act also instituted a numbering system for the chemical substances used to color these goods.

## The Debate Goes On

Despite regulation, there continues to be a justifiable controversy surrounding the use of food coloring. After all, their entire purpose is to change the colors of food to be more acceptable to the consumer. Manufacturers fear that if they were discontinued, few people would be interested in purchasing a white stick of margarine, a grey hot dog, or a brownish-grey maraschino cherry—even if these are the real colors of these processed foods. Because the public persists in holding perfect coloring as an ideal, it's only "natural" that the consumer buys those foods that look best—no matter whether that look came from nature or science.

# Fat Substitutes

*Is faking it the way to go?*

## Fooling Mother Nature

A low-fat diet is one mark of a healthy lifestyle. The recommendation has been to cut back on fatty foods and eat fruits, grains, and vegetables in their stead. Through food technology, though, we have some other options. Rather than abandoning all your favorite fat-laden foods, you now can select from an assortment of similar products that have been reformulated with fat substitutes. But are these phony fats good nutrition, or do they serve to conceal the need to make better food choices?

## Faking Fat

Before food scientists could replace the fats in a food, they had to identify how the fat contributed to the taste of that particular product. Usually, the role of fat has to do with "mouth feel." This term refers to a slippery, slide-over-the-tongue sensation that coats the mouth and carries the food's flavor. To come up with practical fat substitutes, technologists had to find one or more ingredients that would give this sensation, carry similar flavors and not add fat calories to the product.

## It's Only Natural

Many companies first began looking at naturally-occurring food materials to replace the fats. This made sense as it's likely that any new synthetic substances would be closely scrutinized by regulatory agencies. No one wanted another ingredient that needed a warning label. The most promising has been, of all things, dietary fiber. Talk about a win-win situation: What better than to have a health-promoting, zero-calorie fiber to replace some of the taste pleasure of fat! It's also a plus for food companies, as they can avoid the maze of regulatory approval.

Fiber now being used as fat substitutes includes vegetable

gums, such as agar, locust bean gum, tragacanth, xanthan gum, and pectin. Other fat substitutes include dextrins, gels, glucomannan, and carrageenan. These ingredients contribute no vitamins or minerals and they act as binding and thickening agents, adding texture and a slippery "mouth feel" to foods such as yogurt, salad dressings, sauces, jellies, puddings, sherbets, and ice cream. And although they're built like a carbohydrate, because they are not digested or absorbed, they add no calories.

## What's Available Now?

One fat substitute now at the supermarket is called Simplesse. It was developed from milk and egg proteins by the same Nutrasweet company that gave us the sugar substitute of the same name. While not calorie-free, it is fat-free. A gram of Simplesse has less than one sixth the calories of fat.

Simplesse, and a similar product called Trailblazer, are not heat-stable. When the temperature rises, the mixture begins to fall apart. As a result, the only practical application for these fat substitutes is in cold or frozen foods.

Also, in an effort to reduce the fat in ground beef Auburn University and McDonald's came up with a ground beef containing a plant gum, named carrageenan, that comes from seaweed. Why seaweed? Previous attempts at making low-fat meats were rejected as dry and flavorless. The poor taste is not surprising, as most of the flavor we associate with meat comes from the fat. With carrageenan, though, you have a food additive with an ability to hold in moisture. So to the meat/carrageenan mixture, scientists add a bit of water, a pinch of salt, and a dollop of meat flavoring. Voilá, a juicier burger containing 13 grams less animal fat than the regular one.

## Dried Fruit Can Work Too

Fat plays a variety of roles in different baked goods. Most, however, rely on fat's slipperiness to weave its way into the structure of the dough. Once there, fat not only contributes to the mouth feel of the baked product, it shores up the physical structure and keeps the food from falling flat.

By virtue of their high content of "slippery" carbohydrates, prunes and other dried fruits can, to a degree, mimic this effect. Their water-holding fibers and carbohydrates can shore up the structure of dough and provide the needed mouth feel.

## Then There's Formulated Fats

Rather than a fat substitute, a new ingredient called Caprenin is a formulated fat that provides fewer calories. It is now being tried out in candy bars, including the new Milky Way II. Caprenin accomplishes its calorie reduction by being made from fats that the body is not able to digest efficiently. As a result, a gram of Caprenin provides only 5 calories, compared with the 9 calories per gram we get from other fats.

Caprenin is made of about 50 percent capric acid and caprylic acid, two fatty acids found in coconut and palm-kernel oil, both tropical oils. The other half is made up of behenic acid, a poorly digested fat taken from hydrogenated rapeseed oil. Keep in mind that although you save a few calories with Caprenin, it's still a fat, not a fat substitute.

## A Word of Caution

Keep in mind that switching from fatty to fat-substitute foods is not the answer to good nutrition. These pseudo-foods pale in comparison to fresh fruits and vegetables. But for those looking for ways to indulge dessert cravings while remaining on a fat budget, they are certainly worth a try.

# Biotechnology Heads to Market
*Friend or foe?*

## It's On the Way

Most people have heard of biotechnology, but have only a vague idea of what it is. To some folks, biotechnology is a new way to improve the food supply, our health, and the environment; to others, the very idea evokes fearful images of unknown dangers from bizarre creations. Whatever your views, one thing is certain: This important new technology is coming, and it's vital that you understand what's at stake.

## We're Talking Gene Splicing Here

Our body is made up of millions of cells that all look remarkably similar when they're first created. Inside each cell is a set of instructions, or genes, that commands it to become the type of cell it's supposed to be. Biotechnology makes use of genetic engineering, or gene splicing, a technique that makes subtle changes in these instructions. The process can add to or change functions in a cell with a speed not previously possible. The changes, once made, remain a part of the cell that gets passed on to future generations.

You can begin to appreciate biotechnology's tremendous potential by looking at its use in agriculture. In the past, improving a food crop via plant breeding was a hit-or-miss process that took years to achieve any measurable success. Biotechnology removes much of the guesswork by identifying the specific genetic code associated with a desired trait. This code is then added to the genetic instructions of a target plant.

For example, the gene for good taste in plant A would be added the genes of plant B, a variety with poor taste but a longer shelf life. From that point on, future generations of plant B would have a better taste *and* a longer shelf life.

## Biotechnology at its Best

Biotechnology has the potential to create crops that are less dependant on chemical fertilizers and pesticides, and are tastier, more nutritious, and have a longer shelf life. Many grains, for example, would be excellent sources of protein if not for the fact that they were missing an essential amino acid. Through biotechnology, the ability to add missing amino acids to grain, could turn inexpensive, easy-to-grow foods into sources of complete proteins. Plants might also be modified to grow in soil and water conditions where they previously could not survive.

Such a development would have little impact in the U.S., where we already eat too much protein. It could, however, be a lifesaving change to developing countries where single grains are often the main food eaten.

Biotechnology can also produce crops that remain fresher longer. Unless you shop at farmers' markets, or a store that buys directly from nearby growers, the produce you eat has been picked unripe in order to get it to market before it spoils. With few exceptions, when produce is picked before ripening it will never develop a home-grown flavor. Varieties made through biotechnology would ripen on the vine and then last long enough to get to the store.

Biotechnology can also give us more options in food processing. For example, lactose intolerance, the inability to digest the carbohydrate in milk, can cause digestive problems in about 70 percent of the world's adults. Through genetic engineering, a bacteria could be developed that would digest the lactose in a fluid milk.

## Is It Safe to Fool With Mother Nature?

With such power and potential, the question of safety arises. Now that science has begun work on reprogramming the way things grow, is it just a matter of time before a mistake is made that opens a Pandora's box of new diseases, bugs, or even super weeds? Although unlikely, the possibility does exist.

There is government supervision of biotechnology through the FDA, EPA and USDA, but there is little practical control over experiments conducted in individual laboratories. As experiments continue, a host of questions need to constantly be asked: Is this research necessary? Will this development feed more people? Will it provide a higher quality of life for a greater number of people? But who is going to ask these questions? And who will determine the answers? It is because of these unknowns that at this point biotechnology should be regarded only with cautious optimism.

## Money May Decide the Future

Unfortunately, as great a potential as biotechnology may have, the forces that may decide its future will be those who control the purse strings of research. Government coffers are running dry and those of private companies are usually salted with economic self-interest, a fact that may not coincide with the good of humanity.

As an example, biotechnology can be used to make food crops that are resistance to a particular pesticide or herbicide. By growing these varieties, more chemicals could be applied to kill more pests without also killing the crop. Rather than a step toward less dependance on synthetic chemicals, such "advances" provide further rationale for their use. This development would not bode well for the environment. If biotechnology is used only for its profit-making potential, there's a real danger that the long-term health of the land and those who work it will become of secondary importance.

## Questions Remain

Few could argue with the use of this science to create varieties of plants with higher nutritional quality, a higher resistance to disease, or greater tolerance to variations in soil and temperature conditions. Such developments could change unfertile regions into productive farmland. This would be invaluable for those parts of the world constantly besieged by drought and famine.

However, will biotechnology chart a course toward the betterment of humanity or will the science become just another industrial tool to use and abuse in the interest of profit? It's in your best interest to follow this field and make your opinions known with your voice and pocketbook.

# Putting it All Together

# An Eating Plan You Can Live With

*A really simple, no nonsense approach*

## It's There for the Eating

Now that you've had a chance to read through the preceeding chapters, it's time to put the information all together in a eating plan. This isn't as complicated as it sounds as there's been a consistent theme throughout the pages: variety and moderation, with a strong emphasis on fresh fruits, vegetables, and grains. It may be a familiar theme, but you now have an appreciation of the science behind its wisdom.

## Making it Happen: Basic Principles

• Your diet should include all the food groups, but the foundation should be grains, vegetables, and fruits—foods that are high in complex carbohydrates. Aim for at least 5 servings per day of fresh fruits and vegetables. (A typical serving is a medium piece of fruit, 1 cup of a leafy vegetable, ½ cup of fruit or cooked vegetables, ¼ cup of dried fruit or six oz. of a fruit or vegetable juice.)

• Everything you eat does not have to be bursting with good nutrition. So instead of thinking about good food versus bad food, direct your thinking toward good diet versus bad diet. You can enjoy most foods if you follow the principles of balance, variety, and moderation.

• You don't have to include animal-based foods (meat, poultry, fish, dairy) to have a healthy diet—but having these foods is not incompatible with good health so long as you don't overdo it.

## Know Your Fat Facts

• Be aware of your fat allowance. This information can help you assess how different foods can fit into your daily menu. Aim for a fat intake between 20 percent and 30 percent of your daily calories. Here is a chart detailing the fat grams and calories for different total calorie intake levels.

## Daily Fat Grams (calories)

| Calories | 20% | 30% |
|----------|-----------|------------|
| 1,400 | 31 (279) | 47 (423) |
| 1,600 | 36 (324) | 53 (477) |
| 1,800 | 40 (360) | 60 (540) |
| 2,000 | 44 (396) | 67 (603) |
| 2,200 | 49 (441) | 73 (657) |
| 2,400 | 53 (477) | 80 (720) |
| 2,600 | 58 (522) | 87 (783) |
| 2,800 | 62 (558) | 93 (837) |
| 3,000 | 67 (603) | 100 (900) |

(An average, light to moderately active woman, 25 to 50 years of age, 5'4" tall, weighing 120 lbs would require around 2,200 calories a day. A man of similar age and activity, 5'10" tall weighing 174 lbs. would require around 2,900 calories a day.)

## Food Planning, Preparation & Serving

• When planning meals, keep in mind that soups are excellent way to add flavors and fullness with a minimum of fat.

• When shopping for meat, purchase leaner cuts and always trim visible fat before cooking.

• Have no more than 2, 3-oz. servings of meat, poultry, or fish a day. Try to have fish on the menu at least twice a week. A 3-oz. serving of meat is about the size of a pack of playing cards.

• Aim for one meatless (vegetarian) day a week.

• Broil, bake, roast, stir fry, or steam instead of deep-fat frying. When you bypass deep-fried foods you not only make a significant dent in your fat intake, you avoid potentially harmful elements (See Fried Food Facts).

• In poultry most of the fat is in or just under the skin. It's okay to cook poultry with the skin on, but remove the skin before eating.

• Cook stews and meat-containing soups in advance so that there's enough time to cool the dish and skim off any excess fat before serving.

• When at the table, practice portion control. Have a high-bulk/

low-fat foods (grains, vegetables, and fruits) at every meal. Remember: if you keep eating until you feel full, you've had too much. It may take up to 20 minutes for the mind to realize that the stomach is full.

## Simple Substitutions
• By using lower-fat foods instead of traditionally high-fat products, you can make significant dents in your fat/calorie intake. For example, substituting one cup of skim milk for whole milk, saves 23,000 calories over a year's time (2% low-fat for whole milk saves 10,600 calories).
• Try dried figs, apricots, pretzels, or cut-up vegetables instead of snack chips.
• Rely on fish or leaner cuts of meat.

## Snack Time
• Plan ahead for snacks. When you wait until you have hunger pangs or for your scheduled break time, you may put yourself at the mercy of convenience foods that often are bereft of nutritional value. At home and work, have fruit and cut-up raw vegetables, such as carrots and celery, stored in water in the refrigerator. Other snacks such as pretzels, rice cakes or air-popped corn can also provide a satisfying treat.

## Other Elements
• Activity is a key element to good health. Even if you haven't the inclination for a regular exercise program, you should be able to find something that fits your lifestyle. Studies show that even when activity is at moderate levels—such as a brisk daily walk—there can be a significant payoff in better health.
• Drink at least 8 glasses of water a day.
• Learn how to read the food label. This tool can help you choose between comparable products and ensure that you get the most nutrition for your dollar. (See Old Label/New Label.)

## Why So Healthy?
What is it about such an eating plan that can make it such a

boon to health? The answer is very basic. Such a diet gives your body all the nutrient-rich foods it needs, *and* it limits those that are potentially harmful. In other words, when a disease such as cancer attempts to invade a healthy body, it has to find its way to the door, force its way in and then overwhelm an ornery immune system that's primed to fight. With a less-than-optimal diet you have unbarred the door, lit the entryway and sent the guard away.

Therefore, it's no wonder that prevailing research continues to connect good health with diets based on hefty amounts of vegetables, fruits, and grains.

## Clues from Our Ancestry

You can get further testimony to the healthfulness of such an eating plan by examining nutritional history. About 90 percent of the time humans have been on this planet, our diet was high in fiber and low in fat. It wasn't until the last two hundred years, following the Industrial Revolution, that the American and Northern European diet began its shift toward higher levels of fat and lower fiber.

Although the palate was quick to embrace this change, the body apparently hasn't had the same success. Research points to the lower fat, higher vegetable, fruit, and grain diet as the best way to avoid heart disease and cancer, now the top two killer diseases in Western societies. In countries in Africa and Asia where a change never occurred, these diseases are almost nonexistent. Undoubtedly, there are other factors involved, but the connection between diet and disease cannot be ignored.

## Other Factors Play a Part

Whether a person actually gets heart disease or cancer, for example depends on family history, diet and lifestyle factors such as activity level and exposure to harmful substances like tobacco. In addition good health care and early diagnosis could make the difference between nipping a potentially-serious problem in the bud or inadvertently allowing one to fester past hope of recovery.

It's important to understand that a good diet cannot guarantee health. But all things being equal, a daily dose of health-promoting nutrients would have to be considered one of the most effective unified approaches against disease. Having a diet based on grains, vegetables, and fruits is an excellent way to accomplish this.

## So Why Don't We Eat More Healthfully?

One answer might be the difficulty in making the connection between eating habits and long-term health. To be sure, those imperiled by a brush with heart disease or another diet-related malady can take to new diets with religious fervor. But many of us heading down the same road are seemingly oblivious to constant reminders that a similar fate lies ahead.

Another reason is that as a society, we haven't looked at the connection between diet, health, and disease through one set of glasses. This can be difficult because today's emphasis on scientific specialization overwhelms any chance for such a holistic view. But in making decisions about what to eat, that's precisely what we need to do.

Consider, for instance, that the American Heart Association and one set of research scientists are focused on heart disease, while the American Cancer Society and a separate set of health scientists have their glasses trained on the big "C." Each group has its own set of scientific societies, journals, and professional meetings where research about "their" disease gets discussed.

No one would question that heart disease and cancer are different diseases, especially where treatment is concerned. Therefore, some specialization is essential. But if you looked at these diseases from the standpoint of dietary prevention programs, you couldn't tell them apart. Both anti-heart disease and cancer diets include a reduction of dietary fat and an increase in the daily intake of vegetables, fruits, and grains. And by strange coincidence, the same eating plan is recommended to stave off arthritis, obesity, diabetes, and hypertension.

The fact that the same type of diet is associated with a lower incidence of such a variety of maladies suggests that they all have something in common; namely, that eating right brings about a higher state of health that fortifies the body's defénses against *all* disease. It's really simple, and there's no nonsense, and it's right there for you.

## Hot Resources

There's no end to the number of available resources. I find the following books, magazines, and newsletters to be of particular value.

**Books:** *The Wellness Encyclopedia of Food and Nutrition* (Rebus, NY, 1992) S. Margen, M.D., *Health & Fitness Excellence* (Houghton Mifflin, Boston 1989) R. Cooper, Ph.D., *Eat for Life* (National Academy of Sciences, Washington, D.C. 1992) C. Woteki, Ph.D. R.D., *The Wellness Encyclopedia* (Houghton Mifflin, Boston 1991) by the authors of the U.C. Berkeley Wellness Letter, *The Healing Foods* (Dell, NY, 1989) by P. Hausman, and *The Mount Sinai School of Medicine Complete Book of Nutrition* (St Martin's Press, NY 1990).

**Magazines:** *Health*, POB 56863 Boulder, CO 80322, *Eating Well*, Ferry Road, POB 1001, Charlotte, VT 05445, *American Health*, RD Publications, 28 W. 23rd St, New York 10010, *Cooking Light* POB 830549, Birmingham AL 35282, and *Prevention*, 33 E. Minor St, Emmaus, PA 18098.

**Monthly Newsletters:** *Environmental Nutrition*, 2112 Broadway, NY 10023, *University of California at Berkeley Wellness Letter*, POB 420148, Palm Coast, FL 32142, *Tufts University Diet & Nutrition Letter*, 53 Park Place, NY 10007. *Nutrition Action Health Letter*, 1875 Connecticut Ave. NW, Suite 300, Washington, DC 20009, *The Felix Letter*, POB 7094, Berkeley, CA 94707, *Consumer Reports on Health* 101 Truman Ave, Yonkers, NY 10703, and *The Edell Health Letter* Health, 301 Howard St. Suite 1800, San Francisco, CA 94105.

See also: Daily Nutritional Checklist and Best Nutritional Sources.

# Appendix

# Commonly Asked Questions

## Aluminum Cookware

*Q. What's your opinion of the safety of aluminum cookware?*

A. Questions about the safety of aluminum cookware relate to Alzheimer's disease, a tragic progressive loss of mental faculties, or dementia, brought about by a breakdown in brain tissue.

In the early 1970s it was discovered that the brain lesions in Alzheimer's patients contained an abnormally high concentration of aluminum. From that information, the idea was hatched—mainly in non-scientific circles—that the disease was caused by an aluminum toxicity. It was a case in which study results were taken out of context and used to form a simplistic explanation of a complex disease.

Aluminum is present throughout the environment. It's the third most common element in the earth's crust and naturally occurs in plant and animal foods. In addition, because it's contained in a number of food additives, it's likewise in processed foods. Aluminum is also used in medications, such as popular antacids, and in deodorants. By comparison, the amount of aluminum ingested from kitchen equipment is incidental.

Despite this, an accusing finger was pointed at aluminum cookware as the potential villain. The sinister aluminum pots and pans were either shoved back in the pantry or sent sailing into the garbage. Sales of aluminum foil took a nosedive.

Since then, scientists have been unable to discover whether aluminum is a cause of Alzheimer's or an after effect of the disease process. It is also unknown why aluminum, and not some other metal, is involved. Until the mystery is unraveled, it's reasonable to err on the side of caution. Other types of pots and pans are widely available. If you use aluminum pans, keep in mind that exposure to acid foods tends to dissolve more aluminum into the food. Therefore avoid cooking or storing high-acid foods, such as tomatoes or citrus, in aluminum containers.

If you use aluminum cookware coated with a non-stick surface, such as Teflon or Silverstone, you need not be concerned so long as the surface remains intact. In addition, a new breed of hardened (anodized) aluminum, such as Calphalon or Magnalite, can be used to cook high-acid foods.

## Buttermilk

*Q. What exactly is buttermilk and what gives it its sour taste? Is bacteria used? If so, is it one that survives in the intestine?*

A. Buttermilk originated as a byproduct of traditional butter making. It was the name given to the liquid left after all the butter was churned out of fresh dairy cream. Old-fashioned churning was not a sterile process; the milk sugar (lactose) in the cream was in contact with the bacteria in the air and in the non-pasteurized cream. The bacteria would change some of the milk sugar into lactic acid, giving the final fluid a distinctive, tangy taste.

Dairy companies must follow a general recipe to call a product buttermilk, but there are no guidelines about the specific bacteria that must be used. The bacteria *acidophilus* and *bifidus* are the ones that survive digestion and become a part of the beneficial flora in the intestines. These, however, are not commonly used to make buttermilk. It's likely, though, that some smaller brands contain them. Check the label or call the manufacturer to find the culturing bacteria present in the buttermilk you're considering.

Incidently, while the *butter* in its name gives the impression that buttermilk is a high-fat food, most commercial dairies use skim milk to make their product. An 8-ounce glass of a typical buttermilk contains 92 calories and only 2 grams of fat.

# Canola

*Q. Exactly what is a canola?*

A. Canola is type of vegetable oil which, by food standards, has come on the scene rather suddenly. What's unique about canola is that, unlike other vegetable oils, it doesn't originate from a plant or seed of the same name. Canola stands for *Ca*nadian *O*il, *L*ow *A*cid. It's derived from the seed of the rape plant, a member of the mustard family and common crop in—you guessed it—Canada.

Common varieties of the rape plant have a high concentration of erucic (ee-ROOS-ik) acid in their oil—a substance suspected of having a toxic effect in large amounts. Because of this, the oil was mainly used for industrial applications. Plant breeders, though, were successful in developing a variety of rapeseed in which the erucic acid was virtually eliminated. Taking its place was a high concentration of oleic acid, the monounsaturated fat found in olive and many nut oils.

Given the growing body of research on the health advantages of using monounsaturated fats in a low-fat diet, this turned the new hybrid rapeseed oil into a perfect product for foods. But who would buy a product named, "rape oil or rapeseed oil?" And the name "low erucic acid rapeseed oil" was thought to be too much of a mouthful. This set the stage for the name, "canola."

In 1985, the oil received GRAS (Generally Regarded As Safe) status from the U.S. Food and Drug Administration. In 1988 the name canola was given approval for use in this country. Presto! A new word was added to the food vocabulary.

# Carob

*Q. Could you please give me some information on carob?*

A. Carob, a relative of the pea, comes from the seeds of the carob tree, originally found in Mediterranean regions. Carob is also called locust or St.

John's bread for its fabled role as John the Baptist's source of sustenance as he wandered in the wilderness. The powder from the carob bean is similar in color and fragrance to cocoa. But compared to cocoa, carob flour is lower in fat and higher in carbohydrate and calcium. Cocoa, on the other hand, is higher in niacin, vitamin E, iron, zinc, selenium, and phosphorous. Neither carob nor chocolate, being vegetable foods, contain any cholesterol.

Many people have experimented with carob flour as a low-fat cocoa substitute. (Because of its milder taste, use about 3 parts carob to replace 1 part cocoa.) Although carob candies, chips, and coatings may start with low-fat carob powder, they're far from being low-fat foods. These confections are made by combining carob with coconut oil or hydrogenated vegetable oils, which result in a final fat content comparable to chocolate. They provide no "fat" advantages over their chocolate counterparts.

## Kicking the Sweetened Cereal Habit

*Q. I'm having breakfast problems with my children. They insist on eating only super-sugary cereals and they go from one movie-fad cereal to the next. Any suggestions on how to break the habit?*

**A.** When a popular kid's movie hits the screen, it's now common for a cereal to follow in its wake. We find Ghostbusters, Batman, Dick Tracy, Ninja Turtle, Addams Family, and even Bill and Ted's "Excellent" cereals on the shelves at the same time the movies begin to pack them in at the local theater. So, after seeing the movie or just watching it advertised, young shoppers come face-to-face with the cereal promotion in a well-timed, highly visible, end-of-the-aisle supermarket display.

Despite the variety in colors, shapes, tastes, and textures, fad cereals are quite similar in composition. It's almost as if there were a master computer that takes the theme of the promotion, shuffles a few shapes, colors, and textures and voila! Out comes the latest product.

A 1-ounce serving is about one cup in volume, depending whether it's puffed or flaked. Each serving usually contains about 110 calories, and the super-sweets contain from 9 to 15 grams of sugar (4 grams of sugar equals 1 teaspoon). There's a small amount of protein and fat (often from partially hydrogenated vegetable oils) and little, if any, dietary fiber. The added sugar usually represents 33 to 55 percent of the cereal's calories. With such paltry nutritional assets, it's not surprising that the cereal companies fortify their products with vitamins and minerals. This, along with milk's major contribution of protein, calcium and other nutrients, rounds out the food value of this type of meal.

There's no question that you can save money and provide better nutrition by serving a basic grain cereal. See if you can switch from the pre-sweetened types to ones having less than 8 grams of sugar per serving. Try using a high-fiber cereal based on whole grains, and then add your own sweetener in the form of dried fruit, such as diced figs, prunes, raisins, dates or apricots. In this way, you get the complex carbohydrates from the cereal, along with fiber, vitamins, and minerals, and you can control the amount of natural sweetness from the dried fruit. By having a variety of fruits available, you offer a choice. Your children might even be able to taste the cereal grain.

If your child is a hopeless fad-cereal addict and can't understand your concerns, consider using these cereals, but only in small amounts to "sweeten" an un-sweetened cereal. It's better to start the day with food than to leave the house with an empty stomach.

## More Chips at the Store

*Q. I continue to see a growing variety of snack chips at the store. We have shifted from plain potato chips to tortilla chips, but wonder if any of the colored, corn, or bean varieties are any better for you?*
A. The chip family is in the midst of a definite population explosion, but unfortunately the new members have not strayed far in nutritional composition. Aside from potato and corn chips, there are now chips made from vegetables such as black beans, carrots, spinach, taro, plantain, bell peppers, and beets. These are present in small proportions, usually in combination with corn, and their strong colors tint the chip and give it a novel eye appeal.

Fruit chips are also heading to the market. To date, there are apple, pear, peach, and banana chips, but if these catch on, bits of the entire harvest may find their way into the deep fat fryer. Consider all of them snack foods and, with the exception of a few "light" chips and a new brand of no-oil tortilla chips that are baked, all are quite high in fat. Try to stick with brands made with non-hydrogenated canola, peanut, or high-oleic safflower oil. If there's no nutrition panel present, you can assume there are approximately 7 to 10 grams of fat per 12- to 15-chip serving.

## Fertile & Vegetarian Eggs

*Q. I recently saw a brand of eggs from vegetarian hens. Will this make a difference in the nutritional value of the egg? Also, is there any nutritional difference between fertile and non-fertile eggs?*
A. Laying hens are normally fed a meal that contains meat scraps as a source of dietary protein. Vegetarian-diet hens are given vegetable protein sources, such as soy. The vegetarian diet is more costly and this is usually reflected in the price of the eggs. Fertile eggs come from hens having had sexual contact with roosters. The eggs, if properly incubated, could develop into chickens. Typical eggs found in most stores are infertile. There are no nutritional differences between any of these eggs.

# Eating Before Exercising

*Q. I ride an exercise bike 5 days a week for about half an hour. I always wait two hours after a meal before starting my workout. Is this necessary or may I begin sooner, say one hour after eating?*

**A.** There's a good reason for delaying exercise after you eat. During the initial stages of eating and digestion, the body shunts its blood supply away from the muscles to the organs of the digestive system.

If you begin strenuous exercise during this period, the body's priorities shift and the blood flow changes back toward the muscles. This can also happen when the body is under stress, an event that triggers a chain reaction that prepares the body for strenuous activity (the "fight or flight" reaction). The worst-case scenario often cited involves swimming too soon after a meal. Then, not only is the blood supply required for the muscles and digestion, it's needed to maintain body temperature in the water. The classic result is an insufficient blood flow to the muscles and the onset of a cramp that impairs the ability to swim.

The optimum delay between the end of a meal and the start of exercise depends to a great degree on the nature of the meal. Other factors are age, degree of conditioning and the intensity of the exercise. I will assume that you're an average individual in your middle years.

If your pre-workout meal tends to be large and is high in both protein and fat, your delay should be closer to two hours. If you eat smaller meals of primarily carbohydrates, the delay can be cut back to anywhere between 30 minutes and an hour. It's best to make any changes gradually, and be ready to back off if you experience any untoward muscular or intestinal problems.

# The Lowdown on Food Irradiation

*Q. There's a lot of conflicting stories about food irradiation. Could you give me a little background and explain what all the commotion is about?*

**A.** Food irradiation is a 40-year-old food preservation technique that exposes food to very low doses of ionizing radiation. The commotion you refer to involves the ongoing debate over the safety and wisdom of using irradiation on our food supply. Radiation is used to kill insects, microorganisms, and other pests that can destroy fruits, vegetables, or grains. It also can inhibit sprouting in root crops such as potatoes, and reduce or eliminate the bacteria, yeasts, molds, and insects that can cause food-borne illness in contaminated meats, poultry and seafood.

Irradiation has been suggested as a better alternative to current chemical preservation methods. The fumigant ethylene dibromide (EDB), for example, used to control insects on fruits, vegetables, cereals, and nuts, was banned by the EPA as a suspected carcinogen. Irradiation could serve as a replacement. Because it destroys the organisms responsible for spoilage, irradiation could also be used to extend shelf life in produce. This could be of great value in countries where a warm climate and poor refrigeration facilities threaten the safety and adequacy of the diet.

It appears as though poultry, however, is the food that could best use irradiation. In the retail market, at least one out of every three packages of poultry contains salmonella or campylobacter bacteria. Despite advisories on proper food handling, thousands die and millions of others suffer from food poisoning every year as a consequence of this contamination. The problem shows no signs of going away. Given the increasing incidence of immune disorders and the steady advance of the average age in this country, those most vulnerable to food poisoning will continue to be a growing segment of society.

The poultry industry seems unwilling, or unable to tackle the more important issue of why such contamination occurs. Given this unfortunate situation, irradiation could serve as a band-aid approach to eliminating the unwanted bacteria. The advantage is that food can be irradiated after it is packaged. The rays go through the packaging material and the treatment leaves the poultry (or meat) free from bacteria and less subject to re-infestation.

The defenders of food irradiation include a broad array of scientists, the Food and Drug Administration, the United Nations Food and Agriculture Organization, and the World Health Organization. Those against irradiation, though, believe that exposing foods to irradiation makes them unsafe, if not downright dangerous to eat.

At the center of the argument is the fact that irradiation can affect nutritional value and create substances called "radiolytic products" in food. These points are not disputed, but those against irradiation believe these substances threaten our health. Those who favor food irradiation respond that similar physical effects occur with other forms of food preservation such as canning, as well as cooking or exposure to sunlight. The changes, they say, do not represent a significant health risk.

Arriving at the truth between such divergent views is not an easy task. Let's face it, the idea that we would allow our food to be exposed to radiation and that anything good could come from it is a challenge to one's instincts. Nonetheless, in the particular case of food safety, an argument can be made for the value of irradiation.

## Food Combining

*Q. I've read that certain categories of foods should not be eaten together. For example, because proteins and carbohydrates are digested differently, eating them together is bad for the body. Could you please comment?*
A. The theory of food combining is based on the idea that the way foods are combined (or not combined) is the key to digestion and health. As this questionable theory goes, an easy-to-digest food, such as fruit, should

never be eaten with proteins or fatty foods, which take longer to digest. To do so would delay the digestion of the fruit and allow the fruit sugar to ferment and putrefy, thus causing health problems. Other forbidden combinations include starchy foods, such as bread or potatoes, together with protein foods, such as meat or fish.

There's no physical reason to believe this theory. The beauty of the human digestive system is that it's specifically designed for a mixed diet. The different types of foods in our diet are each handled in a specific part of the digestive system.

While it's likely that some people have found that certain foods or food combinations don't work for them, this is more an indication of personal preference than a digestive defect of the human species. There appears to be no physical reason that we have to refrain from including a variety of foods at every meal.

## Gluten

*Q. My doctor told me I can't eat any gluten. How common is it to have a problem like this?*

A. Gluten is a type of protein found in wheat, barley, rye, and oats. An acute intolerance to this protein gives rise to celiac disease, also called non-tropical sprue. Symptoms of the intolerance, which affects about one person out of every 2,000, vary from mild upset stomach to a serious condition where the digestive system can no longer digest and absorb food. Medical tests can confirm gluten intolerance. The only known treatment is to avoid all food containing gluten.

There are several gluten-free cookbooks and mail-order companies that supply gluten-free foods. For more information, contact the Gluten Intolerance Group, P.O. Box 23053, Seattle, WA 98102-0353.

## Ice Crystals on Ice Cream

*Q. The ice cream in my freezer forms crystals regardless of how well the container is sealed. It seems to happen more than it used to. What causes this and is there any danger from eating the ice cream once this happens?*

A. The harmless water crystals that form on the surface of frozen foods during storage develop as the product's temperature fluctuates above and below freezing. Normally, water freezes into large crystals of ice. Such crystals in a frozen desert would lend an undesirable coarse texture. To prevent this, ice cream and other frozen desserts are constantly stirred while the temperature is lowered below freezing. This allows only small crystals to form, which gives the dessert its smooth texture.

As ice cream in the carton is used up, the increased air space allows the water in the ice cream to evaporate and then refreeze during the normal temperature fluctuations in the freezer. The longer it takes to use a carton, the greater the crystal formation. These crystals can be prevented, however, by putting wax paper or some other moisture barrier on the top of the ice cream before returning it to the freezer.

Larger water crystals can also form if the frozen product is allowed to defrost and then refreeze repeatedly. It starts when we take the carton out and then use a room temperature scoop to serve the ice cream. Allowing more to melt by leaving the carton on the table further contributes to the process.

An increased prevalence of ice crystals is likely due to one of the newer types of ice cream that are lower in fat. These low-fat frozen deserts typically contain a significantly higher percentage of water.

## No Lactose in Most Spreads

*Q. I am lactose intolerant. Where can I find a spread that contains no milk solids?*
**A.** With few exceptions, spreadable fats, including margarine and butter, get 100 percent of their calories from fat. This means there is no carbohydrate and, therefore, no lactose in these products. (Check the product breakdown on the nutrition panel to verify the absence of carbohydrate.) Even if there were a couple of grams of carbohydrate, it's doubtful that would be enough to cause a reaction in people susceptible to lactose intolerance.

You shouldn't be surprised to find a partially hydrogenated oil high on a margarine's ingredient list. Partial hydrogenation is the process that changes the liquid vegetable oil into the spreadable semi-solid we call margarine. Unfortunately, this same process creates the *trans* fatty acids now connected with a number of negative health effects.

If you keep your use of a spreadable fat to a minimum, butter may be a reasonable alternative. You also might consider adopting the European practice of using olive oil (with added herbs for flavor) as a bread spread. If, however, you're set on using margarine, look for a tub or liquid product that list partially hydrogenated oil no higher than third on the list, after water and a non-hydrogenated vegetable oil.

## Meat & Dairy in the Diet

*Q. Doesn't good health demand cutting out all meat from our diet?*
**A.** Epidemiological studies, those that examine health trends in populations, often find a relationship between increasing meat consumption and such diseases as colon cancer and heart disease. As a result of this research, an incorrect assumption is made that any amount of meat is the direct cause of these killer diseases.

Meat becomes a negative health factor not when it's merely part of a diet, but when it *is* the diet—when all meals are designed around a hefty portion of beef, pork, or poultry, with a paltry presence of fruits and vegetables. Because meat contains a higher proportion of calories from fat, the diet as a whole becomes skewed in that direction. This type of diet tends to be the norm in the U.S., which helps explain why many diet-related diseases are so common.

Abolishing meat, a convenient target by virtue of its typically high fat content, is not the silver bullet to end our health problems. If your intake of dietary fat, fiber, and other nutrients are within recommended guidelines, there's no evidence that your health would be any different if your fat calories come from tenderloin or tofu.

## Freezing Milk

*Q. I usually buy more milk than I need and freeze part of it. I haven't noticed any great change in taste, but was wondering what this does to the milk?*
**A.** Although not common, freezing is a safe and acceptable way to store milk. The method, however, can produce a few minor changes. For example, freezing can cause a breakdown in the homogenization—the process that distributes the milk fat evenly throughout milk. Although this does not apply to skim milk, an occasional drop of fat may be seen floating in whole or low-fat milks. Giving the container a few shakes will solve the problem.

Depending on the speed at which the milk is frozen, changes in nutritional value, slight alterations to taste, and some loss of color are possible. In addition, a small amount of sediment may develop. These changes are minor and the milk remains a wholesome food. A good rule of thumb is the faster the freeze, the smaller the damage.

It's best to use small, well sealed containers placed next to a wall of the freezer or on a metal shelf, where they'll freeze quickly and remain solid for the duration of their storage. The frozen milk should be defrosted in the refrigerator.

Keep in mind that freezing will not change old milk into fresh. Because milk is a rich source of nutrients, it is an ideal food for growing microorganisms. Pasteurization helps destroy most —but not all—of the bacteria that are present at bottling. The quality after thawing will be no better than the milk was at the time it was frozen.

## Pasteurized Versus Ultrapasteurized

*Q. At stores I have seen dairy products that are both pasteurized and ultra-pasteurized. How do these differ?*
**A.** Both pasteurization and ultra-pasteurization are heat treatments designed to reduce potentially harmful microorganisms. The two differ in the amount and duration of heat used.

Pasteurization heats a dairy product to 160 degrees F. for 15 seconds, while ultra-pasteurization heats the product up to 280 degrees F. for up to 3 seconds. The higher heat used in ultra-pasteurization eliminates more bacteria and actually results in a shelf-stable product. Once opened, however, both requires refrigeration.

Ultra-pasteurization is not more widely used because high heat often affects flavor. The process is usually used on products such as half-and-half or whipping cream, but ultra-pasteurized fluid milk can be found in remote areas, or in stores that don't sell a high volume of product.

# Non-Stick Sprays

*Q. Please give me some information on the safety of non-stick cooking sprays, such as PAM. What is the propellant used and how do the sprays work?*
**A.** Cooking sprays contain vegetable oil, such as corn or soy, plus lecithin, an ingredient from soybeans traditionally used to keep oil-and-water solutions together. Most of the non-stick sprays use compressed hydrocarbon gas, such as propane or iso-butane, as the propellant. The main safety concern with these products is that the gases are highly flammable. Because of this danger, use these sprays only on cold surfaces, away from all flames.

The sprays keep food from sticking by forming a thin oil-lecithin film between the cooking surface and the food. Because they use a minimum amount of oil, little fat is contributed to the meal. A 1.5 second application—enough to cover a 10-inch skillet—contains less than 1 gram of fat.

Make sure you shake well before using, as the ingredients have to be thoroughly mixed to work properly. An often-ignored drawback of these products is the waste contributed by the empty can.

## The Case of the Cloudy Oil

*Q. Could you explain why oils get cloudy when stored in the refrigerator? Should oils be kept in the cupboard with my other foods?*
**A.** The cloudiness comes from the harmless formation of small crystals—the first step as an oil "freezes" from liquid to solid—and should disappear when the oil returns to room temperature.

It's degree of saturation helps determine the temperature at which an oil turns solid. Olive oil, which is mono-unsaturated, will normally begin forming crystals at refrigerator temperature. A polyunsaturated oil, such as corn oil, would have to be put in the freezer before such changes could be seen. Highly unsaturated fish oil remains clear and liquid well below zero.

As a rule, oils keep longer when stored at cool temperatures. But keeping an unsaturated oil in the cupboard is perfectly safe provided the container is tightly closed and stored away from light and heat. Air, or more precisely the oxygen in the air, is the primary enemy of unsaturated oil. Oxygen turns an unsaturated oil rancid, and light and heat hasten this breakdown reaction.

Rancidity not only affects taste, it also is unhealthy to eat. Nature protects its oil-containing seeds with layers of bran. Often, there's some vitamin E present to serve as an antioxidant. When oils are refined, not only is the protection removed, the oil is often packaged in clear containers. Also, there are some large tins of oil that have no practical way of being resealed. If you purchase your oils in quantity, consider filling smaller containers that can be well sealed and stored away from light and heat. Wherever stored, a frequently-opened container should be sealed promptly after use.

# Psyllium

*Q. I have been adding oat bran to my daily diet, but have read that psyllium is much more effective. Which is better way of adding fiber?*
A. After scientists reported that the soluble fiber in oat bran had a cholesterol-lowering effect, the hunt began for other sources of soluble fiber. Psyllium was a natural candidate. It comes from the seed of the Plantago plant, a native to India and the Mediterranean. Used as a laxative in India for centuries, psyllium is also the main ingredient of over-the-counter laxatives in the U.S. On a weight basis, soluble fiber makes up 75 percent of the psyllium seed—compare this to oat bran's 8 percent soluble fiber.

Recently, several studies reported how the addition of psyllium to the diet helped lower elevated blood-cholesterol levels. Similar to the period following the initial oat bran studies, psyllium began to appear in commercial breads and cereals. Unlike oats, though, psyllium has little to offer besides soluble fiber. By contrast, oat bran is a good source of protein, magnesium, iron, zinc, thiamine, and phosphorous.

Using supplemental fiber also can have its downside. When you add concentrated fiber to the diet, there is a greater chance of side effects such as bloating, cramps, diarrhea, and gas. In addition, loading up on fiber can interfere with the absorption of nutrients. This is a particular problem with supplements such as psyllium, which provide no nutrients. Medications may also be affected, so consult your health professional before you add quantities of fiber to your diet.

While oat bran would be my choice between these two fibers, it's not the best approach to increasing one's daily intake of fiber. A gradual shift to a diet based on fresh foods, with plenty of fruits, vegetables, legumes and whole grains, is generally preferable to getting fiber from a supplement.

# Why the Refrigerator Ruins Bread

*Q. I live alone and am rarely able to use an entire loaf of bread before it turns stale. I have tried storing it in the refrigerator but find that once I do it never tastes the same. What is it about refrigeration that ruins bread?*
A. Bread turns stale as its starch undergoes a change in structure. Although stale bread has a dried-out appearance, loss of moisture is not the complete explanation—a loaf will turn stale even in a well-sealed, unopened package. Temperature, it turns out, is the key.

There are two main types of starch, or carbohydrate, in bread. Over time, each changes from a random to a more rigid arrangement. The first of the two starches changes as freshly-baked bread cools to room temperature. The settling of the second starch takes about a week. As the second starch changes, the texture of the bread shifts from soft to hard, or, as we call it, stale.

It's reasonable for you to consider refrigeration as a way to extend shelf life, as it is useful to slow down many of the ways by which food goes bad. For example, mold, another spoiler of bread, grows slower at refrigerator temperatures. With bread, however, refrigeration is a mixed blessing, as the starch tends to settle faster. Your bread won't get moldy, but it will be stale in about a day.

Freezing may provide a solution. Freezer temperatures not only inhibit mold, but the settling of the starch comes to a halt. If you are unable to get through an entire loaf before it goes stale, consider splitting your loaf after purchase and storing half in the freezer.

Another possible solution is to look for breads that use preservatives, called emulsifiers. They can slow down the settling of starch and effectively extend shelf life. The most common emulsifiers in bread, the mono- and diglycerides, are effective yet harmless additives. However you decide to store your bread, make sure the package is always well sealed.

## Iodized Salt

*Q. How essential is it to use iodized salt?*

**A.** Today it's rare for anyone eating a varied diet to suffer from an iodine deficiency—whether or not they use iodized salt. Incidently, because your salt comes from the sea it's likely that it already contains iodine.

Iodine is an essential element that's needed for the manufacture of the thyroid hormones—the substances that help regulate the body's metabolism. The Recommended Daily Allowance (RDA) for iodine is 150 micrograms, a trace amount. Iodine is plentiful in the ocean, but not on land; foods containing iodine are limited to seafood, those crops grown in coastal areas, and dairy or meat products from animals that have grazed on feed containing iodine.

Once there were vast areas in the middle of the country without a dependable supply of dietary iodine. Such regions were nicknamed the "goiter belt," because of a symptom of iodine deficiency—a noticeable bulge in the lower throat area. That's why in 1926, as a public health measure, the government legislated that iodine be added to table salt—a move that drastically reduced the incidence of goiter. Iodine, in fact, was the first nutrient substance purposefully added to foods. Iodized salt contains 76 micrograms of iodine per salt gram, which means that the RDA for iodine can be met with as little as one-half teaspoon.

# Nutrition Credentials

*Q. There are many people going around with a "Ph.D." after their name. How is one to know whom to believe?*

A. This question offers an opportunity to discuss the use and misuse of credentials, a thorny problem in the health area. It's likely that anyone who has opened a magazine has seen advertisements for non-resident colleges. These are mail-order institutions where one can get a bachelor's, master's or doctorate degree, at home, in his or her spare time. Some offer correspondence classes and require that you submit a project before being credentialed. Others are nothing more than diploma mills, where the only effort required is the writing of a hefty check.

One man had little difficulty getting a Ph.D. for his dog. There's also a company that for $50.00 will sell anyone a fancy-looking certificate proclaiming the bearer's professional status as a nutritional consultant. Consumers should also pay attention to where credentials are from and how they're used. One common problem involves health-related authors, counselors, or lecturers using a Ph.D. or some certificate as evidence of their competence. Often there is no mention of any educational background. For all you know, their degree could be in a field unrelated to the health area in which they are claiming expertise.

Whenever you are relying on expert advice, make sure you're in fact dealing with an expert. If your instincts tell you something is not right, or you are simply curious about someone's training, politely ask. If you ever uncover health fraud, report it immediately. In the white pages of most phone books, under Consumer Complaint and Protection Coordinators, is a list of numbers you can use to contact the oversight agencies for most of the professional areas.

It's deceitful to claim expertise without training. And when the practice involves a health-related area, it can be dangerous as well. As there is no efficient way to purge all health areas of fraudulent practitioners, it always falls upon the consumer to be alert.

# Sorbitol

*Q. Please explain why sugarless gum or mints give me cramps or diarrhea. Could I possibly be allergic to the artificial sweetener sorbitol?*

A. While it's doubtful you're allergic to sorbitol, it's likely the cause of your problem. (Sorbitol, by the way, is not an artificial sweetener in that it occurs naturally in many fruits.) Sorbitol is used as a sugarless sweetener because it has a sweet taste but doesn't promote tooth decay, and it's not absorbed from the digestive tract like other sugars.

The downside of sorbitol is that it attracts water when it's in the digestive tract, leading to diarrhea in some people. In addition, the bacterial flora that live in the large intestines will digest the sorbitol and create gas in the process. With small amounts of sorbitol, there are no symptoms. With larger quantities, as with several mints or sticks of sugarless gum particularly on an empty stomach, the result is the upset stomach you describe.

If you have problems with sorbitol, or the similar synthetic sweetener xylitol, it's best to either limit intake or consume only after a meal.

# Tofu

*Q. What's the nutritional content of tofu? How long can it be kept in the refrigerator and how can I tell if it's gone bad?*
A. Tofu is made from soybeans that have been soaked, crushed, cooked, and filtered. Calcium sulfate is then added, causing the soy pulp to form a gel. The water is then removed as the soy is pressed into cakes. Unlike other legumes, the soybean is relatively high in fat content. About half the calories in tofu come from fat. One 4-ounce piece of tofu supplies 20 percent of the daily protein requirement, 12 percent of the RDA for iron, 14 percent of the daily requirement for phosphorous, and 15 percent of the RDA for calcium (this nutrient coming primarily from the calcium sulfate used to form the tofu into cakes).

Because of its relatively high content of polyunsaturated fat, tofu quickly turns rancid when exposed to air—the warmer the air, the more rapid the change. As such, most tofu is kept refrigerated underwater or is vacuum packed. When you purchase tofu, make sure it's stored in a similar manner.

Tofu should be discarded if the storage water becomes cloudy, if a slippery film develops on the surface, or if you notice any unusual smells. Also, it should be discarded if it takes on a pinkish tinge—usually the effect of exposure to air. If the water is changed every day, fresh tofu can last up to two weeks in the refrigerator.

# Mexican Vanilla

*Q. Is Mexican vanilla safe? How can it be so inexpensive? Is there a way to know if it's fake?*
A. There is nothing inherently wrong with Mexican vanilla. Much of the vanilla sold in the U.S. comes from Mexico, as the beans grow well in the hot Mexican climate. If purchased south of the border, it's likely these products would cost significantly less.

At one time, however, a Mexican product labeled vanilla was banned because it was found to be made not from vanilla beans, but from an extract of the tonka bean. This less expensive bean extract resembles the odor and flavor of vanilla, but it also contains a high level of coumarin, a toxic food additive that can damage the liver and other body organs.

Is there a way to know if your vanilla is the genuine article? Unfortunately, aside from a laboratory analysis, there's no practical test. If you have no way of checking the origin of the product, I would pass up the bargain and purchase the flavoring from a name you trust.

## Chlorine & Water Safety

*Q. A salesperson trying to sell me an expensive water purification system told me my tap water was dangerous. I didn't buy the system, but he left a booklet that listed chlorine as a hazard. As my city chlorinates its water, could you explain what dangers, if any, are posed by drinking chlorinated water?*

**A.** For over 75 years, chlorine has been used to disinfect public water supplies. At present, chlorine is used in about 75 percent of the drinking water in the U.S. Chlorination is credited with the virtual disappearance of diseases such as typhoid and cholera that spread through contaminated water.

But chlorination is not totally benign. Besides disinfecting water, chlorine is known to react with natural organic material and other pollutants to create compounds such as chloroform, which is a known carcinogen. Population studies have linked the presence of chloroform to a slightly higher incidence of certain cancers.

However, most scientists agree that the risk of drinking water that has not been disinfected far outweighs any danger caused by chlorine. More benign methods of water purification are now being investigated, but at the present time, chlorination represents the most practical approach.

If you have any other questions about the safety of your drinking water, send away for the free booklet, *Is Your Drinking Water Safe?*, to EPA Office of Drinking Water, WH-550, 401 M. St. S.W., Washington, D.C. 20460. The EPA also has a Safe Drinking Water hotline, 800-426-4791. Between the hours of 9am-5:30pm EST, M-F, someone is available to answer your questions about water safety as well as provide information on where water is tested and what to test for.

# Glossary of Food Additives

**Key Classes of Food Additives**

*Acidulants:* Acids that prevent the growth of microorganisms by increasing the level of acid in a food. Examples: acetic, citric, fumaric, lactic, malic, phosphoric and tartaric acids.

*Antioxidants:* Prevents rancidity and other oxygen-related food breakdown. Examples: ascorbic acid, beta-carotene, BHA, BHT, erythorbic acid, propyl gallate (and other gallates), TBHQ, and tocopherol.

*Anti-caking agents:* Absorb large amounts of water without becoming "wet." They are added to foods to keep them free-flowing. Examples: calcium phosphate, magnesium oxide, calcium (and other) silicates, and silicon dioxide.

*Chelating Agents:* Bind metals that can react with foods and destroy texture or appearance (also called sequestrants). Examples: EDTA (ethylene diamine tetraacetic acid), citric acid, phosphoric acid.

*Colors:* Added to make food more appealing, usually designated as natural or artificial. Examples of natural colors: carotene, annatto, carmine and titanium dioxide. Examples of artificial colors: erythrosine, tartrazine, or any using an FD&C number, such as Red no.40 or Yellow no.5.

*Emulsifiers:* Allow ingredients to mix that normally would not be miscible, such as oil and water. Examples: mono- and diglycerides, lecithin, polysorbate 60.

*Flavors:* Added to enhance food flavor. Examples: salt, sugar, vanilla, vanillin, salicylates, or simply stated as natural or artificial flavor.

*Flavor enhancers:* Chemical that brings out or enhances flavors in a food. Examples, MSG (monosodium glutamate), inosinate, guanylate, hydrolyzed vegetable protein (contains MSG).

*Humectants:* Absorb water, keeps foods moist. Examples: glycerol, mannitol, propylene glycol and sorbitol.

*Preservative:* Allows a food to stay longer before spoiling, usually by inhibiting bacterial action. Example: salt, sulfites, nitrites, propionates, benzoates, sorbates and ascorbic acid.

*Stabilizers & Thickeners:* Keeps ingredients mixed, can be used to give food thicker texture. Examples: agar, algin and alginates, carob bean gum, carrageenan, gelatin, gum arabic, guar, modified food starch, pectin, sodium carboxymethylcellulose, and xanthan gum.

For a more detailed listing: *A Consumer's Dictionary of Food Additives* (Crown, NY 1989) R. Winter and *Real Food, Fake Food and Everything In Between* (Macmillan NY, 1987) by G. Harrington.

# Recommended Daily Allowances

*National Academy of Sciences—National Research Council*
*Revised 1989*

## Vitamins

### Vitamin A (mcg RE)

| | | |
|---|---|---|
| Infants to 1 yr | | 375 |
| Children | 1-3 | 400 |
| | 4-6 | 500 |
| | 7-10 | 700 |
| Males | 11 + | 1,000 |
| Females | 11 + | 800 |
| Pregnant | | 800 |
| Lactating | 1st 6 months | 1,300 |
| | 2nd 6 months | 1,200 |

*NOTE: 6mcg beta-carotene = 1mcg RE Many supplements or food tables express their vit.A content in IU, or international units instead of RE, or retinol equivalents. To convert: 1 mcg. RE = 5 IU*

### Vitamin K (mcg)

| | | |
|---|---|---|
| Infants to 6 months | | 5 |
| | up to 1 yr | 10 |
| Children | 1-3 | 15 |
| | 4-6 | 20 |
| | 7-10 | 30 |
| Males | 11-14 | 45 |
| | 15-18 | 65 |
| | 19-24 | 70 |
| Males | 25+ | 80 |
| Females | 11-14 | 45 |
| | 15-18 | 55 |
| | 19-24 | 60 |
| | 25+ | 65 |
| Pregnant | | 65 |
| Lactating | | 65 |

### Vitamin D (mcg cholecalciferol)

| | |
|---|---|
| Infants to 6 months | 7.5 |
| up to 1 yr | 10 |
| Children, males and females up to 24 | 10 |
| Males, females 25 + | 5 |
| Pregnant | 10 |
| Lactating | 10 |

*NOTE: 10 mcg cholecalciferol = 400 IU vit.D*

### Vitamin E (mg alpha-TE)

| | | |
|---|---|---|
| Infants to 6 months | | 3 |
| | up to 1 yr | 4 |
| Children | 1-3 | 6 |
| | 4-10 | 7 |
| Males | 11+ | 10 |
| Females | 11+ | 8 |
| Pregnant | | 10 |
| Lactating | 1st 6 months | 12 |
| | 2nd 6 months | 11 |

*NOTE: alpha-TE = alpha tocopherol equivalents. 1 alpha-TE = 1 mg d-alpha tocopherol, the natural form of vit. E. The synthetic form of the vitamin, dl-alpha tocopherol, is about ¼ less potent. Vit.E content can also be expressed as IU (international units). 1 IU vit.E = 1 mg dl-alpha tocopherol, so 10 alpha-TE = 14 IU.*

## Vitamin C (mg)

| | | |
|---|---|---|
| Infants to 6 months | | 30 |
| | up to 1 yr | 35 |
| Children | 1-3 | 40 |
| | 4-6 | 45 |
| | 7-10 | 45 |
| Males | 11-14 | 50 |
| Males | 15+ | 60 |
| Females | 11-14 | 50 |
| | 15+ | 60 |
| Pregnant | | 70 |
| Lactating | 1st 6 months | 95 |
| | 2nd 6 months | 90 |

## Thiamin (Vitamin B₁) (mg)

| | | |
|---|---|---|
| Infants to | 6 months | 0.3 |
| | up to 1 yr | 0.4 |
| Children | 1-3 | 0.7 |
| | 4-6 | 0.9 |
| | 7-10 | 1.0 |
| Males | 11-14 | 1.3 |
| Males | 15-50 | 1.5 |
| | 51+ | 1.2 |
| Females | 11-50 | 1.1 |
| | 51+ | 1.0 |
| Pregnant | | 1.5 |
| Lactating | | 1.6 |

## Pyridoxine (vitamin B₆) (mg)

| | | |
|---|---|---|
| Infants to 6 months | | 0.3 |
| | up to 1 yr | 0.6 |
| Children | 1-3 | 1.0 |
| | 4-6 | 1.1 |
| | 7-10 | 1.4 |
| Males | 11-14 | 1.7 |
| Males | 15+ | 2.0 |
| Females | 11-14 | 1.4 |
| | 15-18 | 1.5 |
| | 19+ | 1.6 |
| Pregnant | | 2.2 |
| Lactating | | 2.1 |

## Riboflavin (Vitamin B₂) (mg)

| | | |
|---|---|---|
| Infants to 6 months | | 0.4 |
| | up to 1 yr | 0.5 |
| Children | 1-3 | 0.8 |
| | 4-6 | 1.1 |
| | 7-10 | 1.2 |
| Males | 11-14 | 1.5 |
| | 15-18 | 1.8 |
| Males | 19-50 | 1.7 |
| | 51+ | 1.4 |
| Females | 11-50 | 1.3 |
| | 51+ | 1.2 |
| Pregnant | | 1.6 |
| Lactating | 1st 6 months | 1.8 |
| | 2nd 6 months | 1.7 |

## Niacin (mg NE)

| | | |
|---|---|---|
| Infants to 6 months | | 5 |
| | up to 1 yr | 6 |
| Children | 1-3 | 9 |
| | 4-6 | 12 |
| | 7-10 | 13 |
| Males | 11-14 | 17 |
| | 15-18 | 20 |
| Males | 19-50 | 19 |
| | 51+ | 15 |
| Females | 11-50 | 15 |
| | 51+ | 13 |
| Pregnant | | 17 |
| Lactating | | 20 |

*NOTE: 1 mg NE (niacin equivalent) equals 1 mg niacin or 60 mg tryptophan.*

## Folic Acid (mcg)

| | | |
|---|---|---|
| Infants to 6 months | | 25 |
| | up to 1 yr | 35 |
| Children | 1-3 | 50 |
| | 4-6 | 75 |
| | 7-10 | 100 |
| Males | 11-14 | 150 |
| Males | 15+ | 200 |
| Females | 11-14 | 150 |
| | 15+ | 180 |
| Pregnant | | 400 |
| Lactating | 1st 6 months | 280 |
| | 2nd 6 months | 260 |

## Vitamin B$_{12}$ (mcg)

| | | |
|---|---|---|
| Infants to 6 months | | 0.3 |
| | up to 1 yr | 0.5 |
| Children | 1-3 | 0.7 |
| | 4-6 | 1.0 |
| | 7-10 | 1.4 |
| Males | 11+ | 2.0 |
| Females | 11+ | 2.0 |
| Pregnant | | 2.2 |
| Lactating | | 2.6 |

# Minerals

## Calcium (mg)

| | | |
|---|---|---|
| Infants to 6 months | | 400 |
| | up to 1 yr | 600 |
| Children | 1-10 | 800 |
| Males | 11-24 | 1,200 |
| | 25+ | 800 |
| Females | 11-24 | 1,200 |
| | 25+ | 800 |
| Pregnant | | 1,200 |
| Lactating | | 1,200 |

## Phosphorous (mg)

| | | |
|---|---|---|
| Infants to 6 months | | 300 |
| | up to 1 yr | 500 |
| Children | 1-10 | 800 |
| Males | 11-24 | 1,200 |
| | 25+ | 800 |
| Females | 11-24 | 1,200 |
| | 25+ | 800 |
| Pregnant | | 1,200 |
| Lactating | | 1,200 |

## Magnesium (mg)

| | | |
|---|---|---|
| Infants to 6 months | | 40 |
| | up to 1 yr | 60 |
| Children | 1-3 | 80 |
| | 4-6 | 120 |
| | 7-10 | 170 |
| Males | 11-14 | 270 |
| | 15-18 | 400 |
| Males | 19+ | 350 |
| Females | 11-14 | 280 |
| | 15-18 | 300 |
| | 19+ | 280 |
| Pregnant | | 300 |
| Lactating | 1st 6 months | 355 |
| | 2nd 6 months | 340 |

## Iron (mg)

| | | |
|---|---|---|
| Infants to 6 months | | 6 |
| | up to 1 yr | 10 |
| Children | 1-10 | 10 |
| Males | 11-18 | 12 |
| | 19+ | 10 |
| Females | 11-50 | 15 |
| | 51+ | 10 |
| Pregnant | | 30 |
| Lactating | | 15 |

## Zinc (mg)

| | | |
|---|---|---|
| Infants to 1 yr | | 5 |
| Children | 1-10 | 10 |
| Males | 11+ | 15 |
| Females | 11+ | 12 |
| Pregnant | | 15 |
| Lactating | 1st 6 months | 19 |
| | 2nd 6 months | 16 |

## Iodine (mcg)

| | | |
|---|---|---|
| Infants to 6 months | | 40 |
| | up to 1 yr | 50 |
| Children | 1-3 | 70 |
| | 4-6 | 90 |
| | 7-10 | 120 |
| Males | 11+ | 150 |
| Females | 11+ | 150 |
| Pregnant | | 175 |
| Lactating | | 200 |

## Selenium (mcg)

| | | |
|---|---|---|
| Infants to 6 months | | 10 |
| | up to 1 yr | 15 |
| Children | 1-6 | 20 |
| | 7-10 | 30 |
| Males | 11-14 | 40 |
| | 15-18 | 50 |
| Males | 19+ | 70 |
| Females | 11-14 | 45 |
| | 15-18 | 50 |
| | 19+ | 55 |
| Pregnant | | 65 |
| Lactating | | 75 |

# Nutrients without RDAs, but with an Estimated Safe and Adequate Daily Dietary Intake[a]

## Vitamins[a]

### Biotin (mcg)
*Estimated Safe and Adequate Daily Intake*

| | | |
|---|---|---|
| Infants to 6 months | | 10 |
| | up to 1 yr | 15 |
| Children | 1-3 | 20 |
| | 4-6 | 25 |
| Children | 7-10 | 30 |
| Males | 11+ | 30-100 |
| Females | 11+ | 30-100 |

### Pantothenic Acid (mg)
*Estimated Safe and Adequate Daily Intake*

| | | |
|---|---|---|
| Infants to 6 months | | 2 |
| | up to 1 yr | 3 |
| Children | 1-3 | 3 |
| | 4-6 | 3-4 |
| Children | 7-10 | 4-5 |
| Males | 11+ | 4-7 |
| Females | 11+ | 4-7 |

## Minerals[ab]

### Copper (mg)
*Estimated Safe and Adequate Daily Intake*

| | | |
|---|---|---|
| Infants to 6 months | | 0.4-0.6 |
| | up to 1 yr | 0.6-0.7 |
| Children | 1-3 | 0.7-1.0 |
| | 4-6 | 1.0-1.5 |
| | 7-10 | 1.0-2.0 |
| Males | 11-18 | 1.5-2.5 |
| | 19+ | 1.5-3.0 |
| Females | 11-18 | 1.5-2.5 |
| | 19+ | 1.5-3.0 |

### Fluoride (mg)
*Estimated Safe and Adequate Daily Intake*

| | | |
|---|---|---|
| Infants to 6 months | | 0.1-0.5 |
| | up to 1 yr | 0.2-1.0 |
| Children | 1-3 | 0.5-1.5 |
| | 4-6 | 1.0-2.5 |
| Children | 7-10 | 1.5-2.5 |
| Males & | 11-18 | 1.5-2.5 |
| Females | 19+ | 1.4-4.0 |

### Manganese (mg)
*Estimated Safe and Adequate Daily Intake*

| | | |
|---|---|---|
| Infants to 6 months | | 0.3-0.6 |
| | up to 1 yr | 0.6-1.0 |
| Children | 1-3 | 1.0-1.5 |
| | 4-6 | 1.5-2.0 |
| Children | 7-10 | 2.0-3.0 |
| Males & | | |
| Females | 11+ | 2.0-5.0 |

### Chromium (mcg)
*Estimated Safe and Adequate Daily Intake*

| | | |
|---|---|---|
| Infants to 6 months | | 10-40 |
| | up to 1 yr | 20-60 |
| Children | 1-3 | 20-80 |
| Children | 4-6 | 30-120 |
| Males & | | |
| Females | 7+ | 50-200 |

## Molybdenum (mcg)
*Estimated Safe and Adequate Daily Intake*

| | | |
|---|---|---|
| Infants to 6 months | | 15-30 |
| | up to 1 yr | 20-40 |
| Children | 1-3 | 25-50 |
| | 4-6 | 30-75 |
| Children | 7-10 | 50-150 |
| Males & | | |
| Females | 11+ | 75-250 |

[a] Because there is less information available on which to base an allowance, these estimated daily requirements are given as ranges of acceptable intakes.
[b] Because there is less information available on which to base an allowance, these estimated daily requirements are given as ranges of acceptable intakes. In addition, since toxic levels may be only several times usual intakes, upper levels should not be habitually exceeded.

**Units:**
**mg = milligrams**
**mcg = micrograms**
**1 milligrams = 1,000 micrograms**
**1 gram = 1,000 milligrams**

# Index

combining and **210-202**

Eating Plan **188-193**

Eggs: protein **5,6**, vitamin and mineral content **21,22,25,26**, oxidized fats, heart disease and powdered eggs **37**, and salmonella food poisoning **112,113-114**, fertile **199**

Emulsifiers as food additives **211**, and stale bread **207**

Exercise: diet and the athlete **106-109**, and weight loss **58,59,61,** for stress reduction **74**, longevity and age-related weight gain **83**, eating before **200**, metabolic rate **59**, as part of overall plan **190**

Fat and Oils: **7-12**, digestion of **30,31,33**, determining your fat allowance **10-11,189**, hydrogenated (trans fatty acids) **123-126**, and heart disease **37-38**, oxidized fats **37**, and cancer **47-48**, omega-3 fatty acids (Fish oils) **50-52**, and stress **74,75**, farm-raised fish **121**, fat substitutes **181-183**, cloudy oil **205-206**, fried foods **130-131,132**, Non-stick sprays **205**

Fiber **40-42, 43-45**, fat and **8**, and heart disease **40**, and cancer **40,41**, as complex carbohydrate **13,14,15**, and digestion **31-32**, and intestinal flora **97**, in juice **101,102**, vegetarianism and **65**, and longevity **83**, oat bran **43-44** psyllium **206**, on the food label **162,163,167,168** daily value for **162**, as fat substitute **181,183**, as part of eating plan **191**

Figs **44-45**

Fish: seafood safety (See Food Safety), fish oil (See Fats and Oils)

Flavor Enhancers as food additives **211**, salt as **136**, reactions to **152-153**,

Flora (see Intestinal flora)

Fluoride, function and dietary sources **24,25**, Estimated Safe and Adequate Daily Intake **216-217**

Folic Acid, function and dietary sources **22**,

and immune system **54**, RDA **214**

Food Additives: glossary of **211**, colors **178-180**, preservativeь **169-171**, flavors **175-177**, sensitivity to **152-153**,

Food Allergies **151-153**

Food Colors (see Food additives)

Food Combining **201-202**

Food Flavors (see Food additives)

Food Label **160-168**, calculating percent faι calories on **11**, sugar listing **142**, use of "natural" **172-174**

Food Preservatives (see Food additives)

Food Safety **112-119**, seafood **120-122**, irradiation **200-201**, natural toxins **147-150**, pesticides **154-155**, with HIV or other immune dysfunction **114-115**

Food Sensitivities (See Adverse reactions to food)

Foodborne Illness **112-119**

Fried Foods **130-132**, alternatives to **189**

Garlic **93-95**

Gluten **202**

Grilled foods (See Barbecue)

Heart Disease **36-39**, and fats **7,8-9**, and fiber **40**, and fish **50,51**, vegetarianism and **65**, free radicals and **61-62, 81**, and stress **75**, supplements and **85**, margarine (trans fatty acids) and **124**, and high blood pressure **136-138**, and sugar **141**, and label health claims **167,168**, eating plan to avoid **188-193**

Humectants **211**

Hydrogenated fats (See Partially hydrogenated fats)

Immune System **53-55**, fats and **8**, cancer and **46,48**, omega-3 fats **51,54**, and stress **75**, garlic **93**, and intestinal flora **96**, food poisoning and **114-115**, and trans fatty acids **124**, food allergy **151,153**

Integrated Pest Management **156,157**

Intestinal flora **96-99**: and digestive system **32-33**, and gas (flatulence) **32-33,208**, and buttermilk **196-197**, (See also Yogurt)

Iodine, function and dietary sources **24,25** and goiter **147-148**, iodized

# Best Nutritional Sources

Here's a list of the healthiest and most nutrient-dense foods in every food category. It's designed to help you select the best foods for your daily menu. (Note: some of the fruits and vegetables may not be available in all areas.)

## DAIRY

Skim Milk ,1% Milk
Low-Fat Acidophilus Milk
Non-Fat Yogurt, Buttermilk
Sherbet, Fat-Free Frozen Desserts
Low-Fat Frozen Dessert
Reduced Fat Cheese
(Fat-Free, Low-Fat or Dry Curd)

## PROTEIN
### Meat, Poultry, Fish, Legumes, Eggs & Nuts

Fresh Fish
Canned Fish (Waterpack)
Pork Tenderloin
Chicken (without skin)
Turkey (without skin)
Beef Top, or Eye of Round
Egg Whites, Beans (Pinto, Navy, Lima, Garbanzo and Kidney)
Black-eyed Peas,  Lentils

## VEGETABLE

Cooking & Salad Greens
(Turnip, Mustard, Beet, Collard, Kale, Romaine  & Leaf Lettuce, Parsley, Arugula, Amaranth & Spinach)
Potatoes (white & sweet)
Corn (fresh & air  popped)
Leeks, Winter Squash, Carrots
Cabbage, Cauliflower, Asparagus
Red Peppers, Broccoli

## FRUIT

Bananas
Citrus ( Orange, Grapefruit, Lemon & Lime)
Melons ( Cantaloupe,  Honeydew)
Berries  (Blackberries, Raspberries & Strawberries)
Tropical Fruits ( Papaya, Guava, Mango) Kiwi
Dried Fruits (Figs, Apricots, Prunes & Dates)
Apples

## BREADS, GRAINS & CEREALS

Grains & Flours (Barley, Oats, Buckwheat, Rye, Bulgur, Millet, Quinoa, Amaranth & Flaxseed)
Hot or  Cold Cereals,
Bread & Pasta (whole-wheat is best)
Rice (brown is best)
Wheat Germ
Bran (Wheat, Rice & Oat)
Baked Goods (Bagels, Pita Bread, Corn Tortillas, Matzos, Rice Cakes & Pretzels)

## FATS & OILS

LISTED IN ORDER OF PREFERENCE
Canola (Rapeseed), Almond, Olive, Safflower, Sunflower, Walnut, Corn Oil
Sesame, Peanut, Cottonseed Oil
**Choose less often:**
Butter, Chicken Fat, Lard, Palm Kernel Oil, Coconut Oil, Liquid Margarine, Tub Margarine
**Choose Rarely:**
Vegetable Shortening, Stick Margarine